C000146697

MEN IN RAGE

Hell is other people. And it is the morning rush hour. And it is a telephone left on hold, and a job you hate, and raw youth, and anyone and everyone who is conspiring to foul up your life. Thus Philip Pickles, insurance clerk and father-to-be.

It is Saturday evening and, in yet another fit of pique, Philip is seeking to lay the blame on someone else for his latest predicament. But wait. There's blood on his fingers. And where is Kath? This is serious. The regrets come flooding in. If only he could turn back the clock. To last weekend, say. Yes, seven days, a single lousy line along the calendar. Is it too much too ask?

So begins an account of a week in the life of this disenfranchised young man, this secret and not-so-secret road rager, supermarket rager, this curser of the aged and the unborn alike, his tale threaded with a second narrative, that of Luke and Darren, two boys whose fate may or may not be linked with Philip's.

Men in Rage is a story of our times in which Paul Sayer once again expertly lifts the lid on a byway of the human psyche, namely the phenomenon of rage, this epidemic of modern life.

MEN IN RAGE

Paul Sayer

BLOOMSBURY

This book is dedicated to David Nicholas,
who left the party earlier than he would have liked.

First published 1998

Copyright © 1998 by Paul Sayer

The moral right of the author has been asserted

Bloomsbury Publishing Plc, 38 Soho Square, London W1V 5DF

A CIP catalogue record for this book
is available from the British Library

ISBN 0 7475 4125 6

Typeset by Hewer Text Ltd, Edinburgh

Printed in Great Britain by Clays Limited, St Ives plc

'As men in rage strike those that wish them best'
– from *Othello*

One

'Hell is other people.' Philip reached for the wine. 'It's just, you know, the way I see it.' He put his hand round the bottle neck, grinning. 'What d'you reckon, Chris? Am I right?'

Chris stood up. 'I'm just off to the other room for a minute. Something I forgot.'

When he had gone, Philip raised the bottle towards the door. 'What's he doing now? Finding out the population of Surinam?' He laughed hard. 'Accessing Buckingham bloody Palace?'

'He's downloading,' said Sheena.

'Well, shit the bed!'

Kath stared at her glass and tutted. Half the night she had been tutting. 'I don't know why you don't get into something like that.'

'What, fucking computers?'

'Oh, stop swearing at everything.'

'We-ell. What do I want with computers? I look at the damned things all day long.'

'Something else, then. It'd do you good to have a hobby. It might stop you getting so mad at everybody.'

'Give over. Who gets mad?'

'You do. You're always mad at something.'

Philip filled his glass to brimming. 'Such as?'

'What about tonight?' Kath turned to Sheena, their host. 'I need a plug on my hair-dryer. Philip used it for the Christmas lights, but when he comes to take it off again he can't find a small enough screwdriver. So what do you do?' she said, looking down at her empty plate.

'I don't know.' Philip put the glass to his lips, warily. 'Tell me, what did I do?'

'You threw the whole lot at the wall, that's what. Then you kicked the hair-dryer across the room. I saw you. I saw you do it.'

Philip wrinkled his mouth. He didn't know Kath had been able to see him. Sheena was smiling, embarrassed. 'It was just . . .' He closed his eyes, pinching the bridge of his nose. 'Frustrating. That's all.'

'It wasn't worth that carry-on.'

'It was nothing. Everyone has their moments. I bet Chris does too, eh, Sheena?'

Sheena rubbed the back of her neck. 'Well, no, not really. He's quite organised when it comes to things like that, you know, practical stuff.'

Philip looked around the room at the meticulous wallpapering, the white coving, the finishing touches of the brass light switch and the stencilled pelmet above the expensive curtains. It was true. Chris was a clever bunny. Very clever. 'Maybe he should come and change the plug on Kath's fucking hair-dryer then!' He laughed, but the silence of the two women was against him. He shifted his legs under the table. 'There's a lot of pressure at the moment, I mean, work, the baby and all that. It's not my fault if I lose my rag sometimes. Like I said, it's just people . . .' He was fishing through his drunkenness for a telling comment. 'They screw things up. They'll give me cancer one day, I swear it.'

Kath was turning her packet of Marlboro Lights edge to edge on the pine table-top. 'That's a stupid thing to say. How could anyone give you cancer?'

'No, it's right,' Philip said, though he was aware of the silliness of his argument. 'It's the things they do. The *stress* of it all.' He was looking at his glass. 'Life in general. It's a tough cow.'

'It's the same for everyone,' said Sheena.

'Ah, but it's not. Though I admit you can *make* things more difficult.' He took a drink, and raised the glass to Kath. 'I mean, take this being a father thing. All right for some, sure, but I don't know. I don't know if I'm ready for it at all.'

'Shouldn't you have thought about that before you did it?' Sheena said, smiling. 'It was hardly an accident, was it? You did plan it, didn't you?'

2

Philip stared at the smooth flame of the candle between them. 'I suppose. After a fashion.' He looked at Kath. 'Eh, pet?'

Kath lit a cigarette.

'Is this your man, then?'

'Yeah,' said Darren. 'This is Luke.'

Luke couldn't think of anything to say. The guy, Mick, was walking round him, looking him up and down. He snorted softly. 'Another fuckin' bairn. Jesus, what do I let myself in for?'

'He's a mate,' said Darren. 'He's all right.'

'Fuckin' have to be, won't he? It's a bit late to start changin' things now.' Mick ruffled Luke's hair, laughing. 'Hey, Lukey, my man! Don't look so worried! Tell you what, we'll have a drink, get a few things sorted about tonight.'

Luke pulled away from his hand. He hated people talking to him as if he was a kid. They were still standing in the hallway of the flat. The door was just behind him. He could turn around and go, if he wanted. And fuck this bloke.

'We've already 'ad a drink,' Darren said.

'Aw, you're joking, Dazzer? What did I say about havin' your wits about you?'

'It was just one.'

'You say that, but how do I know?' Mick shook his head. 'Fuck's sake . . .' He turned into the living room, then turned back. 'Christ. All right, we'll do a bit of something else then. Shit, I'll have to get you two *up* somehow.'

This idea made Luke happier. A bit of whizz, maybe. He'd tried that a few times, and it made him feel great. And after tonight he might be able to afford as much as he wanted, which was one of his reasons for agreeing to this. Mick nodded behind him. 'In here, Luker.' Luke went straight into the living room, too quickly, betraying his seventeen years, while the other two went along the hall to a bedroom. Now Luke was standing there alone, like a tool, hearing them along the hall, arguing the toss. In whispers.

*　　*　　*

3

'If you didn't want to go, you should have said. I could have gone on my own.' Kath was sitting forward, peering at the narrow country road, the trees and hedgerows caught napping in the headlights.

'Don't be like that.'

'Well, honestly. You spoil things, the way you go on at people.'

Philip rubbed at a mark on his trousers, wishing he could have worn his jeans, like he always did of a weekend. 'They're your friends.'

'I've known Sheena for twenty years. We were at school together. They could be your friends too, if you'd try a bit harder.'

'I don't want *friends*. I want mates. That Chris, what a bloody bore.'

'That doesn't mean you have to start pulling him to pieces.'

'I wasn't. I just made a few observations. No one has to take them seriously. All I was doing was stating things the way I find them.'

'All you were doing was getting drunk and being obnoxious. It's bad enough when you're sober. Why do you have to get so, I don't know, so *basic* all the time?'

'We-ell, I hate all this. Being nicey-nice, going to each other's houses. God, dinner parties. Why couldn't we just go up the pub like we used to?'

'We can go to the pub. It's just that sometimes it's good to have a change from all that.'

Philip settled himself lower in his seat, the flat black countryside seeming to go on for ever. They went silent until, at a deserted junction, Kath stalled the car. Here, Philip thought gloomily, in the middle of fucking nowhere. Now he could have a go at her, get his own back, legitimately. He looked at Kath, the seatbelt across her pregnancy, the lights from the dashboard giving her face an unearthly orange tinge. She was wrestling with the gear stick, near to tears. *You're always mad at something.* What a

4

night this had been. And all his fault, really. Best keep the mouth shut, he thought, closing his eyes as Kath crunched the engine, jolting the car back to life. Yes, shut it. Best way, for Christ's sake.

TWO

Blood on the fingers. Who to blame?

Someone, some place, perhaps way back, at the very beginning with that famous slap of the midwife, the first act of a lifetime of people putting on him, fouling up the game with their meddlesome ways? The world. He never had a chance. Yet you could not change people. Oh no, they still carried on, taking up his space, obstructing with their excremental logic, brains of bone, their hittable flesh crying out for mutilation, disease, the sooner the better. And they never died! Philip did not know anyone who had departed this life as quietly and rapidly as possible. They just stayed, driving him . . . Enough to make your blood boil.

But this is serious.

He looks again at the powdery stain, brown and rehydrated pink. As if there had been strawberries for tea. Now he can hear his own breath, its catch in the sinuses. What should he be doing? It's a moment for following the rules, yet what were they? He takes a couple of steps, nudging the silence, making it dash like a mad angel, away up the stairs where it reassembles, recovers its hovering function. Another stride, a half-step of indecision, his foot shushing on the bristles of the carpet. His own carpet, his own living room. They happen in the home, things like this. He should go back upstairs, but he can't face it. An impossibility. A straightening of the back, a traipse to the kitchen. He looks at the basket of washing on the floor, the pots in the sink, the forks, the spoons, the knives. *You're always mad at something.* When had she said that? Too often for comfort. Poor Kath. Nice woman. Everyone said.

Philip rubs his head, his eyes. What to do? There must be a pattern of behaviour for something like this, a predictability he could ape. He sees his reflection in the window. Greasy brown hair, a paunch, an appalling ordinariness. He pulls the blind, and for a shrewd second there's a temptation to turn back into the house, to look again, make sure there's nothing that can be mended. But it's all a fact. You can't turn back time. If only . . .

Luke broke into a joky lolloping stride, the way he used to walk behind the teachers at school, taking the piss. He pushed into Darren, but his friend shoved him away. Miserable bastard. With a smirk, Luke resumed his normal walk. He still felt good, up, but there was a hint of the drug diminishing. Already. And he didn't want that. The last time he'd tried this stuff he was left in a shag-nasty mood for days, wanting more as soon as he could get it. For a moment, he wondered if the gear Mick had given them had been laced with talcum powder, or chalk dust. He had heard of such things.

Mick, ten yards ahead, looked back. 'Come on, for fuck's sake.' Darren broke into a little trot to catch up with him, but they had to wait for Luke, who refused to run, ambling along, looking up at the roofs of the terraced row, lips pursed in a soft whistle.

'We're round here,' said Mick. 'Next street.'

As they walked together, Luke kept pace – close to them, feeling glued to their company, for some reason. They reached Mick's car, an old blue Fiesta, and got in, Luke sitting in the back on his own. 'Hey, Micky, mate,' Luke said. 'This sherbet's a bit feeble, old son. 'Ave you brought it with you?'

Mick groaned. 'You're supposed to be concentrating on what we're doing. It's for sharpening you up, not getting fucking high. Maybe after.'

'Aw, come on. Jesus, I'm on a fucking downer already! A fucking bum trip! It weren't enough!'

Mick had his hand on the steering wheel. He turned around. 'All right. One more taste. But you fuck this up and you're for it. Right?'

7

'Hey, steady away, mate! Steady away!' Luke watched Mick take the prized little packet of powder from his jacket pocket, but instead of putting it on the back of a spoon, like before, he just wet his finger and dipped it in.

'Here.'

Luke scowled. 'I'm not lickin' your fucking finger. You might've wiped your fuckin' arse with that!'

'This is all you're getting. Take it or leave it, Lukey.'

It meant a severe loss of face. Luke felt himself blushing badly, but he had to have a hit, a maintenance dose, however small. He sucked on Mick's salty finger. 'Mmmm.' He grimaced, peevishly.

Mick offered the packet to Darren. 'Daz?'

'Nah,' said Darren.

'Right,' said Mick, putting the dope away. 'If we're all sorted then. All,' he looked pointedly at Luke, 'our little needs seen to . . .'

'We're right,' said Luke. 'Cushty.'

'We'll be on our way, then. It's going to be a busy night.' He started the car, looked behind, and pulled carefully away.

Can you put the plug on my hair-dryer? Do you mind? When had that been? Seven days ago. To the hour, more or less. Dear God, then to now. If he could retrieve the time, how different things would be. Yes, if they would only let him turn back the clock seven days. Not so much to ask, was it, from a world that has caused him such aggravation? A week only, a single poxy line on the calendar, the Sunday in red. Seven, that loved number, the spiritual three, the material four. Seven seals, seven veils. A lottery line, plus the bonus ball. A quaint idea, but time is against him, its hand on his neck. No getting it back, not without a miracle, one of those things at such a premium these days.

Philip opens the back door to the stock-still cold of the evening. This fucking winter. He'll be stuck in it for ever now, frozen by the balls. The closing of the door, a tug to make it catch. Yet the sound is gratifying – Philip has an ear for its normality, and with it a tiny hope for a return to his senses. He locks the door, a brilliantly mundane action, the clink of the key connecting with the hubbub of the world. There. Drop the key in the pocket and away, a hook to be slung, and no looking at the little huddled shapes beneath the kitchen window. Then, as he ducks under the leaning cypress, a branch catches his forehead like a jabbing finger, dripping water in his hair. 'Bastard! Bastard!' He kicks at it, punches, in the dark, where no one can see. *It's the slightest thing with you. Honestly* . . . Kath, love. She saw through him so well. Forget the tree. Fuck it.

Round to the front and across the empty drive. At a house opposite, a family is arriving home, the kids shouting, tumbling out of the car. The father gets out. 'What have I said about slamming the doors?' Then he sees Philip. They have only spoken once before. Shortly after Philip and Kath had moved in he came over to ask Philip if he wanted to join the neighbourhood watch scheme. 'What,' said Philip, 'so if an alarm goes off we can all rush out with our brushes and shovels to see off the rascally interloper?' It was not funny, not even original – something off the telly. And the man had not taken it at all well, choosing to ignore Philip ever since, though now he was watching him, bearing witness, as if catching something reckonable about his hunched and scruffy air. A chance to even the score. Philip ignores him, walks on.

Down the sloping avenue, with sidelong looks to see who else might be watching, but seeing only the shoe-box houses, semi-detached starter homes, evidence, if any were needed, that life has no meaning at all. Hard to think that he had agreed to live here. But then it had all been Kath's idea anyway, territory, with carpets, a three-piece suite, roses, fucking roses, in the back garden. And yet, to think of her now, just lying there . . . It cannot be thought about. It will send him mad.

At the end of the avenue, there's a fresh purpose to the planting of his heels. Waking up a bit, the ideas livening, details to add to this departure, this kind of flight, not least of which is the fact that he will have to get a bus. A bus! He's not been on one in years. But there's a modesty about this task that warms him, and it's simple

9

enough, the doing of it perhaps bringing a shape to his problem, scaling down its mountainous size. More of this and his mind may right itself of its own accord and he can prepare a defence of his part in all this, an argument filched from the recent past, with a little ancient history thrown in for good measure, that slag of a midwife perhaps, and the whole long list of individuals who had delivered him to this regrettable episode, sending him . . .

Up the wall!

He is feeling better already, until, at the opening of the estate, three youths appear, in oversized clothes, plodding along with that forced laughter, and the giant feet, of the teenager.

Philip stops and strokes the stubble on his cheeks. Footsteps on his grave . . .

'Hey, Mick. Put some sounds on, can't you? It's too quiet.' Luke laughed. 'Like a fuckin' morgue in here.'

Mick looked in his mirror at Luke, then switched on the radio.

Luke listened to the song until he knew what it was. 'Ah, Jesus. U2? U shitbag 2? Can't you find anything better?'

'No.'

'Shee-it. Well at least turn it up, then.'

'It's loud enough.'

'Like a fuckin' monastery in here. I mean . . .'

To Luke's surprise, Darren spun round, showing the whites of his half-caste eyes. 'Just cool it, Luke. Get your head straight. Right?'

'Whoo-ooh! Hey, Daz, sorry, mate. Didn't know you were so worried, like.'

'I'm not worried. I just wanna keep my mind on what I'm doing. If that's all right with you.'

'Jesus . . .' Luke shook himself on the back seat. He was blushing again and, sure as fuck, Mick could see him in the mirror. Half-covering his face, Luke looked out at the passing streets, sulking, deciding to say nothing else until they spoke to him.

*   *   *

The boys slope off across the road, no interest in Philip. He walks on, trying not to think of the old memory they have stirred. This very day he had been told not to think about it, but for two back-to-back moments he considers that night, its contribution to his present regrettable existence. How long ago was it? Six, seven years back? Again that number. How about, dear Lord, a day for each of those seven years? A man passes, a jogger in vest and shorts trying to stave off a heart attack, looking for credit from the same God Philip is pondering. By freezing his nuts off. The sap. Why do we bother believing there might be anything or anyone else but this here and now?

In the old village there is a horse trough on the green, the curving grass banking of the High Street, white-door cottages above, the immutable church at the other end. The air here has a pleasant tarry tang, as if a warm front is arriving. He passes the newsagent's and Sylvie the hairdresser's. In the telephone box by the Spar, a woman is making an animated point, to a boyfriend perhaps. Outside the shop there are a few more youths, but Philip has had enough of being afraid of them. A man leaves the shop with two bottles of wine, getting into his car on the cobbled parking space, off to make something of the evening. Another night and it would have been Philip. Not now. Never again, it looks like.

Standing there, like a penis, wondering where the bus stop is. Then a woman in a green smock is looking at him through the shop window. Fuck. How could he forget he was meant to be avoiding her? Another pointer to the state he was in. He stirs himself, crosses the road and scrambles up the grass bank to the path at the top. He glances round. She is still watching. The old goat. Why can't she mind her own business? He hurries past the cottages then, with a stroke of good fortune, remembers this is where the bus stop is, near the first houses of the village. He rushes round the corner to stand on the bare cracked concrete.

He recalls one of the locals talking in the White Ox about how erratic the bus service is, especially at weekends. But it does not

11

bother Philip. For once – the first time ever? – he's happy to be waiting, standing there, anonymous since he hardly knows anyone, despite having lived in the village for a year. Truth is, he's in no hurry. The later, the better, really. It will be his excuse, and a little piece of freedom snatched before he does what he has to do. Which is? To confess? To say how much he regrets what has happened? But, already, the bus is here, swaying off the High Street, Fate itself in its timeliness, the chug of its engine.

'Boar Lane.' He counts the change for the driver and takes his seat. As the bus lumbers off, empty to the point of sadness, Philip rubs his rough chin with his wrist, looks at his fingers. The blood is still there, grey now. He could have washed his hands at least. He could have . . . He puts his hand in his pocket and looks out at the dark gardens on the outskirts of the village. Roses. She had wanted roses. Corny, really. Yet was it so much to ask? He settles again to his fantasy about going back in time, seeing himself in the garden, good old Philip, a decent chap, truth be told. And there he is, setting prickly bushes in their holes. Roses ready for summer. Yellow and white ones. Red ones too. He could have done that one tiny thing, couldn't he? Going back. On the hoof. Seven . . . Brides for seven brothers!

But it's no joke. If only it was. If only . . .

Three

'You were up early.'

'Heartburn. Must have been all that pasta. And the wine was filth.' Philip chuckled. 'Typical Chris. Don't save a penny if you can save a pound. Wow, is he tight!'

Kath was looking down at the mug in her hands. 'Sheena was nice.'

'Yes.'

There was work to do here, Philip knew, a good humour to apply, like a bandage. Last night he had been out of order and now was the aftermath, a vacuum sealed with regret. Exactly what he had been saying, he could not be sure, though he remembered feeling he was so right, every word licensed and compelling: *People, fucking up the game. They'll give me . . .* Stupid. Kath's aunt had died of cancer, only last year. But it had only been the booze loosening his tongue, surely she would know that. *I hate nights like this. Being nicey-nice . . .* They were merely things he *said*. He didn't mean them. He was breathing steadily, wanting to be allowed to explain himself, but Kath was subdued, perhaps wary of him resuming his bizarre lines of reason.

The radio on the kitchen windowsill was turned up high. Philip had put it on an hour ago, when he got up, when he had wanted Kath to get up too so he could begin his rationalisations. When he woke, the set phrases had boiled in his head, and their relation was a matter of grave importance. But now they had no sense at all. He had made a prick of himself last night, and it would have to stay at that.

He turned the radio down. Kath looked up, and Philip braced himself for some damning remark about his behaviour. But all

13

she said was, 'I want a shower before we go. I have two a day now. I feel such a mess.'

'Sure,' Philip said. 'There's no hurry.'

Kath put her arm across her stomach. Philip looked at her, at the black hair she had allowed to grow to her shoulders, the fringe she trimmed herself. Her eyes were a good deep brown, rabbity, compounding the innocence lent by her pregnancy. The remnants of mascara were the only detraction from this. At thirty-two, she was seven years older than Philip, and there were fine lines appearing at the corners of her mouth. He had meant to count them so he could rib her about her age, but they hardly seemed to joke about anything these days. They had become routinely serious, Kath keeping everything locked away in her head, feelings revealed only at odd times, with isolated observations, or some incongruous laughter after one of his less than funny comments. She filled her cup again from the teapot, drinking methodically, clenching her muscular cheeks, making a deliberate act of swallowing. These moments were awkward, stiff as boards. If Kath had been as drunk as him last night, she wouldn't have remembered half the things he said.

And he would not have been so high-minded.

She shuffled on to the high stool by the hob, her nightshirt riding up tight round her hips. Philip looked away, not wanting to see her snatch just now. 'I feel tired,' she said. 'Maybe we should give the late nights a miss for a while.'

'You're right there,' Philip said, seizing the chance for consensus. 'It'd do us both good.' He smiled benevolently. 'Why don't you go back to bed for an hour? I could tidy up down here.'

'No.' She lifted her leg to scratch her calf, yawning. 'I won't sleep tonight if I do that.'

'Well, we can always skip Jeff and Tilly's. I'll ring them. They're bound to understand.'

'No. They like to know how I'm getting on. I'll be all right, once I'm on the move.'

'If you're sure.'

'I'll be fine.'

'Good. That's good,' he said, though he could hear the bullshit in his voice. He would have given much to avoid going to Kath's parents' house, the thought of Sunday lunch with them, hours and hours of it, a looming obstacle, cramping his wish to patronise Kath. He loathed going, though it might be minutely preferable to staying here all day when he would be obliged to try and do something to the house, the sort of things modern men – a contemptible breed to Philip – were meant to do: flexing blokish muscles with some inanimate object, like a power drill or, in his case, decorating the back bedroom for the baby. The obligation to learn how to do these things was a cause of resentment. It just was not *him*. So, perhaps a drive out was the least appalling choice, with maybe a stop at a pub on the way back as a reward. But they were supposed to be cutting back on the late nights. They had just agreed. Therefore, no pleasure to be had from this day. Nothing. Well, maybe it would do him good. It was time he sacrificed something. He looked at Kath, wanting her to see his new-found austerity, but she was leaning on her elbow, flicking the mug with her fingertip. Her feet, on the rung of the stool, were puffy, a brownness above the ankles. That's where you start dying, a nurse friend once told him. It's where the system starts to close down. From the feet up. And, oh God, weren't we all going to die one day? He looked away, opening the blind to the morning light.

The back lawn was dotted with dead leaves, luminous patches of moss among the tufts of grass. To the left, by the back door, was the bolting cypress Philip had made a hash of cutting back, the cut branches still in a wilted heap at its side. At the end of the garden was a lap fence, bent by the wind, and beyond this was a stretch of open rubbled ground separating them from a new development of expensive detached houses to which Philip assumed he was meant to aspire. He could muster no such dreams. To him, property was a burden. Even a place as small as this, with its melamine grey kitchen cupboards, the mock-Georgian windows, the cramped length and breadth of it, the seven paces he now measured with his eyes, through the louvre doors to the living room and the little

15

hall, all that constituted the ground floor. A fucking kennel. His fists were clenched in his dressing-gown pockets. The place was just unlovable, three years old with no history, no commentary that could be attached, save that you could hear the man next door going for a pee, an old badger Philip believed listened to every word he and Kath said. Then Philip looked out of the window and saw him, the silver head bobbing above the fence, looking, maddeningly, towards Philip.

'Ah, Jesus,' Philip said, turning away from the window.

'What's the matter?'

'Mr Starey-Man. Up at this time.'

'He's only looking for the cat. He's out there this time every morning.'

'I know, but. . .' Philip bit his lip. He was staring at the cupboard above the oven. It was where Kath kept her cigarettes, not hidden, yet not in view. She was supposed to be giving up the fags, yet last night she had gone through most of a packet. *You smoke like you've got a date with your own coronary.* Something else he had said. Oh, for fuck's sake, let her smoke, if she wanted to. What did he care about the damned baby anyway? His face was colouring with these sudden thoughts. Then he was taking the side of the baby. It was *his* foetus too, wasn't it? What sort of future would it have with arteries like fucking cardboard? And who had wanted the thing in the first place? How selfish can you get? How . . . He gave a little gasp. Nothing said, yet. All in his head, where it must remain. A tune came on the radio, a tinkly new pop song he had heard before. He turned the volume back up, loud, dah-dahing to it, patting a crescent on the floor with his slippered foot. The taps became a thud of the heel, an attempt to work off the beat of his heart, not to let his anger spill out. He was not mad. No, Philip Pickles was a tolerant man, and he loved Kath, for all her weaknesses. In fact, her flaws made her more endearing! And as for their child, he would love that too, when the time came. And one day he might actually marry Kath, conceding her the one great prize she had yet to win from him. Women, one of his uncles once told him, get everything in the end. They just know how to wait for it. It's their strength. But Philip would let her have this victory. Yes, they would marry and live happily . . . If only she would stop the fucking smoking! Just stop it!

Stop . . .

Kath was wincing, as if sensing his thoughts. Or maybe it was just the radio. He turned it off. Kath breathed out softly, the tip of her tongue on her lips. She slipped off the stool, her feet slapping on the cushion-flooring. She ran the tap and rinsed her cup, looking out of the window. 'It would be nice,' she said, 'if you planted a few roses in the back there. A bit of a border down at the end. We could take the baby out to look at them when they start growing.'

Philip was digging his nails into his palms, feeling for the bones. 'Yes, maybe. When the weather warms up.'

'You can plant them when you like. They'll take any time, Dad says.'

It was a titanic struggle for Philip. He did not want to talk about roses, or to hear what her father knew on the subject. 'Didn't I just say I'll do it?'

'Only asking.'

'Right. Fine.'

'It's the garden. All I'm talking about is something to make the garden look better.'

'I know,' he said, his stomach burning. 'I heard you.'

Kath closed her eyes and shook her head. 'God, Phil, sometimes . . .'

'Sometimes what?' Saliva was flowing in his cheeks. He was on the brink of shouting. 'What do you mean, "God, Phil, sometimes"?'

She opened her mouth. He could hear the soft click of her lips parting. But all she said was, 'Never mind.' And she walked bravely past him, closing the door as she left the room.

Four

When he had dressed, Philip hung around in the little back bedroom. He was trying to think of a colour scheme he might suggest to show an interest, however superficial. Pink or blue, he supposed. Or cream, or lemon? How was he expected to know? It was no good, he possessed no natural curiosity for the idea. He would have preferred the place to stay as it was, the junk room, sealed off when it had become filled to the ceiling with the dross they seemed to be accumulating, now they had the space for it.

He shuffled a box aside with his foot and looked miserably around the room, remembering when everything he owned once fitted into six Tesco carriers and an Adidas bag. He bent over the box, finding remnants of his earlier life, books and binders from university covered in dust, a Bugs Bunny clock with a flat battery, a biscuit tin full of old photos, headphones for the CD player he could not bring himself to bother with any more. In another box was a barometer he had not learnt how to set, bought from a gift shop on a rare impulse when he thought he might try and properly invent his new home-owning personality by filling the house with trinkets, projecting himself, somehow. Another stillborn idea. He picked up the heavy box, moved it a few desultory inches, and stood upright again, arching his back. In the corner was a dodgy electric blanket, and behind this the plastic Christmas tree with bits of tinsel still hanging from its bent branches. Then Philip saw the lights in a tangle on the floor, and the hair-dryer half-hidden behind the teeming linen basket.

In the bathroom beyond the partition wall, Kath was cleaning her teeth, spitting in the sink. Philip picked up the hair-dryer.

There was a dent in the grey plastic nozzle. Unhideable. He wrapped the flex around it to cover the dent, trying to think of a line to dismiss his treatment of the thing. What was it about him and electrical goods? Incompatible, that's what! They should try and avoid each other!

He opened the fitted cupboard, warm from the hot-water tank at the other side of the wall, and tucked the hair-dryer away on the shelf. In here was some of Kath's junk, a badminton racket, a cheap white vase, Christmas wrapping paper. Then he saw his old Sega Master. A copy of Interstellar Cowboy was still stuck in the top, where it must have been for four years. Philip thought about the nasty things he had said to Chris about his computer. Maybe Kath was right. Maybe he should learn to play games again. It was a sort of Zen thing, wasn't it? All it needed was a little application of spirit. He made to lift the console from the shelf when he spotted, hidden in the opposite corner, a brown flex sticking out of an Asda bag.

It was a telephone. Something forgotten, *blocked from his memory.*

A few weeks ago, at work, he had made a call from the empty desk in front of his, then – how to justify this? – he had ripped the phone from its socket and, before anyone came, jammed it into his bag. And why? Simply because he had been put on hold. Crazy. He had meant to get rid of it. Or had he, subconsciously, kept it here as a reminder to himself about how far he could go with that temper of his, that gremlin that got into him more often then he cared to think about? *You're always* . . . Kath came out of the bathroom and he hurriedly closed the door on the cupboard.

'I'll be ready in a minute,' she said.

'OK,' Philip said, pretending to brush something off his shoulder.

Ten minutes later he was driving to the mouth of the estate. The sun was out, bright and bold, the brown fields lapping it up, though the countryside around Dabton village was unremarkable

– provincial territory, Philip thought, a place for scurrying around the edges of things that really mattered, the life that went on elsewhere. Yet was it so bad? Could he not see that the world was a worthy place at heart, this England where there was no war, no real hate, no need to get upset at all?

Kath was wearing her woolly maroon coat, and the black leggings that showed off the bulge and her ballooning arse. Philip liked her better in the navy smock she had bought, and the white tights. They gave her an ill-starred, angelic cast, a look he could make love to.

'Can you stop at the shop?' Kath said, as they entered the village. 'Mum asked if we could bring some milk.'

'No problem.' He pulled up outside the Spar. 'I'll get it.'

'A two-pint carton. Semi-skimmed, if they've got it.'

'Right.'

There were only two other customers in the shop. He went round to the fridge display and picked up one of the cartons with the best sell-by date. But when he got to the check-out, the other two people, a man and a woman, had got there first. The woman had a basket full of things and the old woman serving was taking off her glasses and squinting at a tin of fruit. 'I can't see a price on this. Oh dear, must be free, this one!' She laughed, turning the tin around. 'No, I'll have to go and look.' She shuffled out from behind the till and disappeared into the rows of tinned food.

Philip tapped his thumb on the carton. A few seconds earlier and he could have been served and away. He looked out of the window at Kath. She was fluffing her hair behind her neck. The old woman came back. 'Sorry about that.' She took her seat and Philip relaxed. Progress. Another minute and he would be out of here. Then, when it was the man's turn to be served, the woman picked up the packet of biscuits he was trying to buy, took off her glasses and held it to her nose. 'No, there's nothing on this either.' And she was off again. Philip gave a soft sigh, turning away, turning back. He looked at the man's red neck. Why didn't he say something? Why can't people in this country demand better service? How absurd for them both to be just standing there, looking at a vacated till. The seconds were piling up. How much longer were they going to be? And anyway, why did Tilly have to have the milk? They lived in Tadcaster. It was a town, wasn't it? Weren't the fucking shops open in Tadcaster on fucking Sundays? Did they think Philip had nothing better to do? How could people value his time so cheaply? The milk would have to go back. He couldn't stand it . . .

The woman returned, taking her seat in her rustling nylon overall. 'Dear, dear, we'll have to sort out this pricing business.' At last. Philip could pay and leave. And he had not blown a fuse, nor shown himself up in any way. When the man had gone, Philip put the milk on the counter.

'It looks damaged, this one.'

Philip looked at the carton. It was bent where he had been squeezing it.

'I'll get you another,' said the woman.

'No!'

'It'll only take a second.'

'No,' Philip said, the word floating out on a gasp. 'It'll be fine.'

'Yes, but if there's a hole in it . . .'

There was a trickle of sweat on Philip's forehead. 'Really. There's no hole. I can see. It'll be fine. Honestly.'

The woman seemed to be examining him. 'If you're sure.'

'Yes!' Then, more reasonably, 'I am . . . very sure.' He gave her the pound coin. It was wet from the sweat of his hand.

The woman looked at him over the top of her glasses. 'Are you that young woman's husband?'

'Sorry?'

'The young lady outside in the car.'

'Yes. I am,' Philip said, with no energy to contradict the presumption.

'Well, you are the lucky one.' She took the change from the till.

'Am I?' Philip put his hand out for the money, but she was holding it back.

21

'Yes. Kathy, isn't it? We have some lovely talks when she comes in here.'

'Do you?'

'Oh, yes. And you'll be a father soon . . .'

This could not be happening. It was so *unnecessary*. Another second and he would tell her to keep the change. 'Look, I'm sorry, but I have to go. We're running late.'

'On a Sunday?'

'Yes, on a Sunday. We're meeting someone.'

She gave the laugh of an old bag, laced with spite. 'You young people! Always on the rush!' Philip saw the malice in her rheumy eyes. She was doing this on purpose!

'Look, I really do have to go.'

The woman handed over the change. 'You'll meet yourself coming back! Well, goodbye then. Nice to have met you.'

But Philip did not reply, having already achieved the five yards to the door in three bounding paces.

Once they were out of the village, Kath said, 'I was thinking about getting Dad to take my blood pressure for me. He's got this thing for doing it with. Some sort of monitor. He got it from Boots.'

'Is it still high?' Philip asked, hardly listening, trying to forget the woman in the shop.

'I don't know.'

'Don't they check it at the clinic?'

'Nobody offers. I suppose they would if I asked. I'm just frightened of looking neurotic.'

'You shouldn't be. It's common enough, isn't it? In somebody who's pregnant?'

'Only sometimes. Besides, I don't know if they'd be telling me the truth. You think they'll only tell you what they reckon's good for you, so you don't worry. I hate that, people making these assumptions about you.'

Relaxing now, Philip considered the reasoning behind this. Recently he had developed an idea about the different ways men and women think – male logic being structured, arithmetical, whereas a woman's was emotional, depending on how she felt that day. How much simpler life would be if we all lived by numbers! But he could not say this out loud – it might put him in a poor light, and Philip did not believe he was misogynist, nor sexist, nor anything '-ist' in any way. 'Maybe,' he said, diverting himself from his theory, 'Jeff'll check mine while he's at it.'

'It might be an idea,' Kate said, plainly. 'It couldn't do any harm.'

Philip thought this over for a few seconds. There might actually be something in it, a simple solution, perhaps. He puzzled for a while, trying to find a way of expressing his interest in the condition without it looking like an admission that there might be something wrong with him. 'Actually, they said my blood pressure was high, you know, after the attack.' Kath said nothing. She always went quiet when he mentioned the incident of the assault on him. It annoyed him that she had always been cool about it, ever since the day it happened, a couple of weeks before Christmas. Maybe she suspected it had all been his fault? It was a sore point with Philip, but at least the case was coming to court this Friday and, all being well, she would have to take his side then. For now, he would not press the issue. 'They're personality types, aren't they?'

'Who?'

'People with high blood pressure.'

'Not when they're pregnant, they're not.'

'No, I mean the other sort.' He was aiming for a dig against Jeff. 'They're all pent up.' He chuckled. 'Raging loonies!'

'Dad's not like that. He's always been laid back. Nothing much ever bothers him.' Philip glanced at her. She was moving her head from side to side, in some sort of exercise. Then she opened her eyes, smiling. 'Nothing gets under his skin.'

They were heading for the ring road. Just before the turn-off was a new shopping complex, with the lights of Do It All bright against the evening sky, and a hot-dog stand on the corner. 'Here!' shouted Luke. 'Stop here!'

23

Mick wriggled behind the wheel. 'No.'

'Ah, come on. I'm starvin'. Got to keep me strength up, haven't I?'

Darren turned round. 'Just button it, Luke. We can't stop here. What if someone sees us and remembers us later? Use this, can't you?' he said, tapping his head.

Luke sat forward, leaning on the back of Mick's seat. 'Hungry, aren't I? Can't help it. I'm a growin' lad, me.'

Darren opened his mouth to say something, but Mick spoke first. 'Can't you calm him down?'

'It's not my fault,' said Darren. 'You shouldn't have been so handy with the dope.'

'Well, give him these, if he's so fucking hungry.' He reached into the glove compartment and pulled out a half-packet of mints.

Darren handed them over. 'Here, suck these and shut the fuck up.'

'Mint Imperials? A packet of fucking Mint Imperials?' Luke laughed. He was tempted to throw them out of the window, but instead he tore off the paper and shoved four in his mouth. 'Yummy, yum.' He sat back, bored again. 'Jesus, how much longer are we drivin' about? When are we gonna get to do somethin'?'

'Soon enough.' Mick was rolling his shoulders, as if they had gone stiff. 'Be there in no time,' he said. 'Then we'll have plenty to do.'

Luke sank further down in his seat, chewing slowly, watching the passing streets.

Five

'Hypertension. That's the bugger.'

'That's what they call it, is it?' said Philip.

'It sure is.'

Philip felt like a child, wanting to know some great adult secret. But he liked the sound of this word. Its severity. 'So it's still bothering you then, Jeff . . . this "hypertension"?'

Jeff burped softly. 'Once you get it, you're stuck with it. For life, it seems.'

For ever. A permanent victim. A high-octane personality. Super tense! It said something about you, showed the damage life had done. You were special, with an eye for the failings of the world, a vision beyond contradiction. Philip was quietly thrilled by the idea.

'There's a lot of shit talked about it, though,' said Jeff. 'All this about the obsessive personality, stress and such. It's all bollocks, so far as I can see.'

'You're one of the least stressed people I know,' said Tilly, fiddling with the copper bracelet on her scrawny brown arm. 'If anybody should be stressed out, it's me. You're not a worrier. Life rolls off you like water down a grate. When have you ever grizzled about anything?'

Jeff was sucking his teeth, looking out of the french windows. After a few seconds' silence, Kath began stacking the dishes, an action that annoyed Philip. He wanted to keep the subject of hypertension on the agenda, recklessly thinking to ask Jeff if he thought he might have the same problem. 'D'you take tranquillisers or something, then, Jeff?'

'Do I, shit. Just these beta-blocker things. Snooker players use them. They slow the heart rate or something.' He smiled impishly at the gravy boat. 'Stop you getting a decent hard-on too.'

'You're meant to tell them if you have that problem,' said Kath, leaning heavily on the table to get to her feet. 'I've seen it on the posters in the surgery.'

'Yeah, well . . .'

The two women took the dishes through to the kitchen. Philip felt easier without Kath around. He wanted to ask Jeff about his monitor, or whatever it was, wanting to see it. In his secret intrigue, he was investing the device with the value of a jewel, or something sexually desirable. 'They told me I had high blood pressure,' he said. 'At the hospital.' It sounded lame, but he could think of nothing better.

Jeff shrugged. He was playing with a silver coaster, rolling it from one hand to the other. 'Probably nothing. Probably fuck all. Have you had it checked lately?'

'No. But I get the odd headache.' Philip grinned. 'I had a nose bleed the other day, too.'

Jeff laughed. 'Phil! You're too young, mate! Christ, you kids. You're so glum! It's later when you want to start worrying about this shit. You'll find out, son. For now, you can't do a thing wrong, not when you're young. It's after the age of thirty-five, that's when stuff starts backfiring.'

'How do you mean?' Philip said, sensing a lecture in the making.

'I mean everything. The physical side of things. Your treacherous body. And the rest. Shit, especially the rest. After the age of thirty-five,' he said, pointing the coaster at Philip, 'everything you do is a mistake, d'you know that? Every decision is the wrong decision. You can't get a fucking thing right. And how old are you?'

'Twenty-six in a couple of months.'

'Exactly! You've still got the cradle marks on your arse. Live it up! Expect to die before you get old. It's the best way.'

Philip felt like asking him how he was meant to do that when he was about to spend the rest of his life supporting Jeff's daughter and her baby. But it was unsayable. Philip folded his arms, looking beyond Jeff at the rows of books on the shelves behind his head. The blood-pressure thing had somehow strayed out of their conversation.

These visits were always the same, always ending with some sheathed humiliation he had to endure from either Jeff or Tilly. When he had first met them, Philip was twenty-one, and it pleased him that an adult relationship, particularly with Jeff, might be on the cards. For a while, he felt as if he might get on with these two better than his own parents. But time revealed a constant edge of opprobrium on their part, never quite stated, but always there. Philip also sensed a tacit comparison between himself and Kath's previous boyfriends, particularly the last, Alan, a teacher ten years older than him. He would have been better for Kath, knowing children, and probably all the rules for hanging a roll of fucking anaglypta . . . Sometimes, maliciously, Philip wondered if there was some sexual resentment at the bottom of Jeff's animosity towards him, the older man envious of his youth, of the hold Philip had on his daughter. One day, Philip feared, this was something he might blurt out. And that would be that.

The talk had left Philip deflated. As it was meant to, he suspected. Jeff was sitting back, hands behind his head, rubbing his chin on the open collar of his checked shirt. He was a small man and, in truth, he had a kindly face, with a hesitancy about the smile, the crescents of sweat on his glasses suggesting a world-weariness. But his voice – dusty, with a salesman's drawl – gave the lie to any real warmth. Philip was about to move when Jeff shifted forward, leaning on his elbows. 'When's the court case?'

'This Friday.'

'What's the lad's name again?'

'Stall. Carl Stall. He's Leeds. Richmond Hill, or round there somewhere.' Philip knew exactly where his assailant lived, but there was a certain pleasure in keeping back the precise details.

Jeff picked a tiny thread of beef fat from the corner of his mouth and looked at it. Then he leaned to his side and farted – a little squirt, Philip thought, that becomes the man. 'Bet you could think of a few things you'd like to do to him, eh? A good kick in the balls.' He laughed. 'Wouldn't that be good for the blood pressure?'

He was taking the piss. Philip said nothing.

'Come on,' said Jeff, standing. But when Philip did not move, Jeff came round the table and put his arm across his shoulders, leaning on him, his breath smelling of wine and gravy. 'Don't worry so much, mate! Life's too bastard short!' He patted Philip's chest. 'All right, Phil mate?'

A new wave of anxiety came over Darren, a cold burning in the stomach. It would have been better if he and Luke had not had that drink first. Darren couldn't drink much without wanting to throw up. Stupid mistake. Yet Luke had insisted. To him, this was just a lark, like when they used to rip off the shops in town. But it wasn't like that, nowhere near. It was on a scale light years away from that shit. And you needed to be sharp, he knew, though how he knew was a matter of mere instinct. Stuff he had seen on the telly, that was the sum of his knowledge, when it came down to it. He tried not to think about this, considering their agenda, some of which he and Mick had agreed to keep from Luke, in case he went loony on them.

It should all be over by midnight, that was the idea. But it was wrong to think about that. Too relaxed and he might freeze and let everyone down. Minute to minute. Think that way, get the nerves hard as steel. This part of the job first, and then . . .

In the bathroom, Philip lamely sought some sense of himself. He peed, washed his hands, and looked tiredly at the knitted woollen lady on the spare toilet roll, the olive tiling round the bath, the fern plants and umbrella lampshade. It was all being offered against him, the apparatus of Kath's parents' house, a real home, something he could not contrive if he worked at their place for the next five years. He cupped his hands over his nose and mouth, smelling the soap. Imperial Leather. Nothing fancy

28

about that. Except here it *was* special, part of a preserve he could never emulate, true domestic cleanliness. But, what the fuck. Who cared, really?

He went back downstairs, one deliberate step at a time, stopping at the bottom. They were visible through the open lounge door, all three having a smoke. Jeff had his blood-pressure monitor out. He was fiddling with the Velcro cuff, wrapping it round Kath's arm. When he saw Philip he grinned and called out, 'You next, eh, Phil? When we've seen to the serious cases?'

Philip kept moving, along the hall and out into the garden where he pretended to be looking at the scraggy plants, wondering, in bewilderment, how long it would be before they had finished.

They moved off the ring road and by some rough ground. A billboard, advertising the new Rover Series, was standing alone against the ribbony twilight. The change of direction alerted Darren. They were getting to the heart of things. His head ached a little, and he was breathing fast, through his mouth. Luke had said nothing for the past fifteen minutes. Perhaps he had fallen asleep or, more likely, he was faking it. Darren could not bring himself to look round, not now they were getting down to business. He did not feel as if he could do anything. He risked a glance at Mick, hoping for reassurance. But instead of the serious face he expected to see, the guy was grinning. Like a nut! It was all an adventure to him!

Maybe it wasn't too late to say he couldn't go through with this. Be chicken. What did it matter, really? Then Mick turned, the grin softening to a smile. Almost kind. 'All right there, Daz?'

'Yeah. I'm all right.'

'It's gonna be good. It'll be cool. Right?'

'Yeah. We'll be right.'

But Darren still wanted to back down.

'Fancy some sex?' said Philip. 'And I want you to know I mean that in a caring way.' Kath smiled, faintly. 'OK, OK. Just thought I'd ask.' Then he added, spreading his arms wide, 'I'm only inhuman, after all!' He let his arms flop back to his sides. 'Ah well . . . What about the pub, then? The last hour? I do feel I've earned it.'

Kath was sitting on the edge of the armchair, looking at the warming gas fire. 'I'm a bit hungry, to be honest.'

'What, after that big meal Tilly made?'

'Yes. Sorry.'

Philip joined her in staring at the fire, frowning deliberately, thinking to ask her if there was a subliminal message in the flames. Then he looked away. It had been a mistake to put the fire on, to let her get cosy. He should have mentioned the pub on the way home. Yet why should he have to? Once she would have suggested it herself, not so long ago. He looked down at her. The size she was becoming, mammalian, a creature of the sea, the slime of creation. She did not return his look, in fact he could not remember their eyes meeting all day. He sat down on the worn Dralon sofa, a cast-off from her parents whose presence he could feel again, warming his buttocks. He pondered putting the television on, wishing he had bought a Sunday paper.

'By the way,' said Kath. 'Mum mentioned the soap.'

'The what?'

She was actually looking at him, a hint of collusion in her eyes. For a moment this looked hopeful, a chance yet for some untrammelled intimacy. 'The soap in the bathroom.'

'Imperial Leather,' Philip said, mockingly.

'Yes. She reckons you're supposed to put it label-down, so it doesn't move around. One of us left it the other way up. There was soap slime all over the washbasin.' She smiled weakly. 'Sorry. I shouldn't have mentioned it.'

'No, no. Mention away,' said Philip. 'Half the world's starving, the planet's dropping to pieces, we've a spiritual and cultural vacuum like there's never been before, but what does that count against the fucking soap in your mother's fucking washbasin?' It was far more aggressive than he had meant. He had moved towards her while he spoke, finding himself looking down at the top of her head.

'There's no need for that.'

'No need for what?'

'Going on like that. All that bad language.'

'Like fuck there isn't.' Suddenly there was more and more, set lines of pure petulance, aching for delivery. It had been ages since they'd had a proper row. Maybe it would do them good. But Kath had gone pale. She got to her feet with that elephantine rowing motion, newly discovered for the mobilisation of her bulk.

'I'm going to bed.'

A minute later, Philip was pacing the room with his sharp unanswered mood. He might yet go to the White Ox in the village. It would mean going alone, for the first time, but he could see those days were coming anyway. He bided his time with the idea, until it was too late. He sat down, listening to Kath in the bathroom, washing, snapping the plastic tops on her bottles of cleanser, or pineapple fucking hand cream. And he thought how much happier life would be if she was not with him, if all his obligations towards her were to cease. If she was to leave him or, somehow, simply vanish from his life.

Six

After a night plagued with indigestion and dreary unfathomable dreams, Philip woke to find Kath with her back to him. She was way across the bed, almost falling off the edge. He was sure she was awake, but he could not be bothered speaking to her. He got up and went to the bathroom.

Ten minutes later, on his way out of the house, he looked in the mirror in the hallway. The stubble on his chin was two days old and pleasingly thick. He rubbed his hand over it, then stood back to consider his overall appearance. He was getting heavy yet, for some reason, it did not worry him right at this moment. Rather, it enhanced his chosen careless air, like his tie with the crease across the middle, the grubbiness of his grey suit, and the cheap black shoes that had not been polished since he bought them. It was the way he liked it, a wanton scruffiness added to by the old rucksack he used in defiance of the case-carrying conventions of his colleagues. And this Monday morning, like all the other mornings, his sole concession to neatness was to pass a comb once through his hair.

Driving towards Leeds, minutes later, he could see, beyond the horizon of flats and church spires, a sharp blue winter sky. Every day he looked at the state of the sky. And when he saw it, and considered its infinity, Philip was hard put to see why he got upset about anything. God, that party on Saturday night! And all those little niggles yesterday. Why bother? Here we all were, on this fragile biosphere, in a vast empty universe, completely alone, for all anyone knew. This nothingness was the extent of it, a great big total silence. And in the end we all died anyway. So why not love each other while we are here? Make things that much easier?

Right, today he would be well-behaved. A nice person. And tonight he would make it up to Kath. One day of self-control, out of all the thousands of days in a lifetime. He could manage that, couldn't he? He joined the slowed lines of traffic heading into the city. Nothing to worry him here. No one to get his goat. Think of eternal things. Be spiritual. Then a red Volvo shot out of the next lane, causing him to brake.

And it happened. The whole can of worms opened to the skies, the tiny stigmata in his soul that, tickled by a word, a look, flared up into a body-shaped ball of flame. Once again the world was lining up for its piece of him, the old fever, more familiar and caustic every time, rising through the stage floor as he bore down on the Volvo, inches off its tail. *The shit!* All the predicaments of his life had been instantly pointed up, in all their fetid glory, a chip on his shoulder the size of an anvil, hoisted there by the insult of this man taking his space.

The traffic was speeding up, gaps appearing at the roundabout ahead. Philip was sitting forward, his forehead a heat-seeking missile, teeth clenched so hard the roots were burning. *You've no fucking right!* The driver was looking in his mirror, brake lights flashing. He was middle-aged, one of that grasping generation, like Jeff, who trashed the needs of young men such as Philip, blocking the doorway for them in any way possible. They should not be *allowed to breed!* At the roundabout, the Volvo indicated left. He was going to get away with it! Philip trained the nose of his car on the bumper, making the man speed off the roundabout. Then a white Toledo was trying to inch out in front of Philip. No way. *No way!* He accelerated madly, swinging across the lane, the back of his car skidding. *Showing the bastard his arse!* The Toledo stalled, and in his swerve Philip caught it with his rear bumper, feeling a crisp jolt along the frame of the car. Once he was off the roundabout, Philip had to stop at the end of the next queue of traffic. He glanced in his mirror, then looked back. The Toledo was skewed on the roundabout, its driver, an old man, shaking his head, his hands over his eyes. *You were in the wrong! Silly old fucker! That's what you get for*

33

being a fucking old nuisance, a drain on social resources! The knock, its physical contact, had brought a fresh anger, flaring to the borders of psychosis.

Now he was really mad.

Through Gipton, to the next set of lights, he was a fuming cocoon, wanting to burst ahead, crazed over the way everyone just queued there, without question for the stupidity of this way of organising traffic. Didn't these people have any original thoughts? Didn't they have a life? His car was a smouldering shell of indignation. The traffic moved, Philip lurching forward, inch by inch. The horn! Go for it! He pressed twice, hard. A rough-looking woman drew level in a hire van, gesturing to him, screwing her finger into the side of her head, and pointing back along the road. Philip gave her a knuckle in reply. Behind him, a man was flashing his lights. Someone else *raping his soul!* In front of him was an estate car with an absurd decoration of high tail-lights. The back of it seemed an extension of the driver's head, like the large rear cranium of a pre-pubescent boy. Philip's arms were locked on the steering wheel, the rigidity held along the line of his body, screaming to be released on to the accelerator, to fire the bullet of his car into the guts of the world. One second, that's all it would take to blast into this trash, to make the planet a mash of metal and glass. No more than it deserved. Kill. That was the idea. And why not? *It was owed to him.* To his side, the woman was still waving. Fuck her! Make them all die! *That would show them.*

The lights changed and he was away again. Now the frenzy matured into something more cerebral, spiralling from vaguely remembered embarrassments, those little degradations life had afforded Philip, like the time he was hauled up in front of the class at school for flicking ink on the ceiling, or the rejection of his advances to a girl, ten years ago, or, that latest thing, Kate's mother and the soap. The fucking Imperial Leather! Downing him! Everyone *on his case!* And in a new twist against these losses of face, he summoned a litany of moral indignations about the state of the world, the homeless, the sick, the victimised.

These were the things that really *mattered!* Philip cared about these people! He had qualities that no one ever recognised! No wonder he felt the way he did. God, if he could only get his own back, just once, perhaps one day be the man who finds an intruder on his property, someone on whom he could inflict a limitless, legitimate violence, beating him to a pulp. He would be a saint! Everyone's hero! That would show Tilly and her fucking *Imperial Leather!*

He made it through town to the multi-storey, without killing anyone, or himself, or putting into action any of the ideas that railed and fizzed about the spaces of the morning. But he was still mad.

As hell.

On the fifth floor of the car-park, the area leased by his company, he found his usual spot. If anyone else had been there he would have shunted them through the rails to the square below. Nothing was more certain. But he did not. Instead, he took his rucksack, disdained the coat on the back seat, locked the car and clattered down the stairs. Crossing the square with all the hundreds of other workers, he banged his heels down. His throat was dry, his sinuses sore, his shirt wet with sweat. *Someone will have to pay for this.* But the fury had a more settled quality, with a hint at the peripheries of the contrition to come. It was the slower, grimmer phase, the downside when his imagined shrieking turned to mere grumbles, a muttering he might actually make to people about the grief the world inspired in him.

At the sandstone and tinted-glass building where he worked, Philip filed up the steps with his quiet colleagues, walking briskly past Security to the claustrophobia of the lift. The bodies crammed in beside him. Then Howard, Philip's supervisor, was rushing for the doors. They closed before he could get inside. A point scored. It should have soothed Philip. He ought to have been able to share in the giggles of the two girls in front of him. But in the now limping, bizarrely selective nature of his condition, he sided with his supervisor against the women. There should be *respect* here. How else could the firm function?

On the third floor, in the pink-walled vestibule, beneath the tacky heraldic company emblem, Philip signed the 'arrivals' book and went into the big open office to his desk. The sweat had dried on his face, making the skin tight. He was standing by the cubicle, feeling a little dizzy, when Howard came in.

'Morning, Phil,' Howard said, barely breathless from his climb up the stairs.

That bald head of his, the whiff of deodorant. Philip felt a flutter of contempt, but he was too tired for it all now. 'Howard.' It was the first word he had actually spoken that day, and it came out in a whisper. He dumped his bag behind his chair, sat down, put his key in the computer, and entered this week's password – Serenity.

And that was Philip. Ready for work.

Seven

Elvis came on the radio singing 'Blue Suede Shoes'. The sound depressed Luke. His father had been an Elvis nut, Brylcreeming his hair into a duck's arse and wearing a long purple velvet-collar jacket on a weekend. The cunt probably thought he was Elvis. And what did he look like with those front teeth missing! Maybe if he'd spent a bit more time being himself, seeing to the family and the like . . . Luke tensed the muscles in his arms. Yeah, what had the old get ever done for him and his sisters? One day out, that's all he could remember, when Luke was small, a real nipper, and the old bastard took him fishing . . .

They went up on the river above Leeds where, his father said, the water wasn't so full of shit. He had borrowed the tackle from a mate of his up the pub, payment for some stupid bet about football. Fishing, he said, was what he used to do with his father. They used to do it all the time, every weekend, which made Luke wonder why *they* didn't do it all the time. Was it his fault? 'It's not a competition,' the old man said, but from his beery toothless grin you could see that it was.

It was a hot day and neither of them was catching a thing, though Luke was loving it, the surprising lightness of the rod in his small hands, the whirr of the reel, that satisfying click of the bail arm. 'There's nowt in 'ere,' his father said, fed up. 'Water's shagged. Didn't used to be like this.' But Luke did not want to go. It didn't matter that there were no fish. He could have stayed on all night, casting and rewinding, his feet at the water's edge. Then his float bobbed, sank, and the line pulled hard.

'Got one! Got one!'

His father came across, laughing, telling him to take it easy or he would lose it. Luke reeled and reeled. The fish splashed silver on the surface. It was coming. The pull and jangle on the line had a sense of urgency that made his heart race. It was like nothing he had ever felt before. His father picked up the landing net, waded in and scooped up the fish. It was a fat old perch with a big spiny fin on top. His father whooped. 'Hey, matey! Look at that! Must be two pounds! A specimen!' he said, hugging him. Luke was almost sick with pride . . .

When 'Blue Suede Shoes' had finished, Luke felt his mood lift. He didn't want to think about his father. It was a downer. Besides he hadn't seen the bastard since fuck knew when. Missing for years. Gone when Luke's mother couldn't stand any more of him pissing it up, arguing, taking it out on her when Luke had grown too big to be picked on.

He thought about asking Mick for more dope, wondering how he could do it without making him annoyed. But both he and Darren were super-quiet now and Luke daren't ask. It just could not be done.

Mick was keeping to the quieter streets, cruising, staying out of people's way. Then he seemed to be looking for somewhere in particular, watching the street names until he found the road he wanted, in the middle of a knot of dark sidestreets.

It seemed like they had been riding around for hours and Luke could only guess roughly where they were – still Leeds, but strange territory that made him feel cold. He wished *he* could drive. He resented the power it gave Mick over him and Darren. It meant they had to trust him, and Luke did not care for trusting anyone.

At the end of an alley, Mick pulled up and got out of the car, muttering to Darren about clueing Luke in on what they were meant to be doing, and telling him to watch for anyone taking too much interest in the motor. He closed the door softly and disappeared round the first corner.

'Where's he gone?'

'To get some fresh transport.' Darren turned round in his seat. 'Look, Luke, you can still get out if you want to.'

'No way!' said Luke. 'I'm in on it, aren't I? That's what I said.'

'Well, it's not a bloody game. You're gonna have to have your wits about you.'

'I'm all right, mate. Top notch,' he said, not caring for Darren giving him advice, nor for the way everyone had him as the greenhorn round here, though for all that there was a lonely feeling in his skin. 'What am I supposed to do again? I've forgotten half you said.'

Darren, his oldest pal, blew out heavily then scrabbled under his seat. He pulled out a cloth bag, and peeled the top back like an ice-lolly wrapper. 'We use these.' Luke leaned forward and saw the barrel of a sawn-off shotgun, with a pistol resting on top.

'Wha-at?' Luke laughed nervously. 'Fuck me!'

'Get serious, Luke, or you're not comin'.'

'I know, but guns? Jesus, I thought we were just gonna act rough with this guy then get him to open his fuckin' shop for us. Fuck's sake, you didn't mention guns!'

'They'll do the talkin' for us. We get taken seriously with these.'

'Jesus. Jeez-us shit!' He slammed back into his seat. 'Shit, Daz, what've you been gettin' up to with this fucker?'

'He's a mate. I know him off the site. Just trust him. Do as he says. It'll be worth it. Honest.' There was a note of innocence in his voice.

Luke whistled softly. 'All right, all right. But Jeez . . .' He shook his head. 'Let's 'ave a look then.' He sat forward and made to get hold of the pistol.

Darren snatched the bag away. 'Hands off, stupid!'

Luke jerked his hand away. 'Shit, are they fuckin' loaded?'

'Course they are.' Darren was looking down at the protruding barrels, fondly, in a way that made Luke see him in a new light. They had come a long way since the days when they used to jump school together, when they would hang around town all day, thieving chocolate bars, one of them keeping the assistant occupied while the other filled his pockets. When Darren had found a place on a youth scheme on a building site, where he had got to know this Mick, Luke had thought that would be the end of all that. But the site had gone bust and they began their drifting again. It pleased Luke for a while, though there was something sour about it, being older, their lives open-ended. Heading nowhere. Maybe a night like this always on the cards, somewhere along the line. Still, what else could you do?

Darren pulled on a glove and lifted up the pistol. 'This'll be yours. Look, there's the safety catch. You keep it on all the time. Right?'

'Hey, sure, mate.' Luke shuffled further forward, wanting to get hold of the thing, try it for weight.

'But we don't use them,' Darren said, softly. 'Not unless it gets dire.'

'Steady away, Daz. Steady away.' Luke was itching to pick up the gun. A sense of adventure was replacing his dropping mood. Maybe this would be all right, a new high. He laughed. 'Christ! Armed and dangerous! That's us!' Then Darren lurched over the back of the seat and grabbed the shoulder of his jacket.

'I told you what it was! You knew, Luke! You knew!'

Luke looked at him, the film of sweat on his pale brown face, the glaring eyes. 'Most of it. Not everythin'.' But he could not counter Darren's agitation. Luke could see he didn't really want to do this. He was shit scared, underneath. Luke pulled his hand away. There was something about Darren in this moment, some fuck-awful loneliness Luke had not noticed before, not even at those times at school or in the street, when Darren used to get baited for being a half-caste. Nothing odd about that – Luke would probably have said the same things, if they had not been mates. That's the way it was. But, with a sobering insight, Luke suddenly pitied him. A soft feeling, quite grown-up.

' 'Ave you done this before?' Luke asked. Darren didn't answer. 'You 'ave, haven't you?'

His friend turned his head away. Looking down the quiet street. 'No.'

'Well, what about your mate? What's he done before?'

'Enough. Mick knows his stuff.'

'Yeah. Bet he's been down for it an' all.'

'You don't think like that.'

'Like fuck.'

The sound of a car alerted them both, headlights appearing at the end of the road, dipping twice.

Darren closed up the bag and opened the door. 'Come on. We're off.'

Luke sat back, hesitating. Then Darren was outside, tapping on the window. 'Lukey! We're away!' he hissed. 'Now!'

Luke tutted and got out of the car.

Eight

Philip did not *work* for Pilot Insurance, he *achieved attendance*. It was a distinction he liked to make. In reality, he was one of the company's three deputy underwriters in Life and Deaths, a department he had joined for the appeal of its title: his work was a matter of . . . Thus his career aspirations, resting on a joke.

Pilot was a regional arm of a Midlands-based firm with a speciality for the provision of favourable, that is dangerously cheap, life-insurance premiums for company employees and the self-employed. The legal department had, several years ago, devised a dubious tax loophole on which the bulk of their business depended. Philip had never cared to understand this fully, choosing naivety over a knowledge he thought would only add to his misgivings about the work. Insurance was a piss-dull subject anyway. And it had irked him to discover that people demanded so many safeguards in their lives. Were you born with an insurance policy? Why not just take a risk on the way things turned out? Be daring. Trust to Fate. Such were his ruminations, sometimes on a minute-to-minute basis.

Taking the job had been a matter of forgotten imperative. Working, because everyone else was? The done thing? What had been the hurry? There had been five sleepy months on the dole when he had graduated from Manchester University (with his degree in Social Policy and Administration – something else chosen for a laugh: the most useless subject he could imagine). And after that, he had not, in his heart, wanted a career or anything which might ensnare him. He had no wish for a future, knowing only what he did not want, namely a yawningly predictable life like his contemporaries. Like Chris and Sheena, for an instance.

At the time he had been living with Kath in a flat in Cross Gates.

She was out all day, working in a toy shop in Thornton's Arcade while he idled the days away, watching the telly, sleeping, ambling to the pub at a respectable hour. A great summer, he seemed to remember. So why had he given it up? Because it looked bad? *Was that all?* Kath had never objected to his indolent ways, yet maybe it was this silence that made him uncomfortable? Or was it simply because there was *nothing else* to do?

It felt wrong from the start – the suit, the daily trail through the traffic to work. At first he took to meeting Kath for lunch in a café near the toy shop. He used to put his bag on the same chair every day. It seemed the way to behave. But the obvious was not what Philip really wanted, and after a few weeks he began avoiding Kath in the city centre. Yet he still fell for all the traps. They found the house within two months of his starting work, arranging a mortgage with Pilot which was dependent on his remaining with the firm. Another thread that bound him. Like Gulliver. But who devised these rules? What law was there that told you this is what you must do to be happy? Whose hand was on his balls, squeezing and pulling?

Whose? Who, the fuck . . . ?

By ten the ferment had lost its ravishing control. Philip was a lamb now, working diligently. And alone, people seeming to sense when he was not to be approached, Philip with one eye on that square yard of open blue carpet he maintained between him and the aisle by pushing his chair close to the partition of his cubicle. It was his private space, an invisible fuck-off barrier between him and the rest of the office.

He was hunched over his terminal. All around him, between the rings of the fax machine, the polite telephone interventions, the girls and young men were chattering about their weekend and the cheerful trivialities that seemed to concern them constantly. 'It's Monday. It's got to be a King-Size Snickers.' 'He's got this rash on his scalp.' 'We were looking at fridges. I said . . .' Yet, for once, Philip was able to ignore it all, the energy of his irritation burned out in that secret angry start to the day.

For over an hour he dealt with requests from brokers, working out and sending quotes for premiums based on four times an employee's salary, rather than the usual three. It was a new initiative from Pilot Head Office, another gamble to beat off the opposition. But what the hell, it was hardly Philip's money, was it? When he was clear of the new requests, he turned his attention to the Griffiths account, potentially the most awkward claim that had ever come his way. The man was a Bradford garage owner whose secretary, also his wife, had died in circumstances that had suicide neon-emblazoned all over it. Challenging the claim would be a test for Philip, and if he could get a result in Pilot's favour it may even, incredibly, add to his stock within the firm. 'I told her, if I didn't get a full refund I was going to the Citizens' Advice.' 'Did you watch . . .' Philip lifted the file from the stack of green folders on the floor behind his chair.

It was an associate policy, less than two years old. On Christmas Eve the woman had been found unconscious from an apparent overdose. She had been taken to hospital, appeared to come round, then died two days later. Last week there was a tiny local newspaper report, found by Howard, in which the coroner had returned an open verdict, stating that the finding of suicide might carry an unnecessary stigma for her and her family. This was despite the mention of a history of depression which, crucially, had not been offered by Griffiths when he took out the policy. Suicide could only count in a group scheme, not an individual plan. Taking your own life was not *personal*, at least not as far as Pilot were concerned.

Philip sat back, chewing on his pen. According to the company's own terms, they were meant to pay up within forty-eight hours of a claim, but that was merely something written on paper – it did not mean they actually had to *do* anything. Furthermore, since the coroner's report had yet to arrive at Pilot, there was plenty of scope for a delay. Certainly, a challenge looked more than possible. He read everything, making notes, considering the first line of rebuttal, namely a letter he would draft carefully, keeping within the boundaries of the law. He set to work, all of this revealing a part of him seen only in function – and something he would never have owned up to – his competency.

By twelve he had the letter and all the other bits and pieces in place, ready for the afternoon when he would get the thing moving. Quietly pleased with his morning's work, at least as pleased as he ever was with anything he did for Pilot, he took his bag and left the office to stand in line at the drinks machine in the corridor.

No one at the firm ever wanted to be seen taking lunch with relish, but that never bothered Philip. He was hungry, and he had earned a break. He pressed for hot chocolate and went to the rest room. Tom, one of the other deputy underwriters, was the only other person there. He was standing by the window, talking on his mobile phone to a girlfriend. Philip ignored him and picked his way, among the low-backed sofas 'artfully' clustered round the room, to a place in the corner. He sat down and peeled the clingfilm from the sandwiches he had made himself, in one minute flat, that morning. Crunchy peanut butter. And two Penguins. Kids' food. No wonder he was getting fat. He ate, leafing through an old *Woman's Own*, wondering if he might find anything about high blood pressure. Only when other people began wandering in did it dawn on Philip that he had not spoken to anyone in the office, save for his grunt to Howard, all morning. It put him in a certain light, he knew, but what the fuck. Then one of his Life and Deaths colleagues sat down opposite.

It was Sarah.

There had been a long sore silence between Philip and this girl, ever since the Christmas piss-up when he had misread all the signs she appeared to be making and made a lunge for her. *Across the punch bowl!* And at the moment, of course, when the music and all the talk had suddenly stopped. She had avoided him carefully since, leaving Philip to suffer a quiet anguish over his disastrously revealed feelings. Now she was sitting opposite him, when she could have sat *anywhere*! Philip squirmed with the *Woman's Own* in his lap.

'Hi, Phil.'

Hi, Phil! It took his breath a little. How to act? 'Hi, Sarah.' Casual enough. It would have to do.

'You busy?'

'Yeah. Plus some.' He risked a look at her. She was wearing a cream ribbon-knitted top, a flowery wrap-around skirt that sat just-so on her soft hips, and black Nu-Buck shoes with red tags on the laces. She was twenty-two, with long blonde hair and a roundish face, a bit flat, though Philip had to admit she was everything Kath was not right now – young, with a desirability that made him feel bulky, scruffily male. Then he saw that she was smiling at him.

'You're looking well, anyway, Phil.'

'Yes, I'm sound. Tip-top.'

'Good. Glad to hear it.'

He could hardly believe it. She was wanting to make up, to put that sorry little incident behind them! How to capitalise on this? His mind ran through a selection of small-talk comments about work, something on television, the price of property, the weather, the fucking weather, anything to shore up this healing of the rift between them. Think of something! But as he was about to speak Hamid, from General Business, the other department on the third floor, came and sat down next to her.

Sarah sat up a little. 'Hiya, Hammy.'

'Sar-ah!'

Philip watched resentfully as Hamid unscrewed the top from the huge vacuum flask he carried, unselfconsciously, everywhere. Then he was looking at Philip. 'Did I see you this morning, Phil?'

'See me where?'

'Don't you come in along the York Road?'

'Sometimes.' He bit into his sandwich, watching Sarah peel an orange.

Hamid poured a vomit-like soup into his cup, catching a dribble and licking his finger. 'At the Gipton roundabout,' he said, his finger hooked in his mouth. 'I'm sure it was you.'

Philip turned a page of the *Woman's Own*. 'It might have been me.'

'Didn't you clip someone?'

'Not that I remember.'

'You did!' Hamid had lifted the cup to his lips, but he was smiling. 'A guy in a white car! Come on, you must remember.'

Philip felt his cheeks burning. 'Oh, that. It was nothing. The guy didn't know where he was going. Half-asleep, some people, specially at that time of day.'

'God, Phil, you want to watch it, driving like that. And you're not far from the cop shop there. The pigs are all over the place, that time of day. That guy pulled over, you know.'

'He was in the wrong,' Philip said, struggling to appear calm. 'Everyone's the same, trying to get to work.' Sarah crossed her legs, Hamid looking at them. 'Don't tell me,' Philip said, mad for his attention, for the chance to rationalise, 'you don't step on it a bit, if you have to.'

'Hardly pissing likely!' Hamid said, laughing. 'I don't drive! I was standing at the bus stop!'

'You wouldn't know what it was like, then.' The mention of the old man had struck deep, reminding Philip of the mood he had been in that morning. He had been seen! And now Sarah, of all people, knew about it too.

He hated Hamid. He hated his slimness, his good looks, and especially the way he was now chattering to Sarah, making her laugh.

After two hours of dealing with piddling queries and requests for quotes he knew would never go any further, Philip decided, with a sense of luxury, to put off the Griffiths thing until the next day. He was tired, and he kept looking at Sarah, whose desk was at the head of the far open row, next to the windows.

A block of bright sunlight was shining between the pulled vertical blinds. Sarah was cooing at a pigeon outside on the windowsill, and when she turned on her seat, Philip could see the bold roundness of her calves. She had offered to make

47

things up between them, and now she was breaking his heart. He wanted to be close enough to her to feel the heat of her bare arm against his skin. She stretched, a tease, her breasts flat on her chest, resuming their fullness as she brought her arms down in two affected movements. Such femininity, with a touch of the predatory nature he was beginning to find a turn-on in young women, something, now he was older, he could be equal to. Why couldn't Kath be like that? Why did she have to be so – and he hated the word – mumsy? Sarah was not drowning in hormones. She was clear-headed, knowing exactly what she wanted – success, money, sex. Life's tangibles. Why bother with anything else?

The telephones rang, the chatter rattling on. Howard was doing his rounds, making his way up the aisle from the back of the office. Philip could not make any pretence of activity. It was not in him to sham anything. What you see is what you get, he once said to Howard. And, to his surprise, the supervisor had seemed oddly pleased by the comment. A few minutes later, he had reached Philip's desk.

'What's the score with our friend Griffiths, Phil?'

'It'll be sorted,' said Philip, drumming his fingers on the Quality Street tin where he kept his pens.

'We could do with a result this week.'

'I know, Howard. I'll be on to it.'

Howard leaned on the desk. He was in his late thirties, prematurely bald with black crow's-wing eyebrows, and a dent across his nose. But a handsome bastard, and very corporate, known to read the *British Medical Journal* in his spare time to try and understand more about health risks and how they might be taken into account in forming insurance policies. The twat. He put one highly polished black shoe in the sacred square of blue carpet. 'Are you OK, Philip?'

'Yes. Why, shouldn't I be?'

'Oh, nothing much, mate. It's just that someone saw you driving into the car-park this morning.' He was grinning, something Philip could sense. 'Doing sixty, by all accounts.'

'Ah, Jesus. Hamid?'

'No. Louise. From downstairs.'

Philip looked at Howard's hand on the desk, the clear step-cut stone in his wedding ring, the white shirt-cuff. 'Howard, I don't think that pile of shite I jokingly call a car is capable of doing sixty. I was a bit late, that's all. I'd been hurrying since I left home. All right?'

'Hey sure.' Howard lifted his hand from the desk. 'Just thought I'd mention it.' He came closer, drowning Philip with his cologne. 'By the way, Phil, isn't the court case coming up soon?'

'Friday. I'll have the Griffiths thing sorted by then.'

'I wasn't thinking about that. Look,' he said, more quietly, at Philip's shoulder now, 'if you want to take the time on the firm, just go. It'll be OK.'

'Thanks, Howard. It's appreciated.'

'That's all right, Philip. And you know, if you have any other problems, you can always talk to me.'

Philip grinned, staring at the Quality Street lady. 'That's comforting, Howard. It really is.'

'That's all right, mate,' said Howard. And he moved away.

At five-thirty – thank all the angels in heaven – the day was over. A moment gratifying by legend! Maybe it was worth all the hassle just for this sensation of release: if there was nothing to escape from, he could never know this pleasure. There was a profundity in this idea, but Philip could not be bothered trying to work out what it might be. He walked down the stairs, his back aching, his feet sweaty, and in Reception he swung his bag on his shoulder, buttoned his jacket then, almost smiling, scenting the delicious cold air of the outdoors and freedom, he descended the steps between the chrome rails, the six steps to the pavement. Where he stopped abruptly, his eyes taking in a figure across the road, a shape too familiar to be true.

Here? On his own territory?

Nine

The car belonged to a woman, something Luke could tell from the smell, all perfumy, and the box of tissues between the front seats, the big sunglasses on the dashboard. Some rich bird. Or a tart maybe. Evidence like this, of someone better off than him, always gave Luke a bit of an attitude. It was the unfairness of it, the way people just had things and didn't give a fuck about anyone else. Still, tonight might even things up a bit. Nothing wrong with that. Nothing at all.

They had assumed the same seating arrangements as before. Luke had not liked being in the back, but now they were getting close to what they were meant to be doing, he did not think about it. He was wearing gloves, like they all were, and sitting in the middle of the seat, leaning forward, wary of touching the upholstery or leaving any tiny trace that might be linked to him later. His stomach, which had been empty and a bit pukey, was no longer of concern. And his misery over the declining effects of the dope had gone, replaced by a new alertness, an almost childish curiosity for the events ahead. ' 'Ow far now?' he asked, wriggling up to the very edge of the seat.

'Another ten minutes,' said Mick. 'Are you all right then, Luke?'

'Yeah, fine, fine.'

'Daz?'

Darren was looking to his side, out of the window. He turned and nodded.

'Well, keep it like that. Keep your wits about you. You're gonna need 'em.'

Luke alternated between looking at the road ahead and at the back of Mick's head. He was trying to think of something wise to say. He liked Mick now. But nothing came. Silence, it seemed, was the bull's bollocks. For now.

It was a presence greater than its constituent parts. The hair was combed across, a straw cap untouched by the breeze. He was a greaseball, though it did not detract from his self-possession, neither that nor his smallness. What was he? Five foot seven? An intimidating compactness, with that gypsy weathering of the cheeks – someone who knew the elements, and disregarded them. Shit, what a moment. And where had everyone gone? Where was the usual flood of bodies emptying from Pilot, from the solicitor's office next door, people Philip now thought of as allies, whose company he craved? Some friends. Never around when you want them. He watched as the young man crossed the weirdly empty road to the side where Philip was standing. He was flaunting his freedom, here on Philip's patch, a territory marked out in his mind. Had he no reserve?

As he reached the pavement, ten feet on from Philip, he glanced across. And looked again. Had he recognised the tall shape? Philip's soft stomach? His assailability? The city seemed reduced to the dimensions of a village. Philip hunched the rucksack higher up his shoulder, a vaguely defensive gesture. But he could not begin to move away from the steps. So much happening in the space of a few seconds, trashing his peace of mind, that hard-won thing.

Five foot seven? If that?

Walking on, with a new bouncing movement, the lad turned again, Philip able to hear the scrape of his foot on the pavement, atrociously audible above the hum of the Pilot building's ventilation grille, the horns and whines of the traffic, streets away, dashing for City Square. A cheap black trainer on the concrete. The swish of that turn! Philip glared, feeling a perverse need to know if there was a smile, any special humiliation, since the details of the encounter would, he knew, fascinate him for hours.

*   *   *

Mick drove them slowly up to the housing estate. He stopped on the corner, at the mouth of a cul-de-sac. 'It's the one on the right,' he said, nodding at a group of three houses. 'The one with the Escort outside.'

A lightness came into Luke's chest, his mouth dry as dust. What if he fucked it up? Think of the trouble. But it was best not to think that way. Sharpen up. Get the attitude working.

Mick turned to him. 'You OK, Lukey?'

'All right. A bit scared maybe.' He didn't think he was frightened, but he felt a need to admit to some weakness.

'That's natural. It helps, sometimes, as long as you don't let it get the better of you. Just think of it as being like a film. You're play-acting, that's all. Think of the minutes passing. It'll be over in no time, you'll see.'

'How long are we waitin' here?'

'Not long. Not long at all. How about you, Daz? Are you fit? Good an' sharp?'

Darren was breathing rapidly. 'I reckon.'

'Right then.' Mick opened the cloth bag on the floor of the car. He brought out two balaclavas, and a home-made hood which he handed to Luke. It looked clownish, but Luke decided not to object. Darren smeared white cream round his eyes then pulled on the balaclava. Luke put his head in the hood, twisting it round, unable to find the eyeholes. 'Here, dozy get.' Mick twisted it round for him. Then he handed out the guns. 'Are we right?' he said, breathing heavily. 'Are we fit?'

Darren nodded. 'Ready when you are,' said Luke.

Mick breathed in and out, fiercely, like a boxer. 'Right, let's fucking do it!' He reached for the door handle.

'Wait!' Darren was pointing at the front door of the next house. 'Shit!' It was opening. A white-haired man came out with a dog, a black labrador, pulling on the lead.

Mick put his hand on Darren's arm. 'Take it easy.' They watched the man passing by on the other side of the road. He stopped to light a cigarette, glanced at them, and walked on. 'It 'appens,' Mick whispered. 'It fucking happens!'

'What do we do now?' Darren said, his voice dry and squeaky.

Luke could hear Mick's exaggerated breathing. 'We ignore him,' Mick said. 'We get on with it.'

Wanting to appear more in control than Darren, Luke sat back and watched the man through the rear window. 'He's gone.'

'Right, my beauties,' said Mick. 'Got everything? Daz?' Darren nodded, the gun in his arms. 'Right, let's go! Let's fucking do it!'

They jumped out of the car, Luke following the other two, trying to keep the hood from falling over his eyes, the few yards to the house seeming like a mile, as they skipped over the low hedge on to the lawn, the air damp, no wind, the estate quiet as the dead.

He was walking away up the street. Had he actually recognised Philip? Did he think about him? Ever? An upraised finger might have put this whole business in its proper place. But there was nothing, no tiny smile, not the slightest smearing of the eyes and cheeks. And in less than a minute he had made it to the top of the street and disappeared from view.

Philip tried to reason with himself. It was a coincidence, a crappy piece of luck, nothing more. Another minute and he would have missed him and known only sublime ignorance. Why not leave it at that? Why should he take it *personally*?

'All right there, Phil?'

Philip turned, a little too quickly, finding Howard's shiny black shoes skipping down the steps behind him.

'Fine. Tip-top.'

'Er, if you're looking for a bit on the side, you want to be up Chapeltown way. I'll be passing, if you want a lift.'

Philip forced a laugh. 'I'll give it a miss, I think. Just this once.'

'See you tomorrow, then.'

'Yes, Howard.'

Now he had to hang around round another minute to let Howard get away before he followed to the car-park.

On his way, Philip told himself he would forget what had just

53

happened. It was something he could *choose* to do, and in the process he might recover a little of the happiness he had been feeling a few minutes before. He focused on this, trying to retrieve that end-of-the-day gladness as he crossed the dead flat floor of the car-park, not daring to risk its fragile recovery further by acknowledging the torn bumper on the back of the car. In his breath-holding, world-defying cocoon of self-control he looked away, *deciding* he had not seen the rip, that it could not be there. Or if it was, that it must have been caused by *someone else*.

Ten

There were times, it had to be said, when Philip's heart was so light and airy he felt like singing. It was a refinement born of the simplest sensory experiences, the smell of the streets after rain, the sunlight of an early summer evening, or of the most mundane sounds, like the boiling of a kettle, the chug of roadworks in town. Strikingly impersonal, stupidly small, yet containing a hint of so much. And his deepest wish was for his whole life to consist of nothing but these piercing perceptions, though there was no owning up to this without sounding like a dick. He knew that from the time he had attempted to explain it all to Kath, one night in the pub. 'I don't get it,' she said. 'I'm not *religious* at all.' She was missing the point, he said. Then he sulked, vowing never to risk revealing such private thoughts again.

The television was on, Kath sipping Guinness, the glass cradled in her breasts, her legs sprawled across the sofa. When she laughed, it was a sound Philip had not heard before, hearty, with a rasp in the lower register. Maybe she had picked it up from the women at the pre-natal classes, deciding on a different personality, without so much as a by-your-leave. And that skin, shiny, mawkish from losing the tan she had picked up on their trip to the Algarve. Philip watched the screen, trying to work out the plot of the film, but finding himself thinking about that holiday last October.

They'd had a good time, hadn't they? And he liked Albufeira, with its white bucket-shop hotels and the lack of an imperative to seek 'culture', or any of that carry-on. All the cafés had a British menu, plenty of chips and pasties and beer to pig out on. Just the ticket, really. But one day he had a row with a timeshare salesman, a Scouser who just would not go away, and who woke the bad temper Philip thought he had left behind in England. The guy was tapping him on the arm, following them down the street. It was so *maddening*. Philip rounded on him, lifting his fist. Then the guy squared up too, the 'Mother' tattoo on his thick bicep, the prestige of that bronzed chest beneath the denim waistcoat. 'Come on then, yous wank-ah!' Philip knew he had to back down. The disgrace, the white, male, squidgy, insurance-clerk *shame* of it. Kath, seeing this, suggested they went back to the hotel where they sat in the bar. Philip was still angry. Fuming. But Kath was warming with the drink, teasing him out of his mood. Soon she had that languid look he knew so well, suggesting, in her soft voice, that they went up to their room. He didn't feel much better, yet what else could he do? She was happy, he was miserable. Hers was the only agenda they could follow. Thus, later, with other English chaps ripping up the streets in hired cars beneath the balcony of their room, she whispered, 'Let's make a baby. A big fat one.' He hardly heard her. Making love, at that moment, would be such a *cure* he had not *wanted* to hear her.

Something she knew. And had schemed for. A *psychopath*, that was her. And now here she was, sprawled on the sofa, a glass of Guinness sitting on the trophy she had won from him.

'I like him.' She pointed at a head on the screen with her glass. 'He used to be in *ER*.'

Philip did not know who he was. He mumbled a word that was almost 'yes'.

These nights were so long. Not like it used to be when they had that . . . What could you call it? Friendship? Reliability? Whatever, where was it now? It was a tired animal, slumped on the Berber carpet between them. Poke it with a stick, in the ribs, an eye, it would not move.

Was there no going back to the way things were? If so, Philip needed to know. He had a right, he thought, taking a long quiet breath, to be told where he stood.

Once, Philip used to like resting his head in her warm naked groin, staring along the shaft of her leg. Kath used to be a runner, half-marathons, and the honed firmness of the muscles was still there, the skin, in those days, perma-tanned, though there was that unappetising white puffiness above her bush. But he could ignore that, looking along her leg, as if taking aim. Once she took to wearing a gold ankle chain with a tiny padlock. She gave Philip the key. And there was that other time, with the handcuffs she had borrowed. 'These'll hold you,' she said, cackling. It had not meant much to Philip then. It was just another game, among all the rest.

He thought they would go on for ever.

Another night he asked her what really turned her on. 'Language,' she said. 'The things people say.' Philip asked her what sort of things, but she only laughed. 'That would spoil it. I only want to *hear* them.' And he would fantasise about her with another woman, or ache to know when she touched herself, wanting to watch her do it in the shower, to ask her what she was thinking about and how it felt. He still did not know. Would he ever?

Kath entered his life when he was a student. She was working in the accounts office of a furniture warehouse in Manchester. In the mornings he used to lie in the single bed they shared in her flat, watching her dress for work. The details were absorbing, the clasping of her bra and the brisk adjustments to make her breasts point. Next would be the blouse, left open like an overshirt while she put on her necklace and ear studs.

(That blouse. Philip seemed to remember one in white silk. Or had he imagined it? Recently he found himself looking in her wardrobe for that ideal blouse. He could not find it, only something in worn, faded cotton. Similar, but not how he remembered it).

Such a simple pleasure, really, watching her pull a skirt over her black tights, the soft thumps of her feet on the carpet with her little mincing walk, her demure concentration as she fastened the watch on her thin, girlie wrist. It was Kath for the daylight, with the women in the office, and the manager she said stared at her from behind, tilting his head for a view of her black calves tucked under the chair. And why shouldn't he? Kath's sexuality

57

was a reckonable commodity, worth looking at, Philip, at that time, being absolutely interested in it, the whole prism from black to white, with the full range of curiosities in between.

Sex was love. Wasn't it?

Kath was the first woman he had really known, physically. She was older than him. It made it easier. He felt free to help himself to all she had. And why not? What else had she been doing, that night when they met in one of the college bars, other than looking for a man? She was supposed to be attending evening classes about contemporary literature, though Philip had hardly ever seen her with a book. She owned less than a dozen, three of which were the volumes of *The Lord of the Rings*. No, she was looking for something else, drawn by a heartening insecurity to someone with the inflections of a Leeds accent, like her own. Philip was singled out. And grateful. No denying that.

Within a week he was living in her flat, co-habiting with a grown-up woman while the other students, the lads, traded like simpering puppies with girls their own age, or downed the lager, the E's, or patronised the Blues at Maine Road because they couldn't get tickets for Old Trafford. Not for Philip. He was spending his time in this woman's flat, learning how to make lasagne, taking hour-long baths with her, watching her dress for work with that slight lean of her back, the brown eyes that, to this day, never really met his. During the day, in lectures, or about the town, he would reflect on it all. He could not believe what he had discovered, his luck. When the other lads asked him to join them on their weekend binges, ribbing him about his 'wife', he would reply, with pride, 'She wouldn't like it.' To be owned. A privilege.

'Where does it end?' he once asked.

'It doesn't,' she said.

There was always Interstellar Cowboy to try again. But it would take such an effort. Let a simple pleasure like that go and you don't get it back. Maybe it was the same with everything. But why? How come, when two people got to know each other so well, the passion died, and you were left with only its weaker relatives: constancy, politeness?

There was a tickle in his prick. It would be something to do, wouldn't it? He looked at Kath, her bare dusty-soled feet. She still wanted to be fucked, didn't she? Or had she decided she could do without him now? When she had become pregnant she borrowed a book from the library, *Your First Baby – Dodging the Strain of Parenthood*. Philip had only looked at the chapter about sex. It said that women really liked it when they were pregnant, no worries about contraception, and all that. But these days he seemed to have to resort to *asking* her for it. Hardly reasonable, that.

The credits were rolling on the film and Philip, for the first time, realised it was a video. Kath pressed the rewind on the remote control then looked down at her lump, smoothing it with her hands. 'I wonder if I should have the scan? At least then we could stop calling it "it". What d'you think?'

'Whatever you like,' said Philip.

She was staring at the little round hill, smiling. 'Come and listen to it. See if you can hear it moving.'

Philip shifted his legs, recrossing them. 'What, now?'

'Of course, now. Why not?' She chuckled. 'It might say something to you.'

'I'm tired.' He nodded at the television. 'I want to watch this.'

'It's the adverts.'

'So?'

'So it's your baby, Philip. Your child.' Her mouth was open in gentle disapproval. He despised that look.

'Look, I'll see it soon enough. All right?' He was looking hard at the screen, the idea of fiddling with a foetus, even looking at Kath, now out of the question. An impossibility. 'Take My Breath Away . . .' The new Alfa Mondeo. 'It could be you-oo . . .' The fat golden finger pointing out of the sky. A silence. If they had to have a conversation, he might ask her if she would get her figure back when all this was over. But, when he risked a glance, Kath was looking at the blank wall behind the sofa, her head turned away from him. To his side was a spider plant that was shrivelling through being too close to the fire. He picked at its yellowing leaves, squirming with the fact of his indelicacy. 'It's good to talk . . .' It was not his fault, he wanted to say. Didn't she remember what their lives used to be like? Couldn't she imagine his needs? Or see how *he* was suffering?

Eleven

Maybe the stubble should go – a beard might make him look too old. The only time he had tried growing one before was when he was eighteen, and it was pathetic, the thicker bristles sticking like pubes through the down. Regrettable now, like so much of his youth. So, get rid of the stubble, and perhaps consider a proper hairstyle instead. Anything for a change.

Any chuffing thing.

Eight in the morning, and already bored. What a life. He leaned on the washbasin. The bathroom was so small he could push his buttocks against the wall behind him and touch the opposite wall without straightening his arm. And it smelt of urine, the radiator being next to the toilet bowl, cooking the thing up during the night. It could not, of course, be flushed in the hours of darkness for fear of disturbing the stoat next door. The old slug, why couldn't he move? Or die? Philip dabbed the foam on his face and fished his Bic razor from the clutter of Kath's creams and gels, dragging it over his chin, along the lie of the bristles, the way his older brother had once shown him: 'Otherwise you'll take half your fucking face off.' It was the only piece of advice Ian had ever given Philip. Why couldn't he have helped him more? He was five years older. He could have warned him about life, and the way it stitched you up.

He could have.

Fifteen minutes later Philip was driving to work.

It did not come on him every day, the anger, that hot oil of disaffection. It was not a condition, Philip believed, merely a symptom of unfavourable circumstances. It was a transient thing, not his fault. Indeed, he felt he had many good qualities. The week after New Year he had seen a crowd round a man on the pavement outside Marks's. He was dead, heart attack, everyone was saying. It made Philip feel tender all morning, almost tearful at times. And hadn't he cried watching Princess Di's funeral? What was that if it wasn't *caring*? It just couldn't be summoned all the time, that was all. People put themselves in the way, nothing else.

He had the radio on, a record by Everything But The Girl playing. He liked them. Maybe he should go and buy a CD of theirs this very lunchtime. Something to look forward to, an enthusiasm he might *invent*. He drove into Leeds, past the cacked-out warehouses and council estates. He had grown up in Horsforth, across town. His parents were still there, though when he came back from Manchester it seemed right that he should stake out some other part of the city, a territory of his own. Hence the flat in Cross Gates, with the move to Dabton, even further away, seeming a natural extension to this wish. But why? What point was he trying to make? He got on well with his folks. They were a sheet more likeable than Jeff and Tilly. Still, it might have been better if he had used his imagination for once, moving right away, to Sheffield, or Edinburgh, or, even better, abroad. One day, perhaps.

For now, he was here, the skyline a grid of flats and offices, church spires, the Kremlin. It was an intimidation of architecture, a bitty reflection of the society it housed, the big fat sow of Leeds, turned belly-up, half-sick, half-thriving – Harvey Nichols in Briggate and, a mile away, Chapeltown where you dare not even stop to ask for directions. Yet there was something palatable about Philip's home town. In his better view of himself, he felt Leeds mirrored a particular modesty of his own, a struggling mixture he might even dare to love, if he ended up staying here for ever. As was possible, if he was honest with himself.

Passing through Seacroft he nodded patiently at someone trying to shift to the lane in front of him. Philip slowed and let him in without a thought. Twenty-four hours earlier he would have been trying to murder the guy. Why was that? What got into him? Today he was sitting back, watching the other drivers risking their necks on the dash into town and, at a ring road, he laughed openly at two men with their windows down, bawling at each other neck and neck along the packed road. 'Boys, boys! Calm down!' His tranquillity grew, became a virtue. It was the true norm of his existence, he thought as he waited at the lights, drumming his fingers lightly on the wheel, pulling away only when green was absolutely achieved.

Five minutes later he pulled carefully into the multi-storey, getting out of the car with scarcely an eye for the man standing next to one of the pillars. He was thin, middle-aged, wearing a mac, a white shirt and brown tie showing. Hardly a thief. Besides, the car-park's security man was about, evidence of the way Pilot looked after its employees. The way they cared. Maybe he could learn to like his job after all? More optimism, more joy. Philip walked past the man and down the stairs.

The first two hours passed effortlessly, the buzz of the office maintaining its rare appeal. Why did he ever take such exception to his work? What was so difficult about it? Howard came round at eleven, standing with his finger hooked over the dent in his nose. Philip felt a flush of warmth towards him, thinking he should try to get to know him better. Sometimes their cars were parked side by side and he had often noticed a tube of yellow tennis balls on Howard's back shelf. For a moment it was in Philip to remark on this, to start the kind of digressive conversation everyone used to get round Howard. Perhaps he might ask him if he had been back to Newcastle lately? But Howard was frowning at the clutter on Philip's desk. He stood closer. Philip could smell the deodorant, the fabric of his good wool suit.

'Look, Phil, did you get my message? About the Griffiths claim?'

'No, sorry. I'm going to get to it, though. Any minute. In fact, now.' Philip leaned forward – such a sense of duty – to summon up the internal mail on his terminal.

'Well, thing is, I've got this fax from the guy.' Howard bit his bottom lip, showing his perfectly even teeth. 'He's quoting the coroner at us, the open-verdict stuff.'

'We still haven't got a draft copy from the coroner. And I don't see why we should put up with it anyway,' Philip said, buoyed up with his new sense of loyalty to Pilot. 'Hah! Like she takes five doses of paracetamol and forgets each one. Then the brandy just jumps off the shelf and pours itself into her mouth. Plus the amyl nitrate. Jesus,' he said. Righteously!

'I know, I know.' Howard puffed out his cheeks. 'Look, see to it will you, Phil? Speak to the fella. Get the brakes on the thing.'

'Right. I'm on to it.'

When Howard had moved away, Philip dug out the papers he had prepared the day before. In that lax and dreary mood. How did he ever get in such a state? It was unforgivable, really. Still, he could smile about it now. He reached for the phone, but it was ringing before he could pick it up.

'Phil?' It was Shelley, a secretary who doubled on Security when the regular man was not there. 'There's someone here wants to see you.'

'Well, I'm pretty busy right now, love,' he said, self-importantly. 'Who is it?'

'He won't say. He's looking for someone who owns a blue Nissan, registration number . . .' She gave the number, each digit making Philip's heart slow a little. 'Is that yours?'

'Might be.' He sniggered. 'It hasn't been nicked, has it? I mean, I should be so bleeding lucky!'

Shelley spoke away from the phone, then came back. 'No. He says it's nothing like that. He wants to see you in person.'

'Well, not now,' Philip said, annoyed that she was so unaware of the gravity of his work, his underwriter standing in the firm. 'Tell him to come back at lunchtime. He might be lucky then.'

Shelley mumbled away, then said, 'He says he'll be back at twelve.'

'Right. Fine. Can I do some work now?' She hung up.

Philip rang Griffiths' number. It was answered almost immediately. 'Mr Griffiths?'

'Yes?' There were light hammer-taps in the background, and a woman's voice on a tannoy.

'It's Philip Pickles of Pilot Insurance. I'm sorry to bother you at work, but we're trying to process your claim . . .' A pause for effect. 'For the death of the late Mrs Griffiths.'

'Go on.'

'I know it's a rather difficult time for you, Mr Griffiths, but we need an actual transcript of the coroner's report to check against the terms of the agreement.' Normally, Philip hated lying, but his new affection for the company that paid him was now overwhelming. Someone called Griffiths' name and he spoke away from the phone. 'Mr Griffiths?'

'What?'

'If you could supply us with a copy of the transcript, at your convenience, together with any relevant medical reports . . .'

'Look,' said Griffiths. 'So far as I know, medical histories are confidential.'

'Yes, but they would apply when you took out the policy.'

'My wife told you everything you wanted to know. She didn't smoke, she worked out, she'd barely a day's sickness in her life. What else do you want?'

'Just the absolute facts,' Philip said, knowing he had the upper hand, and hanging on to the card concerning Mrs Griffiths' depression.

'We were married for twelve years. As far as I'm concerned she was fit as a fiddle. Anything else you want to know, you'll have to ask her doctor about.' There was an odd drawl to the voice, a comical overlay to the Yorkshire accent, as if he listened to a lot of country and western music. 'Otherwise you'll just have to accept the coroner's findings. In fact, I don't see why you can't just be happy with that.'

'Well, we have to be sure about a few things and, frankly, it may take a while . . .'

'I don't see why it should, my friend. I don't see why it's taken this long, to be honest. It's not what you advertise, you know.'

'Red tape, Mr Griffiths. Being a businessman, you'd understand . . .'

'Do you realise how all this makes me feel? This is my wife we're talking about.'

'Of course. And I sympathise absolutely, Mr Griffiths . . .'

The man groaned. 'Don't be sympathetic. Just get it sorted. Now please, Mr Pickles.' He hung up.

Philip made detailed notes of the conversation and drafted a completely unnecessary letter to the coroner's office. Three days' delay might give the legal people time to put a case together against the claim. He put the letter in the post tray at the front of the office, feeling at the height of his powers, zipping, on the endless up. He was so relaxed! His contentment was an obscenity!

Two minutes later, everything changed.

'Mr Pickles?'

Philip was heading out for lunch, still high, wanting a change from the numbing routine of sitting in the rest room. Wanting to see the world, maybe even going to buy that CD by Everything But The Girl. He had completely forgotten his visitor from an hour before. He looked closely at him, at the green pallor of the fifty-odd-year-old face, the steady grey eyes fixed on Philip. It was the man from the car-park.

'Are you Mr Pickles?'

Philip smiled. 'I might be.'

He stood closer, blocking the way past the reception desk. Shelley was staring fixedly at the two security screens, as if they were a film. What was going on here? 'That's your car in the car-park, isn't it? The blue Nissan Sunny?'

'Sounds like me. So?'

'Did you hit another car, yesterday morning, on your way to work?'

Philip frowned, affectedly. 'No.'

The man shook his head. 'Well, maybe you could explain the tear on your bumper. It looks pretty fresh to me.'

'That?' said Philip. 'It's nothing. Happened ages ago. What's it got to do with you, anyway?'

Three of the girls from Personnel came past, on their way to the pub for lunch. Shelley smiled at them, as if trying to distance herself from the conversation. 'Look, Mr Pickles. My father was involved in an accident at Gipton roundabout yesterday morning. Someone I know says you were responsible. He was behind you. You were out of control. He says all the way into town you were driving like a madman.'

66

Philip looked back towards the stairs, thinking to turn around for the sanctuary of his newly adored Pilot premises. 'Balls.'

'Oh no. It's true all right. And the thing is,' the man said, following Philip's half-turn, 'my father pulled over. The shock of it, you see.' He moistened his lips. 'He had a stroke, Mr Pickles.'

Philip was looking at the shiny tiled floor, feeling hot under his jacket. 'I don't think he did.'

'He did! Of course he did!'

'Then I don't see that it's my fault.'

'Of course it's your fault!'

A couple came in and Shelley ushered them to the far side of the reception desk. 'Look,' Philip said, keeping his voice low. 'I don't know you. And I don't know what the fuck you're talking about.'

The man reached into his inside pocket, an action that made Philip start, stupidly. He pulled out a pen and a piece of paper. 'I'm going to give you my name and address. I don't know if my father will survive this incident. But what I do know is that you,' he said, wagging the pen, 'are responsible. I've found you. I've caught you out, and I have a witness. And if my father does not pull through this incident, I'm going to the police. Got that?'

'Hey, hang on a minute . . .'

'No, you hang on, Mr Pickles.' He scribbled the note and held it out, his hand trembling to the wrist. 'I know who you are, and I know where to find you.'

Philip looked at the name, Andrew Merrick. He wanted to screw up the note and throw it at the man's feet. 'You know what you can do with this.' But Merrick was already on his way to the glass doors, getting tangled in the company of the departing couple, rushing out and down the steps. Philip looked at Shelley and held his arms out wide. 'Who the bugger was that?'

Shelley shook her head, and attended to an incoming call. Philip dithered between going back up the stairs or following this man Merrick. In the end he simply remained where he was, a hollowness in his chest and head. This was unfair. The day had started so well.

Twelve

The bodies were agitating like bees, making phone calls, ripping paper, talking in competition. Making themselves *seen* to be moving. They were doing it deliberately, a post-lunch revival, none of their activity *necessary*. Hell . . .

Is other people.

If only Philip had a volume knob under his desk, something to lower the racket, to spare him from their excesses. The noise came in a new wave, stirring his filthy juices, the chatter rising, up, up: 'It's old data. It's no good . . .' Or, 'We need to know age attained, not . . .' An appalling *application* of politeness and industry. Then Lilian, a 'cluck' – the office term afforded to women over forty – was fussing with the photocopier, squeaking about how it would not work. Why was she here? What did she need with a job like this? Did it ever cross her vacuous mind about any younger, needier person she might be keeping out of work? After an 'Hurr!' from her, the machine began working, probably of its own accord, no doubt one of its chips alerted to the user's profound imbecility. Then she was wandering again. For something to do! What was in it for her, for them all to rip Philip's arteries from their channels, flay his innards to shreds?

He could not *exist* in this.

He ran from the noise, along the corridor to the toilet where he shoved open the door and kicked the wall, leaving a dent in the plasterboard. He slammed open a cubicle door, backheeled it shut and sat on the toilet lid, banging his head on his knees. The beast had roared from its sleep, pawing the ground with its heels. No escaping it. Someone came into the toilet. No! *Go away!* Philip yanked open the door, his teeth clenched, to find Hamid standing at the urinal, holding his tool. 'Hiya, Phil.' Philip could not speak.

It was inconceivable. He went out, banging into the baskets of paper put out for shredding, running along the corridor, away from himself, down the back stairs, three at a time, four flights. Then back again, wanting exhaustion, collapse, yes, a heart attack, complete cardiac demise, to let everyone know what they had *done to him*. On the top floor, above Life and Deaths, he could see, through two fire doors, Howard coming his way. If Philip stayed here, if he booted open the doors that separated them, he would hit Howard. No questions asked. He rapped the wall, the soulless corporate wall, with the side of his fist. Howard had seen him. He was coming to speak to him! Philip turned and ran back for the stairs, down again, all the way to the fires of hell.

To burn, burn.

It was not always like this.

There were his quiet moments, those little oases of faith and absolute perception. An anonymity, a floating peace. It was above speech, yet not silent, everything still save for this soft flowing motion, each human being made into a vaporous unlabelled ecstasy. And if there had to be contact – since it could never be truly ordered – then it would only be through the occasional collision, when a soft explosion would take place, a sunburst of millions of atoms, red, blue, gold, electric white.

Yes, to be Philip Pickles, the man with no name.

'I just thought you might like to swap chairs. That's all right, isn't it?'

Philip, speechless, watched Lilian's fantastic activity as she wheeled his chair out into the aisle and round to her desk, bringing her chair in replacement.

'There!' she said. 'I'm sure this'll actually suit you better, since you're quite tall. OK, Philip?'

He watched as she shuffled the chair under the desk, his glare fixed on her peaky nose and her stupid black curls. But she ignored him, mired in her human mediocrity, incapable of natural contact.

69

Pleased with herself, she breezed across the office to chatter with Sarah, remarking now on the dust on the windowsill, then leaving the room to find a cloth.

Philip pulled out the chair and sat down, reduced to a silence made of bricks. Until Sarah came by his desk. 'There, Philip. Does that suit you better?'

'What?'

'The chair.'

'Er . . . yeah.'

'Good. Wouldn't want you to be uncomfortable.'

Philip looked up at her. She was smiling. On his side! Oh God, the balm of association. If only Sarah knew what this meant to him. The fizzle of his temper began dying, somewhere behind him. Sarah went to her own desk, turning with that neat pose he liked so much. He nodded, vaguely.

When he thought no one was looking, he took Merrick's note, the cause of all this, from his pocket, hoping to rationalise its details. The address was out Keighley way. Did the old man live there too? If so, what had he been doing in Gipton? Honestly, the way people sought Philip out. And his driving was bad, was it? Witnesses, were there? He would produce witnesses of his own, and a flawless driving record. It was not his fault. *Always someone wanting to have a go . . .*

'All right there, Phil?'

It was Tom. 'Fine.' Philip put the note away and shuffled up to his screen, but his knees were too tight under the desk. He got up and fiddled with the screw under the chair.

'We're away up the pub, if you fancy it,' Tom said behind him. 'It's Jayne's birthday.'

'I'll be there.' Philip slid the chair under the desk and pulled it out again.

'Right.' Tom was still hovering in the aisle. What was he looking at? 'Right, Phil.'

The hours passed numbly, the afternoon laid to waste with little of value achieved. When the others began leaving, Philip toyed around with his keyboard, for effect, then followed, trailing at a distance, letting them huddle into the lift while he took the stairs.

Out in the street they walked ahead in the brisk, tight-arsed office fashion. Snow was falling, light and swirling, a film of slush on the pavements. To Philip's surprise, Howard had agreed to join them, walking at the head of the mob, joking with Mike from Personnel, kicking bits of slush into the road. Sarah was there too, walking with Jayne.

The pub was called the Crack, a revamped place with bare floorboards, barrel stools, the male staff wearing stick-on sideburns and long white aprons. Howard and Mike pushed two tables together, commandeering the territory, for Pilot, that renowned, important company. As if. Philip joined his colleagues but, being the last in, he was stuck near the draughty doorway.

There were six men, and Jayne and Sarah who were sitting at the far end. Howard had taken his jacket off, revealing the shirt gaiters that matched his gold cuff links. They were all uneasy with each other until Tom and Hamid brought the drinks. Philip read a brass notice above Howard's head: 'On this spot, on 17th May 1687, nothing happened at all.' He thought about commenting on it, to ingratiate himself with what he felt was everyone else's superior humour. But Tarquin, a boy of eighteen who had only been with the firm two weeks, was already pointing at a blackboard announcing that night's entertainment, a country singer called Colin Commanche. 'Must be good,' he said. 'His name's in coloured chalk!' Everyone laughed, including Jayne who insisted on calling him 'Tarkers', the mere sound of which got up Philip's nose. 'Hey, sorry, Phil,' he called, half to the group. 'I was forgetting. Jokes are only all right if you like laughing!' The rest smiled politely.

'Very good, Tarquin,' said Philip.

They splintered into twos and threes with sudden conversations that left Philip isolated, pretending to listen to the booming music. Workers from other offices came in, a flurry of snow making it through the door, a few flakes settling on Philip's knee. Why had he come here? He brooded over his Grolsch as Andrew from Accounts, recently famous for having been a reserve on *Blind Date*, took a huge swig of lager and began recounting something he had seen on television the night before. 'Me name's Jake,' he said in a cod Yorkshire accent, tugging invisible braces. 'Jake Botherington. I'm a self-made man, tha' knows. An' I got where I am today, mark my words, with 'onest graft. Aye, aye, graft and leadership.'

'It's what t'country needs,' said Tarquin, who must have seen the same programme.

'Tha's reet, tha's not wrong. There's been nowt since Mrs Thatcher, an' I'm not an 'appy man on that count.'

'Ooh, aye,' said Tarquin.

'Bring back floggin' . . .'

'An' hangin'!'

'Aye, 'anging. For everybody! At least them as not's from t'West Ridin'!'

The laughter was aggressive, a deliberate surge towards a collective good mood. 'Tha sees,' said Tarquin, trying to take over, 'tha gets these soft southern bastards comin' up to Leeds, an' they can't cut the bloody mustard! An' I likes a drop of mustard meself. Nay, not a drop, a bloody shovelful!'

Philip was watching Sarah, her smile hearteningly faint. Next to her, Howard, everyone's senior, was laughing as competitively as the rest. Then he was looking at Philip. 'Come on, Phil. No stories to tell us?'

'Fresh out, Howard.' The reply was bright enough, Philip thought, but Mike was making some comment in Howard's ear.

'No-oh,' said Howard, loudly. 'He tells a good story, does Phil.'

Then Tarquin reached across the table and grabbed Philip's cheeks. 'You need to smile a bit more, old son! It's dead easy! You get the fucking mouth,' he said, squeezing, 'and stretch those lips out. Like this!'

Philip knocked his arms away. 'Get off, twat! Arsehole! Who

the fuck do you think you are? You're nothing, you! D'you know that?' He glared, panting, hardly believing what he had said. He was not even in that bad a mood.

The others were watching with careful amusement. Tarquin sat back, trying to grin his way out of it. 'Hey, all right, Phil mate. No harm meant.' He blew up at his fringe. 'Christ, I didn't know you were that touchy.'

'Well, I am, all right?'

Howard was studying him, one eyebrow raised. Sarah, an inevitable, regrettable witness, was puffing on a cigarette, talking to Jayne. No doubt about that time Philip had made a pass at her! Over the fucking punch bowl! The rest melted back into small groups. Philip took a long drink of lager and left without saying anything.

So now he had done it, let fly at last. God, such a day. How did they end up like this? Yet, driving home, he was smiling. What was so wrong with a little outburst, a siphoning of the gas? It had been brilliantly spontaneous, something he should do more often. Let the bastards have it! Who cares what they think?

It was nearly seven o'clock, the traffic thinner than usual, no doubt many having headed off early due to the snow that could snarl up Leeds in an hour. It was heavier on the outskirts, piled on the roofs and privet hedges, lending an improbable virtue to the council houses and flats of Harehills. Philip was feeling pleased with himself. It was as if he had just had his first shit for a fortnight! He drove out of town, along the empty roads, reaching Dabton High Street, and the white-powdered estate, within ten minutes, half the time it usually took.

But it could not last. It never did. A minute later: 'Please, Kath. For Christ's sake. Stop crying!'

Thirteen

'Goals,' said Mick. 'You've got to have a goal in life. Otherwise, what's the bleedin' point?' He picked up the spirit level. 'You've got to aim that bit 'igher than you think you can go. Shoot . . .' He trained the level on Moonie, like a rifle. 'For the moon! Ker-bang!' He put the level down, a big grin on his dusty face. 'What's your goal then, Moon?'

'Get this bloody 'ouse finished. Then the next.'

'Then we're out of work, old son.'

'Yeah, well, that's the way it goes.' Moonie was Mick and Darren's gang-mate. He was getting on a bit, the plaster dust making his skin permanently dirty, and he always wore the same wool hat and his jumper tucked in his jeans. He wet his trowel and brought the edges of his plaster swipes smooth. 'One job, then the next. For ever and ever, Amen.' He stood back, took a drag on the roll-up pinched between his thumb and finger.

'Me an' Daz, we've got goals.' Mick sat down on a stack of plasterboards. 'Isn't that right, Darren?'

'Have we?' The comment unnerved Darren. He wasn't sure what Mick was getting at.

'Yurr. You bet, my old love.' He laughed, and dragged Darren down beside him, kissing him on the neck. 'You bet, my old china. We're goin' places, you and me. Tell everybody. Tell the whole fuckin' world!'

Darren pulled away. 'Gerroff.'

'Leave him alone,' said Moon. 'He's doing all right. Don't listen to him, Darren. Get a trade and you're fixed for life. It's what my old man said, an' it applies now like it did then. Bloody more so, if you ask me.'

'Get . . . a fucking . . . tray-ade,' Mick aped. 'And where's he gonna get that? Not here. D'you know you're supposed to go to college while you're here, Daz boy? Day release?'

Darren looked at the floor he was sweeping, wary of bending over to get the gobs of plaster and bent nails he was meant to pick from the grooves. 'I know.'

'So, what're they doin' about it? What sort of a fuckin' training scheme's this? They're having you for a monkey, mate.'

Darren had wondered about the rest of his supposed training. He had meant to ask Gayliss, the site manager, about it. But he was no good at things like that – asking for what he wanted. He would come over all embarrassed. Like now, with Mick, this man who had befriended him, and who, at this moment, was getting at him, looking for a way to show him up.

'Look!' said Mick. 'He's goin' red! You can see it, under the fucking khaki! Somewhere, oh-ver the rain-bow . . .'

'For fuck's sake,' said Moon. 'There's no need for that shit.'

Mick stood up and hugged Darren's shoulders. 'Darren doesn't mind! He knows it's only a bit of fun! We're mates, we are. And I'm gonna see you all right, I am. Just stick by your old Uncle Mick. Trust me!' Then he spun away, holding his arms wide. 'There's an aw-ful lot of coffee in Bra-zi-il!' And he laughed.

Three weeks ago, that was. Now they were skipping round the back of this house, this decent-looking place where he did not belong. Could never in a million years . . . He was going faint, as if he hadn't eaten for days. Mick put his finger to his mouth and slid up to the kitchen window. No piss-taking now. Nothing funny . . .

There was a bamboo blind, half up. Inside, Darren could see a woman's hands, fishing in a red bowl at the sink. Mick was just standing there, watching. Nerveless. Could he possibly be feeling the same sickness? Darren wanted to blow it, to say they could turn away, right now. It wouldn't look bad. Only they would know about it . . .

* * *

Two weeks ago. That was when the trouble started. 'Receivership! The bastards have gone bust!' Mick threw his trowel into the corner. 'Knew it! Fuckin' knew it!' He was grinning, wiping drops of rain from his fringe. 'Hah!'

'Are you tellin' the fucking truth?' said Moon.

'Fuckin' Arthur just told me. Go ask him, if you don't believe me.'

Moonie huffed, wearily. 'It's happened to me before, an' I suppose it'll happen again. Jesus, what's happened to the buildin' trade? I thought we were supposed to be in a recovery?'

Mick was pulling on his dust-white denim jacket. 'We're shagged. That's what's happened. Whole country's had it. Buggered.' He picked up his trowel and wrote 'Fucked! Again!' on a freshly plastered wall.

'Aah, don't do that,' said Moonie.

'Why not? There's nobody gonna be livin' here, except for the rats.'

Darren sat down on the floor, his back against the bare breeze-block wall. He might have known it. The way things bloody went. This was his first job, and he liked it. That was the pisser. You find something you want from life and it gets taken away. 'I'm laid off too, am I?' he said, wanting to check the fact.

Mick laughed. 'Course you are, soft get! The whole fuckin' bunch of us. They'll be here with the keys any minute. And out we go!'

'I don't get it. It hardly costs them anything to keep me on. Half the money comes from the government.'

'So what you gonna do then, Daz old mate? Stay here on your own? Build the fuckers all by yourself? Four- and five-bedroomed highly desirable residences, *en suite*, three pissholes, all built by Darren the builder, all on his fuckin' tod?'

Darren looked out of the unglazed window at the bricklayers working in the rain, hoping this was just another bad joke, aching just to stay and be part of it all. Then he saw Arthur, delivering his news, house by house. He picked up a hardened plaster gob and flicked it across the floor. 'The bastards.'

'Yeah, mate,' said Mick. 'The lot of 'em. Come on, we're out of here. We've got our futures to consider. We need a drink.'

Two weeks ago. And now Mick, that same slight shape, hard to take seriously with his head covered, was tiptoeing back along the path beneath the window. He lifted his balaclava and whispered, 'Straight in! Hard! Hard as fuck!' Luke was nodding, taking to all this like it was some prank they were pulling at school. Mick pulled the balaclava down and pointed to the back door. Darren thought he would freeze, just turn to ice, right there. Then Mick had his fingertips on the door panel, the sawn-off raised to cheek-height. Luke copied the action with his pistol.

The silence was unbearable, Darren tensing, feeling as if a hot-water tap was running in his stomach.

The teapot was standing between them, a third party in the tiny flat.

'Are you out again tonight?' Sam asked.

'What if I am?'

'Steady, son. Only askin'.'

Darren looked down, nodding. His way of saying sorry.

'Where is it you get to, you and this Mick?'

'Just about.'

Sam coughed, that groggly throat-clearing that lately had started to sicken Darren. 'Aye. Well, good,' he said.

Darren knew he needn't add any more, but he wanted to reassure his father. 'We muck about with his car a bit. He says he's going to show me how to drive.'

'Drivin', eh? That's good. Useful, that. Something I should've learned.' Sam chuckled. 'Never did, though.'

'Yeah, well. I'll see how it goes.'

It had not sounded convincing, but it was the best Darren could do.

They did not argue much. It would not have been right. There had only been the two of them for as long as Darren could remember, his mother, a Jamaican waitress who had wanted to be a singer, having walked out when Darren was four. He hardly saw her these days, and it didn't bother him. She had a shit-hot temper, and no feelings. None at all. It saddened him that his father always hoped he would get back with her. Even now, after all this time. Just forget her, that's what Darren wanted to tell him. But the moment to say it never seemed right, either.

Sam lit a cigarette, puffing on it, staring into mid-space. Fearing he might come out with some other awkward question about Mick, Darren stood from the tea-table and took his jacket from the back of the chair. 'Well, I'm off.'

'Listen, Darren . . .'

'What?'

His father was smiling. Carefully. 'If you ever fancy going out some time, I mean, if you like, I could take you up the club. Or maybe that'd be borin' for you.' He chuckled. 'Christ knows, it's bad enough for me, some of the funny old buggers up there. Set in their ways. But you know, any time you might fancy it.'

Darren hovered, disarmed. 'Yeah, sure. I'll come up the club with you. Name a night, an' I'll be there.'

'Right. Right y'are.'

Only two hours back, that had been. If his father knew about this . . . Not to be thought about. Ever.

The door was open. They were running into a pine-panelled utility room. Darren stumbled on Mick's heels, catching his elbow on the draining board, Luke shoving from behind. They were falling over each other! But it was only three steps, past a row of coats, and into the kitchen. The woman screamed.

'Quiet!' Mick yelled. He grabbed her arm. 'Where's the old man? Eh? Where is he? In here?' His question was answered by the arrival of a man in the doorway.

'What the hell's going on?'

'Shut it!' Mick shouted, waving the sawn-off. Darren had his gun at his side, his gloved finger on the outside of the trigger guard. As a lame afterthought he raised it, pointing at the man, a middle-aged type in sweater and jeans. The gun felt stupid, like a toy. His arm was weak as a kitten's. 'Right!' bawled Mick. 'In there! Back in there!'

The woman was crying, already. Mick bundled her into the hall, shoving her against the wall, the sound of her stumbling, and the thump of their feet on the floor, upping the stakes. Darren filed into the living room behind them, jig-jogging, for some reason. He wondered if he should be shouting, acting the part. His face was hot behind the balaclava, the cream like a second melting skin. A bead of sweat ran into the corner of his eye. He wiped it with the wrist of the hand holding the gun. A soft thing to do. It might look as if he was crying.

The television was on, a big wide screen on a swivel base. There was a pot plant that reached to the ceiling, a brown leather suite, long gold velvet curtains, a gas fire belching out heat. Mick shoved the woman on to the sofa, picked up a white statuette and smashed the head off against the mantelpiece.

'Pack that in!' shouted the man, in a deep voice that made Darren feel even smaller. 'What do you want? Come on. Tell me what you want!'

Luke was holding his gun up, pointing at the ceiling. Darren raised his forward, holding it two-handed to hide the trembling. He switched his finger to the trigger and aimed at the woman, an action that drew looks from everyone. She flinched, the husband watching, mouth open in plain surprise. That was something, thought Darren. Now they knew he meant business. It made him feel better, the gun no longer a toy, but an object of universal significance. And bigger. Much bigger. Something to hide behind. And if he could keep this up for just a few minutes . . .

'All right, all right,' said the man. 'What is it you want? The video? The telly? Money?'

'We're goin' for a drive,' Mick said, his voice lower, muffled by the wool over his mouth. 'In your car.'

'The car?' the man said, calmly. 'Take it, if you want it. It's nearly new. Worth plenty.'

'That's not it. You know what we're after.'

The man leaned against the mantelpiece, looking pale, the incident catching up with him. 'You'll have to tell me. I don't know what you mean.'

'Your work. We're going to your work.'

'Ah, I see.' He closed his eyes for a few seconds, then looked at his wife who was crumpled on the edge of the sofa, sobbing. 'And no one gets hurt. Is that the deal?'

'If it all goes all right, everybody'll be fine.'

The man nodded slowly, opening his mouth to say something, then closing it again.

Darren looked at Luke who kept pushing the cloth hood up his head. Mick was still as stone. And it was hot in that room. All three of them were breathing fast.

'Right,' said Mick. 'This is the plan, and you follow it to the letter. Got that?'

'Yes,' said the man. 'I'm with you.'

Fourteen

However fat it made him look, the waistcoat had to be worn. Had to be. It was a present from Kath, last birthday, and this was the first time he had tried it on since. He looked sideways in the mirror, his stomach a pot, a baby of his own. Fuck it, what a pair they were going to make. Never mind. Too late to change again anyway. Kath was in the bathroom, re-fixing her make-up, a heartbroken child with a reprieve. So vulnerable. How had he forgotten this evening? He went to her.

'Look, we'll get there. There's plenty of time.'

She was fixing her earrings. She said nothing.

Fifteen minutes after arriving home, Philip was driving back through Leeds. He told himself it was merely an oversight that he had forgotten this. It should not matter. But he was still searching for a mollifying remark for Kath when they reached the theatre. He reversed into a narrow space in the slushy car-park, hoping she would not see the rip on the bumper. Philip still hadn't mentioned it to her, and he didn't know if she had seen it. Then he realised they would have to squeeze their way back round the car to get to the entrance. Kath saw the bumper straight away. She looked at it sadly, turning her head as if nothing Philip could say might explain it.

Before, she had considered him merely thoughtless. Now he was a fool too.

The crowds were already in the foyer, mostly young people, laughing with an uncomplicated anticipation. They were here for the comedy, the chance to put a smile on their faces, an unquestionable pleasure. Philip pushed through to the bar, leaving Kath standing by a pillar. When he came back, he said, 'I really am sorry I forgot. I don't know what I was thinking about.'

Kath took her drink. 'It doesn't matter. We're here now.'

Philip sipped his lager, looking around, the general mood of the place nicely tempered by some jazz impro playing on the PA. Maybe this could be enjoyable. Then, two or three groups of people away, an argument broke out. It was a couple in their thirties, the woman scowling fiercely. The man was looking away, then he turned and said something to her, his words drawing questioning glances from those nearest. The woman slammed down her drink and pushed between the chromium chairs and glass tables, leaving the man shaking his head, vainly looking around for allies.

'God, what a state!' Philip said, when the woman had brushed past them. 'Some people, eh?' He grinned at Kath, wishing she would smile back to emphasise the fact that *they* were not arguing. Standing against the pillar, in her flowered smock and white T-shirt, she was still solemn. Yet it was an almost mythical look, quite fetching and, for a moment, Philip felt secretly proud of her pregnancy, the wholesomeness he thought put everyone else to shame. He had an urge to kiss her, but he resisted, knowing it would look sickly, unfunny. He took a drink.

There was a smell of dope on the air. Kath used to love that stuff, whereas Philip had tried it just once, when she made some hash cakes at the flat in Manchester. He ate six dutifully, watching *Superman II* on television. For an hour, nothing seemed to happen. He was sitting with his chin resting on his hand. Then his heart was going ten to the dozen, and his fingers were growing into his face. A minute later he was sick. 'Drugs do nothing for me.' It became one of his lines, a statement of virtue. 'I've enough trouble with the booze!' Another, a credential of life's victimisation of him.

The announcement came for them to take their seats. With this drink on top of the Grolsch he had in the Crack – an episode slipping from his mind without a grain of guilt attached – he was warming to the buzz of the place. He guided Kath through the crowd from behind, his hands on her shoulders, hoping the touch might mellow her.

The auditorium's wide space made Philip's chest swell, the

murmur of civilised talk floating up to the lighting gantries, the eerie stillness of the air edged with expectation. They found their seats and after a few minutes the lights dimmed and the curtain lifted to a spotlit microphone. The warm-up man, a local guy, walked on. Philip could not remember his name, though he remembered having seen him on television. He muttered this to Kath through the first wave of gentle laughter. The silhouetted heads of other couples nodded in front of him, as if they were remarking on the same thing. Philip felt relaxed, letting himself be drawn into a spiel about Yorkshire Water and last year's drought, the tumbleweeds blowing through Huddersfield streets, the town-hall doors creaking in the wind, the sound of which the man made into the cupped mike. The laughter was polite, Philip sensing a design to the act, a need not to be too good and risk upstaging Sean Tooley, the main event. Then the guy made a joke about Pakistani off-licences which brought hisses. 'Sorr-ee!' he said. 'Wrong venue. Thought I was back at the Young Tories' annual dinner!' A couple more routines followed, and a few disconnected one-liners to make way for the main act.

Tooley, thin as a nail, hair a mess, breezed on to the stage to whistles and loud applause. Again, Philip experienced a rush of pleasure, and a regret that he had not thought more about this evening. 'The snow!' said Tooley. 'The fucking snow in Leeds! Have you been in the car-park there? Have you? Christ, when I came in there was fucking Titus Oates out there! True! He says, Have yous seen a tent anywhere? Only I was lookin' for me mates, like! Jesus!' Philip laughed. It was the time for laughter, its arrival amongst the audience as much a part of the performance as the comedian's. Tooley stalked the stage, using the space, with a pause for everyone to check his designer scruffiness. 'Old Titus. God, he looked knackered, I tell yer . . .'

Philip took hold of Kath's cold hand. It seemed a decent moment for it. And if he laughed enough the tears might roll down his cheeks and she might see it, see him *enjoying himself*. His spirits continued to surge. He wanted to say, This is great, isn't it? And maybe when the baby comes they might still do this sort of thing, once a week say, get Tilly to babysit. What a great idea! The future! Nights out, Saturdays especially, up town, a meal to follow. And a shag! He wanted to say all of these things, all in a hurry. And he would, he told himself, as soon as the time was right. In the dark of the theatre, Philip felt so *happy*.

'The security guy stops me on the way in. A cultured fella. Pronounced the "h" in arsehole . . .' Philip chuckled, thinking he would try to remember the jokes for the office, to show them he could enjoy a laugh, that he was not the miserable bastard Tarquin had tried to make out. 'The things up my arse! Bits of Lego, a twelve-piece socket set . . .' The refreshed memory of Tarquin lent a hard edge to Philip's laughter, as if he was settling the score with it. 'My old man? Tight? He used to save the holes out of the fuckin' Hula Hoops!' Even though it was an old joke, Philip howled, teeth clenched. 'Ah-hah, hah!'

Now he was smiling, wide and toothy, holding it for Kath to see. 'Isn't he good?' he said in her ear. But she was screwing up her eyes, her forehead damp with sweat.

'So. The old man back in Ireland. One step removed from a bogman. In the other direction, that is. D'you not know what a bogman is? What, here in fuckin' Leeds? The Venice of the North? I seen the canal there. I seen it . . .'

Kath leaned over to Philip. 'I don't feel very well.'

Philip was guffawing, pretending not to hear.

'Tell you what, the mentally ill,' said Tooley. 'Is the government supposed to provide for them, or what?'

'Or what!' came a shout from the audience.

'Yeah,' said the comedian, chuckling. 'Right. Well, they did nuthin' for my old feller . . .'

Kath was holding her hand to her head. 'Phil, I'm sorry. I'll have to go out.'

Still staring at the stage, he leaned sidewards to her. 'What for?'

'I feel a bit faint. You stay, if you want to.'

Philip felt a thud of peevishness. She was doing this on purpose.

Getting at him, his pleasure. Couldn't she see how hard he was working to be happy? 'You can't go on your own. What will people think?'

Kath closed her eyes. 'I'm sorry.'

Suppressing a groan, Philip stood, took her hand, and led the way along the row of seats.

A voice spoke. 'Was it something I said?'

Philip did not look round. He knew it was coming from the stage. Round faces, golden in the wash of the stagelights, were turning to look at them. 'I mean,' said Tooley, 'I'm very nearly a professional, you know.' Philip waved dismissively. 'Oh, I see. Well, we all know what you two've been up to. Or was it the hip-and-thigh diet gone a bit wrong, love? Did you have the book upside-down, maybe?' Everyone was laughing. Philip felt his scalp run with sweat. Kath was running up the steps to the exit. As Philip climbed after her he stopped and made a 'V' sign at the stage. 'Two?' said Tooley. 'So it's the twins, then? Mind . . .' He turned to the far section of the audience. 'If it's come from a fat bastard like yourself, it could just be the one.' The laughter was wilful.

Unfair.

In the empty bar, Philip sat next to Kath on a wall seat. He watched a woman straightening chairs, wiping tables, the air reeking of stale smoke. From the auditorium came layers of laughter and Tooley's muffled voice. Had he found someone else to make fun of? Someone who could take a joke? Philip would never be able to watch him on television again. More grief to suppress. Or maybe he should go back inside? Or wait for him afterwards? For one thing, Philip was not that fat. For another, it's not on to make fun of pregnant women. And for another . . .

'I'm sorry, Philip,' said Kath. 'I just didn't feel right. I thought I was going to go over.' She was looking down at the points of her boots, her skin milk white, her hands held tightly together.

'They've got the heating too high,' he said, wrapping the comment around his real annoyance. 'It's not your fault.'

85

He sat up, looking ahead of him. 'If anyone's to damn well blame . . .'

'Please don't go on. I'll be all right, in a minute. We can go back in.'

'You're joking! After what he said?' Without thinking, he snatched up her hand. 'Come on, we're out of here.'

On the drive home, the sleet came down and slithered on the windscreen. Kath was sitting with her head back, her eyes closed. She owed him. When had he ever said they should go home early? When had he *decided* he felt sick? Then through the smeary glass Philip thought he saw a familiar figure leaving a pub on the outskirts of town. His *bête noire*. The smallness of him, encamped behind a ridge of black snow. Twice in two days now. And it probably was Carl, Philip thought as they passed by him. It was part of the way things were going right now, the crappy hand life was dealing him. Back straight, erect against the shiting weather. The contempt of the guy. Here, on top of everything else. Philip drove on.

When they were home, Kath went up to bed without a word. Philip took off the waistcoat and threw it against the wall over the sofa. He would never wear it again. Ever. Then he sat down and stared into the fire, not bothering to turn it on. A few minutes later he could hear Kath getting up, and her quick padding steps to the bathroom, followed by her retching. With each bout of heaving, Philip looked harder into the fire, the man next door seeming to turn down his television. So he could listen too. The old rodent. The . . .

Fifteen

Every detail of the night streets was too real – the Belisha beacons at a zebra crossing, the window of a pet shop, a flickering sign for Budweiser above a closed off-licence. The only people Darren saw were two drunks staggering along, yet even they looked too important, as if they could suddenly come round and pass judgement on what was going on in the car. On a terraced street there were lights in living-room windows that filled him with a longing for normality, something he promised for himself when this was over.

Mick and the man were in the front, the man driving, piss-careful at the junctions. Mick alternated between looking ahead and watching the guy, his pistol under his arm, pointing at his ribs. Darren's gun was in his lap. It felt heavy on his legs. He would be more than pleased if he never had to pick it up again. The car had tinted windows, but he still kept low, pressing the back of his head against the seat, feeling his hair rub against the wool of the balaclava.

Mick cleared his throat. 'The security man doesn't start till twelve. Right?' He had a bone in his voice, sounding corny, like someone off the telly.

'There is no security man.'

'Come off it.'

'It's true. There hasn't been anyone for months. Cost-cutting. We just kept the sign in the car-park. It's a bluff.'

Mick sighed. 'Well, for argument's sake we'll pretend that there is. Just in case. All right?'

The man was making a left turn, the indicator light ticking gently. 'What exactly do you mean?'

'I mean, when we're through, we leave everything neat and tidy. No doors open any place. Got it?'

'Yes. I've got it.' The guy had held himself together pretty well until he rubbed the side of his face, his hand shaking. 'My wife won't be hurt, will she? You're going to promise me that?'

'It's down to the fucking alarm system, mate,' said Mick. 'And everything else. We're back at your place within forty minutes. If not, our friend back there has his instructions. Right? And he's a hard bastard, I'll tell you. Fucking fearless.'

Darren, for all his qualms, couldn't resist a smile. Two hours ago, Luke hadn't really a clue what they were going to be doing that night. It was Mick's idea to keep it from him, and to get a bit of dope into him so he'd just go through with it without thinking.

'So,' said Mick. 'Just get it right. Clean and simple. Fast as you like, and we'll all be OK.'

'How can I trust you?'

'You'll just have to. You've no choice. Now shut it. We're nearly there.'

The man looked across at Mick, trying to see his eyes. He glanced down at the gun, perhaps weighing up the odds about its being genuine or not. What was he after? Evidence? Being a hero? God, not that. Darren couldn't face any more shouting and banging about. He was not cut out for it, and he swore that, when this was over, he would go back to being the quiet kid everyone took him for, not saying boo to a bastard goose.

He resumed his vigil on the passing streets. The houses gave way to a set of white railings and the closed gates of a park. Some sort of memorial place. Beyond this were tall old buildings, one of which was a Barclays Bank, then a wide empty street and an industrial estate. Darren's hands were itching and sweating in the gloves. A minute away. That's all they were.

Sixteen

There was nothing wrong with this idea. He had his reasons, didn't he? For a start, he had barely slept all night. That wasn't normal, was it? In this day and age you had a right to expect a decent night's sleep. And there was that worry about his blood pressure. What was the word? Hypertension? Yes, that was the main thing. Prevention better than cure, that's the ticket. Nothing *neurotic* about that. And anyway, what were doctors paid for if they didn't see their patients once in a while?

Philip pulled into the car-park. Only one space left. Christ, did the planet have enough metal left for the making of all these cars? What were they all doing here? Didn't they work, these people? Was everyone in a permanent state of needing a doctor, a way of avoiding life's changes of fortune? They should get their heads together.

Get a grip.

He eased in between an Audi and beige Reliant Robin. Cursing, he squeezed out of the door, only to step into a puddle of brown slushy snow. When he had sidled and tiptoed between the cars, he stopped to look at the bumper. It was the first time he had examined it in open daylight, the bright torn lips of the nine-inch gash jolting his heart. It was worse than he had thought. Yet it had only been a clip. The thing must be made of paper. What else could explain it? He touched it with his finger. It would have to be fixed, then maybe he could forget the whole episode. A good idea – the tidying-away of at least one piece of recent grief.

A misty rain began falling as he crossed the tarmac to the surgery.

There were three winos in the waiting room. One looked morose, but the others were laughing, swearing, a big bottle of cider on the floor between them. Philip took a corner seat, hoping not to attract their attention. Why were they allowed in a place like this, anyway? What might they do to his blood pressure? He looked out of the window at the dreary Cross Gates roads, trying to spot the roof of the house, two streets away, where their flat used to be. Dear, dear, life was simple then. He had been so free. The buzzer went and one of the winos answered the call of the receptionist with a loud 'Right y'are, darlin' ' before staggering into the corridor.

Philip looked at a row of leaflets. 'Drug Abuse – The Signs in Your Child.' 'Diabetes Counselling.' 'The Management of Arthritis.' They made his presence seem fraudulent, a familiar feeling, the same every time he came. And how many times had that been? Six or seven? It probably said something about him, an uncomfortable indication of . . . One of the winos, a man of unguessable age with a ratty beard and a lumberjack shirt, was watching him. Philip picked up a two-year-old copy of *The Field*, wishing he had not come.

Yet he had imagined a meeting like this so often, fantasising about having someone to talk to, seeing it last for hours as he offloaded some of the millions of words that went through his mind about the state of his health, his life. In minuscule detail he would offer theories about his uniqueness, his wayward concentration, his unsuitability for work as an insurance underwriter, the pressure of impending parenthood and how he *needed* to avoid it. And, at some late point, there might be a frank admission of his feelings of anger and the way he believed them to be the residue of an unreasonably difficult existence. In his imagination a kindly Dr Beauman would clutch his healthy pink chin, nod sagely, perhaps even produce the after-surgery Scotch from a filing cabinet, since the elaborateness of Philip's 'case' would require a period of consultation way beyond the usual ten minutes. Then, at the last, after some great and silent analysis, the doctor would offer a single key suggestion, the answer to everything. Hands would be shaken, absolution guaranteed, a new and radiantly happy life waiting the moment Philip stepped out of the surgery door.

Staring at a picture of a herd of Friesians, he wondered about the raking extent of these secret daydreams. They were hardly normal, were they?

The wino was still watching, smiling. He shuffled across the seats to Philip, nudging his elbow. 'Any sex?'

'What?'

'In thi magazine. Any sex in it?'

'No.' Philip looked imploringly for the receptionist, but she was across the office, on the telephone. He glared at the magazine.

'What's up with yer? Like sex, don't yer? A nice fanny. Bet your wife's got a nice warm one. Bet you could set up 'ome in it. Eh?'

Philip could smell the man's fruity breath. He gave a sigh of middle-class indignation. 'Please leave me alone.'

'Whoo! Hark at this! Please leave me alone. Not good enough for you, are we? Not . . .'

The buzzer went. 'Mr Pickles?'

'Pickles? Fuckin' Pickles? Branston fuckin' . . .'

Borne by a relief beyond measure, Philip went through to the doctor's office.

Beauman was flitting about his room. Philip could never remember finding him seated. He took the chair beside the desk, with the doctor standing behind his own chair, looking down at the notes. 'You again!' he said. 'I've seen you sitting out there before with my old ladies and coughing kids. You didn't seem to fit in!' Philip thought this unfair. He had not been here for six months, the last time being for a perfectly genuine chest infection. He considered his rehearsed opening line about the difficulty he was having sleeping. But it did not seem enough. 'So what's it now, then?' asked Beauman, shrugging oddly in his grey suit.

'I was wondering about my blood pressure. I get these headaches. And there's my mood . . .' It was as feeble as it could possibly be. Beauman shook his silvery head, raised his pointed chin to the ceiling, and tutted.

'Anything else?'

91

Philip looked down at his shoes. 'I was hoping you might tell me.'

The doctor had still not sat down. 'So it's just reassurance you're after, really.'

'I don't know.'

Beauman, breathing heavily, leaned towards Philip. 'You don't know?'

'Well, I just thought . . .'

'Never mind. Never damn mind.' He darted over to two cluttered tables by the wall, looking for something, coming back with his device for taking blood pressure, a famous-looking medical device that for some reason made Philip even more miserable. The doctor tapped on Philip's arm, motioning him to take off his jacket and roll up his sleeve. 'I'm not sure if this is the right thing to do. I often ask myself what the point is in telling people they're all right. They're only happy for a day, then they're back with some other piddling thing.' He put the cuff on, inflated it and listened with the stethoscope. Philip watched the mercury fall. '126 over . . . 82. I should be so healthy! God, what's up with you young people? It's every blessed little thing. Honestly, you see something on the television, or in a newspaper and you're away to the surgery like a rat up a drainpipe.' He snatched off the cuff and tipped down the lid on the apparatus. 'Now! What else is the matter?'

Philip could see a network of bright capillaries on his nose and, along his jaw, a line of silver bristles he must have missed when he shaved that morning. Now he was in Philip's face, his chest rising and falling beneath the red tie. A man having a bad day. God, why had Philip come here. 'Nothing. There's nothing else the matter.' He rolled down his sleeve. 'That's all I wanted to know.'

'Maybe in the future you might consider what a consultation like this costs, young man.'

'Yes,' said Philip, making his way to the door.

It had been a mistake. A stupid admission of insecurity. And it made him an hour late for work.

As soon as he arrived at his desk, the phone was ringing.

'Life and Deaths. Philip . . .'

'Mr Pickles?' It was Griffiths.

'Yes . . .'

'I'm still waiting to hear from you. Yesterday you said you'd be sorting out my claim straight away. What's happening? Can you tell me? Eh?' Another man at odds with the world. What was the matter with everyone today?

'It'll take a little more time, Mr Griffiths. I'm sorry. I do understand . . .'

'Like hell you do. Do you know what your sales pitch claims?'

'I am aware of the terms.'

'Forty-eight hours. That's two days, Mr Pickles! And we've been at this for weeks now. Do you know anything about the Trades Descriptions Act? Do you know what I can do here?'

'No,' Philip said, tiredly.

'For a start there's my MP. Then there's the local paper. They know me there. I advertise with them every week. What sort of a story do you think this will make? How will your company look then? Well, Mr Pickles?'

'Look, Mr Griffiths, don't be hasty.'

'Why not? Why the hell not? Something's got to be done!'

'I know. And it will be. Trust me.'

'That's just it. I don't trust you, or anything to do with your firm. You've got till Friday. Right?' He hung up.

Philip put the phone down and closed his eyes. He wanted to sleep. Then Howard appeared, with his bustling, unearthly brightness. 'All right there, Phil?'

'Sure, sure. Just fine.' He rubbed his eyes, simply not being able to take Howard asking him why he was late in.

'Er, I took a call on your phone.'

'Nothing important, I trust.'

'A friend of yours. Someone called Oz.'

'Oh, right.'

Howard was hovering. Philip hoped he would not ask about

the Griffiths claim. He was too tired. It was not worth talking about.

'Are you on for this afternoon still?'

'On for what, Howard?'

'The review. The staff review. Are you on the case yet, Phil?'

'I forgot. Sorry.'

'Well, let's say two-thirty. Right? I'll give you a shout.'

As he moved away, bouncy as a puppy, the telephones about the office seemed to ring in a flurry. There had been a mail shot that morning, a glossy leaflet, a copy of which Howard had placed on everyone's desk. Philip picked his up and looked at it: 'Pilot Insurance – Transporting You to Peace of Mind.'

For fuck's sake.

His phone rang again. He picked up the receiver and dropped it back, looking around, daring anyone to notice.

It was a Wednesday. That was the trouble with it all. The longest day of the week. Philip had been born on a Wednesday. The woe, the woe. It had hung over him all his life. Fucking nursery rhymes. Who invented them? Didn't they know what they could *do* to people?

He closed his eyes, wanting to sleep. For a long time. Such a long time.

Seventeen

These thick carpets, the smell of money. Probably not the smartest place in the world, but still better than anywhere Luke would ever live – a fuck-off house, two fingers up to dogs like him. He'd spent all his life in a council maisonette, with crappy furniture, heating they couldn't afford to turn on, the phone cut off every other bastard week. How did people get the cash together for somewhere like this? How come they *deserved* it, and not him? Maybe he should level the scores a bit. Right now, he could do whatever he liked, couldn't he?

Power, for once. Neat.

He went into the kitchen, opening cupboards, looking for anything that might drop into his pocket. In a narrow cupboard beside the cooker he found a bottle of sherry. He had never tried sherry before. He took the top off and drank. It was sweet, sickly, though the hit was instant, a good warm feeling in his empty guts. He strolled around, swigging from the bottle. There was a radio next to the microwave. He turned it on. Fleetwood Mac. Radio Two-type wank. But he jacked up the volume and did a little jig to it, all the same.

The drink was making him smile. He looked in the other cupboards, leaving them all open, then thought about the upstairs. There must be cash somewhere. And jewellery. A biddy like this might have plenty of the stuff. But how would he know what was worth having? Better find it first. Or why not make her tell him where it was? He left the radio blaring and went back along the hall, feet bouncing on the springy blue carpet.

Mick had taped her hands and feet, blindfolding her with one of her own scarves. Luke was meant to stay with her, saying nothing. But she wasn't going anywhere, lying on the sofa, head on a pink

95

velvet cushion, shit scared. He took another drink, watching the thin legs, all still, the dyed blonde hair with the roots showing, the lines on her neck. Middle-aged. A privileged cow.

'Are you there?' Her voice was like a girl's.

'What d'you want?'

She cleared her throat. 'What are you going to do with us?'

'Nothin'.'

'Don't hurt John. He's a good man. He doesn't deserve bad things happening to him. Neither of us do.'

Luke watched her mouth, the dry lips, her worn yet unblemished teeth. She sobbed a little, taking in a gasp of air. He had left the gun and hood in the kitchen. A vague urge told him to go and get them, but his head was feeling light and lazy. He wanted a bit of fun. He sat down on the armchair by the fire, cursorily looking round for drawers, fancy boxes, stashes of treasure.

'Do you mind if I talk?' she said. 'I'll go mad if I don't.'

Luke shrugged, despite knowing she could not see him.

'You're very young.' She gave a quivering half-smile. 'I can tell.'

'So?'

'So, nothing.' She tried to moisten her mouth. Her fingers wriggled. 'How long do you think your friends will be?'

'Not long.'

'They will come back here, won't they?'

Luke felt a spasm of annoyance. What was she saying? That they'd do a runner? 'Course they will.'

'And then you'll leave John and me in peace?'

'That's t'plan.'

'We won't ring the police, I promise. You'll have plenty of time . . .'

'Look, just shut it will yer, missus?' He stood up, feeling angry. The insinuation that Darren and Mick might not come back was needling him.

'All right. If you say so . . .'

'I do say, missus. I do fucking say.'

Her mouth wrinkled. Crying again. A crappy sound.

96

Luke crossed the big white rug. He stood over her, watching, then, with a childish curiosity, he touched the raised veins of her blue, bound hands with his fingertips. She jerked and sobbed. Luke stood back. Look at her. He could do anything he wanted with her. His prick was up like a brush handle. Maybe . . . She was not such a bad looker. Dog old, but what the hell. When would he get a chance like this again? And it would mean so much. At long last. For it was Luke's guilty secret that, at seventeen years of age, he had never done it with a woman. It was his Big Shame. He touched her ankles in a pretence of checking they were still fast.

'What are you doing?' Her voice was dry and old now. Like a teacher's. 'I'm not going anywhere.'

A flush of sweat came over him. She was helpless. A slab of meat. But how to do it? How to get it right?

'What are you doing now?'

'Nothin'.'

She licked her lips and swallowed. 'You're not going to hurt me, are you?'

'For fuck's sake, will you shut up!'

'I will! Yes, I will!' The skin on her cheeks had gone grey, like she was really frightened, descending through layers of fear.

He looked around for something to cut the tapes on her ankles. The body of the smashed statuette was in the hearth. It had a sharp edge where the neck had been. He picked it up and began cutting at her bound feet, the idea of what he was going to do getting him in a frenzy.

'No! No!' She was kicking her legs.

'Keep still! Stupid bitch!' He straddled her, sitting on her knees, his arse to her head. It was brown parcel tape, six layers thick, making a binding like leather. She carried on moaning and wriggling. He could not cut through the tape. Mad as hell, he threw the statuette across the room. It would have to be something else. But as he turned, pulling at his belt as she bucked and groaned beneath him, it was over.

He had shot his load. It had emptied and emptied in his pants.

He rolled off her, dropping to the floor. For a moment he closed his eyes. The woman was sobbing above him. 'Oh, dear God. God . . .' Luke looked up at the ceiling. He had fucked it up. The first time in his life he'd had a chance. And what a chance. Fucking gilt-edged. He sat up, looking at her. A broiler. Could be his granny. A tired relief came, a gladness that he had not done it with such a poor specimen. She was still weeping and groaning. He stood up and bawled in her ear. 'Quiet! For the last fucking time!' He went back in the kitchen.

There was still time for a bit of thieving. But his heart was not in it any more. He opened the fridge and took out a slice of ham, stuffing it in his mouth. He looked blankly at the still-playing radio then went back into the hall. To his left was a pair of glazed doors, a darkened room beyond. He pushed one of the doors open and switched on the light. It was a dining room, with shelves and shelves of books, a small television in the corner, a big chrome and smoked-glass table in the middle. He looked around for what might be valuable, but that plan had gone now. His bowels curdled with the ham. Then, with a grin to himself, he had another idea, something born of an ancient angry heritage. He stood on one of the chairs and tested his weight on the table, one foot, then the other. He positioned himself carefully in the middle, dropped his trousers and squatted. This would give them something to think about when they had Sunday dinner. 'This'll teach 'em,' Luke muttered, going red with the effort. But, while he was still in the process, he looked back through the open door.

Someone was there. Watching him.

Eighteen

'Phil, lovey!'

In an instant part of Philip's past came visiting – lower sixth, him and Oz, bright lads idling away the summer holidays, taking the piss out of soft porn videos at Oz's house in Farley, drinking his old man's beer allowance from Tetley's where he worked. Just for the laughs. Everything. Did they even look at a clock in those days? 'Darlin',' said Oz's mother. 'How are you?' Philip could have dived into the mouthpiece and kissed her. Oz's family were like his own, only more so, surrogate, easy to please.

'I'm fine! I'm great!' Philip said loudly, for the benefit of Tarquin who was hanging around, two desks behind him. 'Is Oz there, Mrs D?'

'Listen to you, Mrs D! You can call me Joyce, now you're all grown-up!'

'But I don't want to be grown-up!' he said, tapping the desk with his pen. 'I prefer Mrs D. All right?'

She laughed politely.

'Is Oliver there then?'

'He's out somewhere. I think he's after meeting up with you on Friday. He's looking after his sister's flat. Do you know it?'

'Course I do! Over at Headingley.'

'Well, he's been away a bit . . .'

'I know! I know!'

'And I think he wants a bit of company.'

'And why not, Mrs D? Why not? A chance to talk over old times. Has he got a job, then?'

'Sort of. Well, you know what he's like. Just drifting along. Seems he'll never stick at anything. Not like you. You're doing so well, I hear.'

Philip laughed. 'Wouldn't put it like that. Just following the crowd, doing what's expected. Boring as buggery, really.'

'Oh, come on. And you've got that baby on the way too, I'm told.'

'I know! Somebody told me about it too!'

She cackled. A golden nature. 'You lads. Our Marion's got two now, you know, Oz's other sister.'

'Two! Fancy! One's unlucky. Two's downright careless!'

'Give over. I'll tell him you called then.'

'Do that,' said Philip. 'Tell him Friday's just fine. I'll meet him at the flat. Tell him six o'clock, and don't be late!'

The call lifted his spirits massively, recalling a life beyond this drudgery, a time of *promise*. But as soon as she rang off, Shelley came on the line. 'Two callers waiting. A Mr Hyder and a Mr Merrick.'

'Great!' said Philip. 'I'll take neither! Out to lunch! Sorr-ee!'

'Come on, Phil . . .'

'Another time, Shell!' And he put the phone down and sprinted from his desk before it could ring again.

'I've just come out of the bog. Somebody's kicked a hole in the damned wall.' Howard fingered his Adam's apple, pondering. 'Who'd do a thing like that? What gets into people?'

'Pass, Howard,' said Philip.

It was two in the afternoon and they were back in the rest room where Philip had idled away an hour and a half for lunch, happy to spend the rest of the day there, if he could get away with it. He slouched in his chair, arms folded, legs sprawled and crossed at the ankles.

'You know, one day I'd like to catch someone pissing about like that. I'd give them bloody hell.'

'Good luck,' said Philip.

'Anyway, let's get on to skill sets.' Howard looked down at the papers in his lap, switching his fingers from his throat to the dent in his nose. 'By the way, how's the Griffiths thing going?'

'Oh, you know . . .' Philip grinned.

'Well, they think they've got a handle on the bugger, down in Brum. It's this history of depression. As you know, Griffiths said naff all when he took out the policy. They're going to try and find out if she had a breakdown, at some point.'

'No such thing,' said Philip.

Howard looked up. 'Come again?'

'I've read about it. There's no such thing as a nervous breakdown. There're extremes of things, but no one ever actually goes over the top. It was in the Sunday paper the other week. Fascinating.'

Howard looked away, frowning over this challenge to his assumed expertise on medical matters. 'Well, you know what I mean.'

'Yes, Howard.'

Philip took a sip of the coffee Howard had paid for himself. A contrived gesture, Philip thought. Dreary. He looked at the papers in Howard's lap. The staff review. It was the most pointless exercise in the whole of the company's routine. If you were any good, it showed, and that's all there was to it. This was mere ornament, something to make the hierarchy believe they had a hold on you. But, what the fuck, if it made them *feel* happier . . . Philip sat back, pinching his chin, making a cleft. Maybe he really should try to grow a beard.

'Now . . .' Howard had a sheet of paper in each hand, looking from one to the other.

'Howard, do you mind if I ask you a question?

'Fire away, Phil.'

'Your nose. What happened to your nose?'

He laughed, surprisingly loudly. 'Isn't it obvious?'

'No!'

'Boxing. I used to do it when I was a lad. A boys' club, near where I grew up.'

'You had to be tough in Newcastle, then?'

'Sort of. It helped if the other kids knew you were handy. I won a couple of trophies. Then I found my conk was made of paper. Had it broken twice.'

101

'Wouldn't once have been enough?'

Howard laughed. 'What, to make it this shape?' He actually seemed to be enjoying this, failing to spot Philip's flippancy. The sap.

'Sorry. I shouldn't have mentioned it.'

'Hey, no worries, Phil. You're the first person that's asked me in nine years of being here. And there's me thinking no one had noticed!'

'Like I said. Sorry.'

'No, mate,' Howard said, more seriously. 'We should talk about things.'

'The interaction and all that.'

Howard smiled, weakly, as if realising Philip was taking a rise. 'Maybe.' He shuffled his papers again.

Philip was dangerously bored. He looked about the deserted room, the clutter of mugs by the sink, the Twix wrappers and balls of clingfilm that had not made it to the bin. On the wall was a poster from their eunuch union, urging the workers to complain about any injudicial working practices. As if. Through the window Philip could see other offices, the clean lines of the buildings, hard against the ivory Leeds sky. No life there, not even a pigeon, nothing doing that was natural, or human. Jesus, the tedium of it all. Columbus had got it wrong. The world *was* flat. He had sailed to the edge and fallen off. There was no America, nowhere else but this one-dimensional, squashed-dead here and now.

'Diplomacy, OK. Motivation, friendliness . . .' Howard was reading from a copy of the review form Philip had filled in just ten minutes earlier. He had still been ticking his way down it when Howard called him from his desk. 'Tact . . .'

'There's no box for sense of humour.'

'No. And you need it working here, let's be honest,' said Howard. 'But if there was, you'd get top marks, I reckon.' Philip considered the outburst with Tarquin in the pub the night before. Howard was being kind and he should give him credit for it, if he could be bothered.

'Consideration? Yes, very considerate . . .'

Columbus was a cunt. Why couldn't he just leave the native Americans alone? Why couldn't he have pretended they weren't there, just turned back and said the place wasn't worth discovering? Why couldn't everyone simply be left alone?

'Response to pressure . . .'

Why, oh why, oh why . . .

'By the way, I've had Dick from Supplies on to me. Apparently he's done an inventory and there's a phone missing. From the desk next to yours. You wouldn't know anything about it, would you, Phil?'

A pang of guilt. The fucking phone. A stupid trick, no question about that, though he was sure no one had seen him. Or did Howard know something? Deny it. Easy enough. 'No. Can't help you there, Howard.'

'Just thought I'd ask.' He shifted foward on his seat. 'You being closest, like.' He was looking directly at Philip. Those eyes, seeing *into his soul.*

'Sorry, Howard. Not guilty.' He stared back at the supervisor, yet it did not seem enough. Howard had something on him, though he could not just bring it out here, surely, when there were only the two of them, alone in this big empty room? In cold blood? It wouldn't be human.

'OK. Well . . .' Howard flipped the page over. 'All OK, really. You're all right, Philip.'

'Am I?'

'Yes.'

'Great. That's good to know,' Philip said, putting his hands behind his head and closing his eyes. 'I can die unhappy now.'

Howard rustled his pages. 'There's just one grey area.'

'And what's that?' said Philip opening his eyes.

'Concentration. A bit of a tendency to let the old mind wander. I spotted it the other day.'

'Did you?'

'You were staring out of the window.'

'That constitutes a grey area, does it?'

103

Howard smiled. 'A bit grey. But with a few pink tinges.'

Philip stretched his arms and looked towards the window, deliberately, using his boredom as a defence. 'Pink tinges, Howard?'

Nineteen

Darren caught the cuff of his jacket on the window catch. How stupid could he get? He put the gun on the seat, Mick and the man waiting for him as he untangled himself. Six years old! He felt six fucking years old! Behind the two men, real grown men, the big red Save-U-More sign was lit by a single spotlight. The car-park was empty, the streets beyond spookily quiet, as if the city was thinking, holding a big secret, ready to burst into laughter as Darren unhitched his sleeve.

It was not how he remembered it from that day they had come here. Then it was daylight, with people everywhere, the cars coming and going, families with kids, clanking trolleys, no one taking a blind bit of notice of the two young men in a car with false plates, Mick pointing carefully at the staff entrances, explaining the internal geography, which Darren could not follow, and the times and movements of the security staff, one of whom he said was a mate. How reliable was that? Hadn't this guy just said they didn't use a security firm any more? Darren looked around. He hadn't thought it would be this quiet. In his dumb head he had imagined it would be busy, the same as during the day. He leaned back inside for the gun. Mick had said to have it wrapped at this point, but the bag had slipped on to the floor. He could not see it. In a teenage panic, he shoved the gun beneath his jacket, the nozzle pointing up at his chin. Mick and the man were still watching. Darren wanted to say sorry, guessing at the words on Mick's tongue. But all Mick said was a whispered 'Come on', tapping the man on the shoulder and nodding towards the supermarket.

They walked quickly, breaking into a half-trot, keeping to the shadows near the shrub borders, avoiding the covered walkways where the security cameras were pointing. For ram-raiders, Mick had explained. Though what would anyone want to ram a supermarket for? The fucking corned beef? They passed a ventilation grille. Its humming suggested life might be going on inside as normal, unsettling Darren even more. At the side door he was rocking with impatience as the man searched among his keys. He wanted to take charge and tell him to hurry the fuck up. Mick was watching, cool as you like. Then they were inside.

It was an ante-room, dimly lit. Behind the door was a tiny wall cupboard. The man opened it, Mick watching inches from his face as he pressed a combination and turned a small key. 'That's it,' said the guy. 'It's off.'

'You're fucking sure about that, aren't you?' whispered Mick. 'On my life.'

'Right.' Mick tapped his shoulder with the butt of the sawn-off. 'Come on.'

They went along a short corridor and through a fire door to the open supermarket itself. They were in the booze section, the shelves and empty aisles stretching ahead and to the right, lit by night lights. Its hard familiarity struck Darren. In another life they could just get a trolley, pick up a few things and make their way to the check-out. Like anyone normal. He blinked the sweat from his eyes. As Mick had planned, they doubled over, covering their faces as they followed the man to his office. All this would be on camera. The pictures would not be so hot, but every detail would be scrutinised, their build, clothing, the colour, Mick had pointed out, of Darren's rainbow eyes. Hence the cream, though Darren feared he might have sweated it all away. He kept his arm over his forehead as they made the short journey across the floor, watching his feet, fearful of knocking bottles off the shelves. Of, even at this rarefied instant, looking an even bigger tosser than he had already shown himself to be.

Once inside, they ran through a set of swing doors, an inner security door, and up a flight of six stairs. To the right was a room full of blue staff lockers. A white hat and a crumpled overall lay on the floor. In front was the office which the man unlocked, readily. It smelt of new wood, and some kind of oil. The strip light flickered on, revealing two desks in an L-shape, filing cabinets, shelves of box files, a drawn red venetian blind and, in the corner, a safe almost as tall as the door. It was the first safe Darren had seen in his life. The man went straight to it, then stopped, looking at Mick.

'This is really it? I mean, this is what you want?'

'What the fuck d'you think?' Mick revealed his sawn-off and threw a canvas sack on the floor. 'Get on with it.'

The man looked at the bag. He was pale now, looking like a heart-attack job. From another pocket he produced a tiny cloth purse. He picked out a long chrome stem on the bunch of keys and took a key head from the purse, screwing the two together. With a plain Yale, he unlocked a dial, worked in the combination then opened the heavy door with the chrome key. He picked up the bag and kneeled down, slowly. 'I can't see you'll have much use for the cheques.'

'Everything. The lot.' Mick waved the gun at the safe.

Darren shifted round to see inside. The lower half was stacked with till drawers, a small mountain of coins bagged up at the side. On a shelf above were the notes, in hard parcels. A genuine rush of pleasure came with this actual sight of what they were after. The point of it all. He wanted to get the stuff himself, help out, speed it up. But Mick was leaning forward and looking, shaking his head.

'Is this it?'

'Yes,' said the man.

'There's nowhere near enough! Supposed to be a day's fuckin' takings, this! Where the fuck's the rest?'

'It's all there is, I swear. It's as much as there ever is.'

'Lyin' bastard!' Mick cuffed his head with the butt of his gun. The man took the blow stiffly.

'Look, there's nothing else, I promise you. I mean, what do you want? There's over six thousand here . . .'

Mick banged him on the shoulder. 'Get on with it!'

The man began working, removing the stacks four at a time and dropping them in the bag.

Darren dared a look at Mick, not liking the way he was coming on to this guy. Six thousand was less than half the amount he said would be here. But was it that bad? Two thousand apiece? It was way more than Darren had ever had in his life.

When the shelf of notes was empty, the envelopes of cheques and other shit all away, the man began dropping the bags of silver into the sack, shaking it to get the weight to the bottom. When he had finished he looked up at Mick.

'The tills!' Mick yelled.

'We only leave copper in the trays. The rest of the floats are made up in the morning.'

'Empty the cunts!'

The man nodded and began scooping coins from the stacked till trays. Darren wondered about this. It would take another two minutes at least. Didn't they have enough? But he said nothing.

When the man had finished, he got up slowly, groaning like his knees hurt, rubbing his back. Mick gestured to Darren to pick up the bag. As arranged, he dropped the gun inside and gathered up the top. It was heavy, but not as heavy as the sacks of plaster at the building site – and he had lifted plenty of those. He swung it confidently over his shoulder, a display of his growing competence. Mick tapped the guy on the shoulder. The man seemed reluctant to move. Was he thinking about resisting them? Was that moaning about his knees a bluff? For all his grey hair, he might be a handful. Mick, sensing his hesitation, grabbed hold of his arm and shoved him towards the door. 'Away! Bastard! Let's fucking go!' He stumbled forward and began walking.

They filed out of the office, Darren's heart lifting with the relief of being on the move. Now he was calm as could be, skipping down the steps as if he had been let out of some piss-boring lesson at school. The open space of the supermarket was liberating, every step across the tiled floor a glad one. The fresh air would be even better. Passing the rows of booze, he actually felt like dropping a bottle in his pocket for the old man. But that was not in the plan, that brilliant scheme of Mick's that was working so well. Only one part of it left now – back to the man's house. And in another fifteen minutes they'd be out of it. Free as birds. And loaded, with it.

Twenty

Hyder had said be there at six. Philip checked his watch as he passed through the empty market. Ten minutes late. Poor form, really, when you were dealing with the police.

It should have been a pleasure walking into the station, into the arms of institutional protection. So what was he feeling guilty about? Weren't all the *facts* of the case in his favour? Hopefully, though there was so much against him in so many departments of his life. It was a losing streak he felt powerless to halt. And there was Merrick, that black stalking dog. He had rung the office three more times that afternoon, Philip refusing to speak to him, getting Shelley to say he was out, though the bastard must have known he was there. Philip felt his spirits cloud with the thought that Merrick might actually have been here to the station to make a complaint. How would that make him look?

A uniformed man led the way through a series of swing doors to a big open office.

Detective Sergeant Hyder was a little older than Philip, with short fair hair and a thin cadaverous smile. He asked Philip to take a seat with that creepy patrician air Philip had noticed before. This would not be a pleasure, in any way. Philip sat down, Hyder shuffling closer to examine the papers on his desk.

'I saw our friend the other day,' Philip said with a timid cheerfulness.

'Oh?'

'Passing the office. Monday night. It felt quite intimidating.'

Hyder shrugged one shoulder. 'I don't see how he could know where you work. And there couldn't be anything in it for him . . .' He paused. 'If he bothered you again.'

'No. That's what I thought.'

The policeman studied his papers. Philip looked around at the men in white shirts, the neatly arranged desks. Telephones were ringing, the air was filtered, and a man in a brown overall was emptying wastepaper bins into a black polythene bag. It could have been any ordinary day at Pilot. Was this what they did with crime these days? Market it? Provide customer care? Was there regional competition, mail shots about their services? Hyder looked up. 'Well, we're near the end of this, you'll be pleased to know.'

'Good.'

'Yes, it is good.' But Hyder seemed cool, as if in receipt of fresh news about Philip, the revelation of an aspect of his character. Something poor. Had Merrick really been? 'Things like this,' he said, 'well, they can get a bit hellish. The incident's over in minutes, but the ramifications go on for months.'

'Yes,' said Philip. 'I know what you mean.' He looked down at his knees, the office grime on his grey trousers. When he glanced up, the policeman was looking directly at him. Into his worried heart.

'Are you all right?'

'Sorry?'

'You look a bit pale.'

'Oh, it's just a bit warm.' Philip smiled weakly. 'After the cold.'

'Right. OK.' He picked up a form with a City of Leeds coat of arms on the top. 'So, as you know, we've got the video evidence of Stall running away. It's not perfectly damning, but his statement is, and on that alone it should be cut and dried. Robbery with violence.' He looked up. 'I think you know the score.'

'Yes.'

'The thing is . . .' Hyder paused, lifting back a little.

The thing was what? That Andrew Merrick had been here? That Philip had no right to innocence? There was a heaviness in his stomach. This was going to turn out badly.

Hyder coughed and patted his chest. 'Sorry. The thing is,

I've heard on the grapevine that they're trying to make a case for provocation, some earlier incident involving a barman, and some old woman.' A dreadful twist. An avalanche of culpability. Philip had told him virtually nothing about what had led up to the incident. Now this was it, his exposition as a liar and cheat. When you die, it's always *the thing you least expect* that jumps up and gets you. 'Do you know anything about that?'

Philip's mouth had gone loose, a trickle of saliva in his cheek. The thing you *least expect*. Why was he thinking that? Because today he was going to die. 'News to me. I told you everything that happened. Simple robbery. What else could it be?'

'Well, you'd think that, certainly. But, as I say, we may have to consider the complication of a counter-allegation.'

'It'll be crap,' Philip said. 'I've done nothing wrong.' It was a juvenile reflex, a denial of his discomfort.

'Umm . . .' Hyder was looking into mid-space. Had he heard these last words? 'Well, it could be a diversionary tactic, though it seems a bit elaborate. Normally a guilty plea would be the thing, you know, saving the court's time and so on. But they will have seen the possibility of a prison sentence . . .'

The man in the overall, an old man Philip thought might be some kind of reformed criminal, was at his feet, scratching about for Hyder's bin. It was too much to bear. He wanted to kick the man out of the way. You *fucking prole*! But he could not say this. Must, must not. 'Look,' he said. 'What are they trying to say about me?'

Hyder was watching the man, waiting until he had moved away. He sat back, tapping his thumb with a pen. 'They're implying that you were upset over something.'

There was a rush of blood to Philip's face. 'What, that I'm a rager?'

'I didn't say that.'

'But that's the idea, isn't it?' he said, the secret demon stirring inside him, flailing its arms, screaming for confrontation. Here, of all places.

'We only have the facts as produced by our investigation. The theft clearly makes you the plaintiff . . .'

'I'm the victim!'

'If you like.'

'What do you mean, if you like?' Philip said, trying to hide his fast breath.

'Well . . .'

Philip clenched his teeth. He had one wild card to play, almost unthinkable. Yet he had to save face, his need desperate. *Primal*. 'Look, this has happened to me before, d'you know that?'

Hyder sat back, biting the pen. 'No.'

'Well, it has.' Philip leaned forward, chasing the man, *chasing him*. 'When I was eighteen years old, my parents were attacked and held hostage in a robbery.' At the Save-U-More supermarket. Do you remember? *Do you?* 'It happened in our own home, you know, the place where you're meant to feel safest? And I was there at the time, upstairs, frozen to the spot. But I heard everything. I heard what they did to my mother. And I saw them take my father away at gunpoint. At bloody gunpoint! Do you know what that can do to someone? Do you?' The blood was pulsing in his head. 'Then I was chased by one of them. Can you imagine that? Do you really know what it's like to be on the receiving end of shit like this? Well?'

The two men were staring at each other, in silence. The sweat formed into droplets on Philip's temples.

He had made a complete arse of himself.

Hyder rested his head on his chin. 'Did you receive counselling?'

'No. What would be the point? It's useless.'

'Well, I'm sorry for what happened to you.' He leaned forward, recovering the territory of his desk. 'But I'm afraid a *victim's* history has no bearing on the outcome of cases like this.'

'It should. It should . . .' Philip sat back, folding his arms, coiling into his own stupidity. He had been playing for sympathy. What a first-class fool! He never talked about that night. *Ever!* He had always been Mr Cool about it. To his parents, and everyone. A

112

deliberate modesty! And now he had betrayed that virtue. What a plonker. If only he had kept his mouth shut.

If only he was dead.

Hyder licked his lips. 'Look, er, anyway, what we're about on Friday is pitting your version of the event against his. And, frankly, it's a bit late in the day for us to be dealing with any new angles.'

Philip put his hand over his tired eyes. 'What does that mean?'

'It means we proceed with the case as we originally intended. There's no other way.'

'You've got Stall on video.'

'I know we have.'

'And, Christ, the guy owned up to it, didn't he?'

'Yes.'

'Well, isn't that enough?'

'It should be. Normally, it should be. But you have to realise a court case is an abstraction of the true detail. It's down to presentation. Who seems the most believable.'

Philip rubbed his head. 'Do you mean I might not get a result here?'

'That's for the magistrates to decide. I can't say, either way.'

An officer at another desk was answering the phone. Philip watched him, feeling tired, so *weary* of Hyder's company. This day, this life. All the things he had done and said. The buffoonery of it. A little weep might have been on the cards, if it would not have shown him to be an even bigger tit than he already looked.

Twenty-One

Luke clattered off the table, the glass top bending and rattling on its chrome supports. He pulled up his trousers, struggling with the top button. Flapping. Fucking panicking! In the hall he heard the kitchen door banging open, followed by footsteps on the patio. It was a kid taller than Luke, maybe his own age, with a crappy little beard. Still fastening the belt on his trousers, he ran after him.

In the dark back garden there was only a breeze, and the rustle of shrubbery. The cunt. He had to be here somewhere. Luke took a tentative step on to the neat square of lawn, an extension of the grass that ran around three sides of the house. He stood there looking, trying to get his eyes used to the gloom. To his right was a brick barbecue, and to the left a copper-beech tree. In front was a mass of bushes, a tall lap fence behind. Two bats were weaving about the eaves of the house beyond the fence. He hated bats. Just did not like the fuckers.

He took a few paces about the grass, wanting to appear calm in case he was being watched. But his hands were shaking, his heart was going fast. Then he heard a voice.

'Hello? Hello?'

It was the woman. The stupid fucking cow. Was she loose? And what about the gun? Why hadn't he kept it with him?

'Are you there?' The voice was coming clear as fuck through the back door. Half the bastard street could probably hear her. Jesus, shit. He felt light-headed. What a fucking mess he was making of this. Where the fuck were Darren and Mick? And what if they found him pissing around like this? The woman shouted again. 'Young man?' He would have to shut her up.

He ran back through the kitchen, and along the hall where

114

he could smell his own shit. The woman had wriggled on to the floor, sitting with her back against the settee, the blindfold slipping up her head.

'Is that you? Are you there?'

Luke grabbed the gun from the chair. 'There's some fucker out there! Who is it, missus?'

'I don't know.'

'Course you fuckin' know!' He was shouting on to the top of her head. 'You know who's in your own bastard house, don't you?'

She simpered. Her nose was running. 'Where is he? Have you hurt him?'

'So you know who it is, don't you?' He hit her with his knee, shoving her over. 'You cow, you fucking cow!' He was squeezing the gun tight, ready to use it like a cosh, to beat the brains out of that privileged blonde skull.

Crying heavily, she tried to push herself up on her elbow. 'It's my son . . . I didn't know he was in the house.'

'You did! You fucking knew he was here!' He was going psycho. Losing it.

'I didn't know, I swear. Please don't hurt him. Just get what you want and leave us all alone.'

Luke was standing over her, itching to beat the guts out of her, to see the blood, to smash and kick and lay waste, to let free every frustration that had ever been foisted on him, by his missing father, the shit-faced teachers at his school, the tease of television, the adverts that told him about everything he could never have, the people with their fuck-off houses, just like this one, and their fuck-off jobs and cars, and this whole bastard world, here in a split-second poison pinnacle in his head. He was standing there, gasping, baffled by it all.

The radio was still on in the kitchen, otherwise all was quiet. He lifted the safety catch on the pistol grip. The woman was completely still. And calm. You had to hand it to her. He lifted the gun to his face, resting his cheek against the butt, scratching at an itch, breathing on the trigger, as he heard a car pull up in the street.

* * *

115

On Briggate a giant Irishman was selling copies of *The Big Issue*. 'Jay-sus wept! Come on, will yer! Only twelve copies to go and I can get me head in a fuckin' pint!' Twenty yards away, Philip could smell the smoke from his cigarette. He walked on, among the late shoppers and office workers making their tired way home. At a bus shelter a kid was swinging from the roof, trying to kick in the clear Perspex wall, the little queue inside taking no notice. On Albion Street a man in a donkey jacket was shouting drunkenly at passers-by, wobbling on his feet with his indecipherable argument. Philip crossed the road to avoid him.

Snow was falling in large lazy flakes, the air with a coldness that smelt of soot. Philip slobbed along, the ghost of a thousand problems about him, his mind disconnected. He looked at the streets around him. What was he doing here? He was not yet twenty-six. He could have been anywhere in the world. But here he was, his arse parked in the city he had known all his life. Fucking Leeds. Not like it was. It had a new language now, its soul candid with everyone but him. Manchester had been better. He had been someone different there, anonymous, learning the pleasures of urban life with the freedom of a tourist. It had been so *small-minded* of him, coming back here.

Yet, at first, it had been good, that summer when he and Kath hired a boat, down by the new wharf developments, Tetley's and the Armouries. They had eaten and drunk at a café with a palm-court band playing outside. He wanted to think the city *had* changed while he was away, that Leeds might be a place to *believe* in.

A naivety. Dumb mistake. That Sunday afternoon with Kath seemed to mark an end to something. Happiness, probably, a thing you never realise you have until it's gone. It was enough to make your blood boil.

Philip made his way across the empty square to the car-park, fists clenched in his pockets, the city at his shoulder, a cold version of himself.

*   *   *

Mick was getting flustered. 'This light was off!'

'It was on,' said the man. 'It's always on. It's a night light. Look at it.' They all looked up. It was a tiny blue bulb in a disc beside a turned-off fluorescent strip. Darren wasn't sure either, but what did it matter? Couldn't they get out now?

'I still want it off!' hissed Mick.

There was no sense in this. They were by the side door, one wall between them and the outside, and what he knew would be the sweetest air he had ever breathed in his life. Yet he was still amazingly calm, the reason for doing this – the new future it would bring – unfolding inside him. They might even do it again! This internal triumph made him want to giggle, though he held it, watching the man as he shook his head and turned off the light. Quite right too. He *needed* to know who was in charge round here. Darren hitched the bag higher on his shoulder and followed the others across the dark floor.

As the door opened the relief was inexorable, still arriving as they made their way into the car-park, even as they halted, blinded by the big arc lamps Darren momentarily took to be the supermarket's lighting system. And the residue of victory yet remained, madly, as his eyes took in a row of white cars with stripes of yellow and blue along their sides, and the black hats showing above them.

'Stop! All of you! Stop right there!'

Twenty-Two

Longest day of the week. On and on. Jesus wept. If he was free, if everyone . . .

What if the rest of his life was like this?

Driving out of town Philip made a list of what he might really *want* to do that evening. Some pleasure was *owed*, after a day such as this. So. Rent a video? There was nothing he wanted to see. Films bored him terrifically these days. They went on so long. He had so much to *worry about*. If people only knew that and could see what he went through, day in, day out. Well, what to do? Wipe the dust off the games console? Too much effort. And it would give Kath something else to say when he got bored with it. Which would be right away, if he knew himself at all. Read a book? No way. He had not read a book since university. Ask Kath for sex? Always a thought – every six seconds, or fifteen, or whatever. And wouldn't he give his right arm to find her wearing a short black dress tonight, and for her to be thin again, thin and young, with those honey-olive legs and breasts, like the Portuguese girls . . . It would not happen, of course. He was reduced to asking for it these days. On his fucking knees. Bastard begging. Yet why should it be that way? It used to occur so naturally, so *mutually* . . . Which left? Only drink, that dangerously available solace. Though why should it be a problem? Everyone drank, didn't they? Every . . . body. And his body was no different to anyone else's. It needed its comforts. He had a right to drink. He was an adult, wasn't he? And the booze made him amenable. Everyone who knew him would testify to that. 'Yes,' he said aloud, approaching the village. 'I'm a grown man. I can do what the hell I like.' He pulled up outside the Spar. 'And right now, I need a drink.'

The old woman was behind the till, serving two children, the only other customers in the store. The usual irritation came jangling to life. The woman was looking his way. He ignored her and slipped round the back of the central shelves to the booze along the far wall. As he looked along the rows of red wine, he heard the door close. The children leaving. There would be just him and the old bag now. There would be inanities to exchange, but he could manage that, perhaps rehearse a few lines about the baby, the price of fucking tomatoes, things he could say by rote, with no part of himself attached. Wanting something more substantial than wine, he headed for a dump of Stella and picked up two four-packs. Down the aisle, round the corner now. *A tiring day at the office, Kath's husband and father-to-be?* Oh, a *grueller*. I couldn't begin to *tell* you. Yes, that kind of mush. It would be a breeze. But . . .

Where had they come from? Had they been waiting outside for Philip to come into the shop? The children were still there! And now there was a queue behind them. Four people! This could not be happening. There should be regulations, an allotted amount of time for the cretinously simple business of being served. The children were pointing at sweets in a jar. Oh God, something that had to be weighed on the scales. A quarter of bloody rainbow dip! Wasn't that sort of retailing outlawed these days? Weren't there health regulations? 'And this one's yours. And you want the same? Do you want to pay separately?' Unbelievable! 'Six ounces? I don't know if you've got enough there . . .' Philip would pay. He would buy them the whole bastard jar, just to get them out, to get the whole world on its way. Oh, oh, oh . . .

They were leaving. At last. Survival on the horizon. Everything comes to those who . . .

'There's a cheaper one, you know. It's just as good. I've tried it. Why don't I swap it . . .' Never. In a million years. Philip burned a hole in the back of the head of the young woman who was being served. Tell her! For pity's sake, tell her that life has a finite span, that death will be on us before we know it. And at the point of dying, when we reckon up the waste of

119

our precious time on this earth we will remember standing in a queue, in a piddling shop, in a hell-forsaken . . .

'It's OK,' said the woman. 'My husband likes this one.'

Someone rational, sane. Philip should be married to her.

The woman paid and left. Now there was only a couple and the guy standing immediately in front of Philip. Soon he would be delivered. He would not die here. The couple exchanged a few worrying words then put a packet of frozen chicken on the counter. And they refused a bag! Brilliant! Seconds later, they too had gone. This was so simple. Life could be easy. Except . . .

'I think you'll find there's a larger can of these. I know it's there. I spotted one left this morning. Better than buying two small ones, if you're going to eat them all at once. Shall I get it?'

'OK,' said the man.

OK? Philip's insides were burning. The front of his chest had fallen away, exposing his entrails, heart, the dying angel of his soul. It was the end of him, an utter emptying of his being over the two four-packs weighing in his hands like masonry. They would have to go. To save his life! Up in the air, through the window, on the top of this guy's head, or brought on to the old woman's face, smashing it to a pulp! Now she was coming back round the aisle, asking Philip to make way for her! She shuffled back on to her stool, picking at the shoulders of her overall, putting the fucking glasses on. The glasses! She has to die. Suddenly and violently. Now . . .

Now, now. The man had gone. Philip put the lager on the counter. She looked at one of the four-packs, found the label on top, rang in the price. 'Eight ninety-eight, please. Do you want a bag?'

She was looking at him, eyes watery, chin wattles beneath the weak smile. Fragile as a spider's web.

Somebody's grandmother. Somebody's child, once upon a time.

'No,' Philip said. He picked up the cans. And left.

*　　*　　*

It would be all right now. For all that he hated Dabton, and the estate, it was home. He parked on the tiny drive and went round to the back door. No one could get at him now, the world at rest from its meddling ways. He went into the kitchen and dropped the carry-out on the draining board. There was a casserole in a dish, waiting to go in the oven. A nice touch. He would be kind to Kath and maybe, without too much drink, the sex option might be on the agenda, in a way that *happens*. But as he went through to the living room, with his fixed smile, there was a knock on the front door.

'I'll get it,' Kath said. 'It's only Dad.'

Philip's resentments revived like chronic indigestion. This time it might be unstoppable. Nowhere to hide his ragbag of loathing.

Jeff walked into the room.

Twenty-Three

He was carrying the rails of a cot under his arms. He swivelled this way and that, then stacked them against the sofa where Philip had been intending to sit. Only ten seconds ago. 'All right there, Phil?' said Jeff. He turned to Kath without waiting for an answer. 'I'll get the rest.' While he was out Philip gave Kath a glare which she avoided, as if it was something she expected. When Jeff came back, there was a heap of parts blocking the centre of the room. Kath was looking down at it all, holding her back.

'Are you going to put it up?' she asked.

'Well, not here, love, Christ. Is the room ready yet?'

The question was aimed like an arrow. What redecoration there had been at the house – the kitchen and their bedroom – had all been done by Jeff, Philip having always found some excuse not to be in when he did it, repelled by the idea of being some kind of an apprentice to the older man. Kath shook her head. 'It's bad luck anyway, putting it up before it's born.'

Jeff took a packet of bolts from his pocket and put them on the floor. 'If you like.' He pulled out his cigarettes, offering one to Kath which she took.

Philip was leaning against the mantelpiece. Was he such a useless piece of shit that no one could bear to look at him directly? Jeff sniffed, looking small in his Driza-Bone coat. He dragged on his cigarette, still breathless from bringing the stuff in. Maybe the cunt was going to have a stroke. That was one thing Philip had over him. No blood-pressure problems here, you tit. It might be worth telling him about his visit to Beauman that morning, even if it did reveal a certain weakness. And what other advantages might he state against him? His cheap mortgage? His university degree? And, of course, he had his daughter. If Jeff had only known the things they used to get up to, particularly at the flat in Manchester. The things he had done to his little precious, banging her up to rights, shagging the living daylights . . . And still no piece of paper to tie them together. What did the weasel think about that, eh? Did he and Tilly ache in their tiny suburban hearts about that pretty point? Did they? Eh? Eh?

Philip glanced up from his poisonous musings. Jeff was looking at him. 'Fancy a pint, mate?' he said.

'I've got fucking rights, you know! A brief. What about a fucking brief? And my bastard telephone call, an' all. What about that?' Mick bawled, kicking at the door.

In the cell next door, Darren sat back on the hard little bench. He wished Mick would be quiet. It was doing neither of them any good, any fool could see that. He stood up and walked the length of the cold floor in his stockinged feet. The walls were plain cream. There was a smell of bleach. He lay back down on the bench, looking at the grilled light in the ceiling. All he felt was tiredness and a dull resignation. What had he been hoping for from all this? What a stupid idea. Wasn't it bound to turn out this way? Everything he'd done had been a fuck-up. Since the day he was born, all the roads had been pointing this way. Well, he'd done it now, hadn't he? And what was the old man going to say? Darren could not think about him. It was too much.

The peephole opened in the door. 'You all right in there, son?'

'Yeah. I'm all right.'

'There'll be somebody along to talk to you soon.'

'Whatever.'

The peephole closed. A few seconds later the guy was saying the same things to Mick, but all he got in reply was a new level of shrieking and kicking against the door. It summed Mick up. The wanker. Darren turned on to his side, closing his eyes. His face was still greasy with the cream he had put on to hide the colour of the skin round his eyes. Daft idea. A kid's stunt. He wished he could have a wash.

*   *   *

123

'Look, I can always have a go at that bedroom for you. This weekend, if you like.'

There was an almost believable kindness in the drawl. 'It's OK,' said Philip. 'I'll manage.'

'If you're sure, mate.'

'Yeah, I reckon. Time I learned, I suppose.'

The White Ox was almost full, the music booming. Kath had not joined them and, for some reason, Philip was half-glad about it. Sometimes all he wanted in the world was to go up the pub, with a few mates. Male ones. But here in Dabton he was a Billy-no-friends. And he could not see that ever changing. Who could he *like* round here? How would he ever get to know anyone if he did not go to fucking B&Q of a Saturday morning, or drive to Temple Newsam for a round of bloody golf? Last summer, though, he had noticed the men from the village playing cricket on the sports field behind the school. That might have been nice, a few beers to follow, the *invention* of an English idyll. Yet it could not happen now – with his attitude it was already too late. He drank, trying to think of something chatty to say to Kath's father, whom he did not like, and who would have made a damned sight better job of ingratiating himself with the chaps of Dabton if *he* had lived here.

The tails of Jeff's coat completely covered the stool he was sitting on, making him look like a hovering dwarf. Philip was waiting for him to take the lead and speak, the silence between them unseemly in the buzz of the bar. Jeff sipped his beer, looked at a card school in the corner, sipped his beer again. Was this a deliberate ploy to show Philip's woodenness in all its glory? Somehow, Philip knew, he would have to force a conversation. 'So how's work then, Jeff?'

'Ah, fucking so so, mate. Fucking so so. In an average week one day goes well, one goes according to plan, and the other three are a complete pile of wank. Another ten years before I can get out of it. I could do with those six numbers on a Saturday night.' He held his beer halfway to his mouth, still watching the game of cards. 'Then I could tell the fuckers what to do with their job.'

Philip smiled, a little startled by the downbeat undertone. Jeff worked in graphic design and Philip always supposed he was keen on his work. In fact, he thought Jeff had some stake of his own in the company, or that it might actually all be his own business. He had never really known if this was the case, and to ask Jeff now, after all these years, would make him look extra foolish.

Two girls in tiny black skirts were standing by the bar. Jeff shifted his gaze their way, eyeing them openly, touching his glasses up the bridge of his nose. 'So how's your place?'

'The usual. Pretty boring really. I fancy a change sometimes, but we're a bit stuck. The mortgage is through the firm. And you get used to the wage.' Philip said this carefully, not wanting to be seduced into Jeff's air of gloom, recognising the rare edge it might give over him.

'We-ell,' said Jeff, turning to him. 'You don't want to let the bastards grind you down. Like you say, just think about the money at the end of the month. Don't be a martyr to the job.'

'I'm not,' Philip said, adding, 'Sometimes I think I could tell them exactly what to do with it. There are days, to be honest, when I get pretty pissed off with everything.' This was reckless, an ill-considered concession of ground. Then a row broke out at the card table, a heavily built young man in a checked overshirt standing and throwing his cards at a gnarled farmer type opposite.

'You're a wanker!' he said, jabbing his finger. 'A fuckin' wanker and a fucking cheat.'

'A-waay, Frank!' said one of the other men.

'Shove it! Stick the fuckin' game! Here! Here's your fucking money!' He picked up his coins, threw them across the table, and went to the bar.

Jeff grinned. 'God, people, these days. You see it everywhere.'

'What's that?' said Philip.

'People losing their nut. Rage. You know, like all this road rage.'

'Maybe it's just the times we live in,' said Philip. 'People are under a lot of pressure these days.'

'Pressure, bollocks. In the street where I was brought up, there was a woman across the road had eleven kids. You never heard her complaining about stress. She just got on with it, like everyone else.' He lit a cigarette. 'If you ask me, half of this rage shit is because people don't smoke enough.'

'Ah, come on. That's too simplistic.'

'Is it, balls! It's the great sedative of our times, nicotine. Very underrated. You should try it yourself.'

Philip watched the young card player bring his drink from the bar and settle back in his seat. He called for a hand in the next game without attracting a word of comment from the others. Philip turned to Jeff, wanting to pressure him with reasonableness. 'I don't *need* to smoke, Jeff. No one does. There are other ways of dealing with hassle.'

'Oh sure. You've just told me you're pissed off with work.'

'Yeah, well . . .'

Jeff leaned closer to him. 'And what about those other times?'

'What other times are those, Jeff?' Philip said, sensing a rise.

Jeff smiled, in a way Philip suspected was usually reserved for when he was not around – tight and knowing. It was a precarious moment. The older man's bad mood was over, and now Jeff was, maliciously, projecting it on to Philip. 'You know, when you're round at our place.'

'I'm not with you,' said Philip, feeling a little pressure in his head.

'When you're round at our house, and you don't say anything.'

They were too close together. If Philip did not sit back, he might want to butt him. 'Hard to get a word in sometimes, mate.'

Jeff laughed. 'Give over. Honestly, the look on your face when you're round there!'

126

'Like I said . . .'

But Jeff was not going to let him get the upper hand. He was a winner. The top dog. And had to be every time. 'You want to cheer up a bit, Phil! Sometimes, old mate, you look,' he said, tapping Philip on the knee, maddeningly, 'as if you could murder someone.'

'Is that a fact?' said Philip.

Twenty-Four

They were sitting on a wall in the exercise yard. The three of them. Philip, barefoot in his baggy gaolbird stripes, was trying to reason with them. 'I mean, it's just an apology. You don't have to take it personally.' None of them would look at him. He wanted to turn away, but his legs were huge rooted oak trees. 'I'm not that upset about it. Not these days. I don't mind what you did before.' The youngest of them flicked a paper pellet which hit Philip on the nose. He could see them stirring, turning nasty. But he could not move. Then he was sitting by Beauman's desk, the doctor writing on a tiny corner of the blanket-sized paper. They were at the foot of a sun-soaked moorland hill, knee-deep in grass. 'You shouldn't be here,' he said. 'They're looking for you back at the prison.' The sheet of paper kept flapping up in the breeze, Beauman knocking it away irritably, concentrating on his writing, laboriously fashioning each word on top of the last one, making a penny-sized doodle . . .

Philip woke up, sweating, his ears ringing. He sat up, looking about the still-dark bedroom for signs that this was not the prison he had been dreaming about. God, fancy dreaming about Beauman. His recent life was pursuing him across the borders of the subconscious. And those three youths. What were their names? Luke Coyne, Darren Murray, and the older one, Michael something, supposed to be the ringleader. They were there in his head because he had blubbed about them to Hyder. What a wanking thing to do. He had never even told Kath about the incident. Was he going mad? Or was his rabbit cowardice of that night catching up with him, the guilt of not having confronted that vicious trio when he heard them clatter into the house? Did his rage stem from those few minutes, from the locked-in *effeminacy* of his inaction? Perhaps . . . Nothing. It was a piece of history. His parents didn't think about it at all. And neither should he. He was dreaming about prison because that's where those three were now, and had been for seven years. It was not a symbol of his own guilt. Psychology was all bollocks.

Yet . . .

He rested his head back on the pillow. Kath's half of the sheet was stone cold. He wondered how long she had been up. Maybe she wasn't feeling well? He looked at the clock and dragged himself out of bed, feeling sapped by his dream, his back especially heavy. He put on his dressing gown and went downstairs.

She was in the living room, in her nightshirt, looking at the bits and pieces of the cot. Philip went up to her and kissed her cheek, his arm round her shoulder. 'Where's it from?' he asked.

'Somebody Dad knows. A neighbour.'

'It's second-hand, then.'

'No point getting a new one. You only need it for a year or so. The baby doesn't know any different.'

Philip felt a stab of inadequacy. If he had a better job, better paid, if he had been more of a provider, they could have had a new one. He picked up the sellotaped packet of bolts. 'Can't be hard to put together. There's only the base and four sides. Even I could manage that!'

Kath smiled, a response that, in the post-lager, post-dream morning, made his eyes go oddly warm. 'I don't want it up yet,' she said, folding her arms.

'No. Of course not. But we can't leave it here.' Another few minutes and he would be late for work. But for some reason, sensing he owed Kath something, he was finding a reserve of unlikely patience. He picked up a side rail. 'I'll shift it. Won't take long!'

Driving into Leeds, fifteen minutes late and caught in the fat girth of the morning traffic, he still felt remarkably sedate. At Gipton, he saw a wheelchair hanging in the branches of a tree by the roadside. He shook his head, laughing. Further ahead was the familiar skyline, the stupid gyroscope sculpture on top of the

129

Kremlin, the blocks of flats and offices interspersed with curlicues of Victorian and Georgian architecture, and the hills beyond the city, capped with snow. To his left the sunlight was dazzling, warm on his hand and cheek. Sharp northern light. Less than alien. He could love Leeds, if he *chose* to.

A tiny shift of perspective. That's all it would take.

Half the morning passed without contradiction of this idea. Andrea, a woman from Accounts, came round with bits of cake wrapped in tin foil. It was her thirtieth birthday. Philip found himself offering best wishes, taking a piece, munching dutifully without any of his usual disdain for such trivialities. And, at a remove, he dealt with the brokers who called, unflustered by their wheedling for impossibly narrow terms. None of it bothered him. He was working at his behaviour, practising an emotional distance. This was going *so* well.

At eleven he went to the drinks machine, actually seeking company, for once. And finding it, joining Hamid, Tom and Sarah hanging around in the corridor.

'This fucking winter,' said Hamid, cradling his cup even though the heating was stifling. 'The pissing cold. I fancy booking a holiday.'

Tom was looking into his coffee, the fingers of his free hand slotted into the pocket of his Paisley waistcoat. 'I fancy Thailand this year,' he said.

'Yeah, well, you want to watch it there,' said Hamid. 'The tourist abroad, and all that. Make sure they don't plant any dope on you at the airport. Look at that woman from Sheffield who got done.'

'She knew what she was doing,' said Sarah.

'And Aids,' said Hamid, ignoring her remark. 'What about Aids?'

'Well . . .' Tom shrugged. 'You must be all right in the tourist bits.'

Philip brought his drink and hovered round them, looking for a way of getting into the conversation. He stood by Sarah who was leaning against the wall, foot pressed up behind her. She was wearing a blue jersey polo top and a long woollen skirt. Her breasts, Philip had to admit, were very perfect. But with a despotic quality. Not for him. Yet why should they be? They weren't really suited to each other. It was better that she had rebuffed him that time. Over the punch bowl. They were simply colleagues, above emotional contact. And that's how it should stay. He would never look at Sarah's chest again.

'The Dominican Republic . . .' Hamid was saying, though Philip was barely listening. God, this talk was so light and airy. They were all young, privileged. Afloat. It was the distillation of civilised life. This talk about holidays, about enjoying yourself, the language rising like helium. It was their prize for working so hard. Their due. Mine too, Philip thought, aching to join in the exchanges, to offer some information about Albufeira, the heat, the fucking timeshare men.

'I can't see us bothering this year,' Sarah said.

'Well, you've got your house,' said Tom. 'It's understandable. You can't do everything. Is Mike still working away?'

Philip felt a lurch, a little salt in his blood. He did not know about anyone called Mike. Nor any house. He had always assumed Sarah still lived with her folks. He checked himself, took a drink, looked at the shiny tiled floor with deliberate inattention.

'Bonn, this week. Then Singapore . . .'

His disaffection seemed to tighten like a circle around him. So that's what you had to do to get breasts of such immaculate quality. To be some globe-trotting, brown-nosing . . . And, of course, being a mere insurance clerk just could not be good enough for getting your hands on those tits! Without his having said a word, Philip was losing it, wanting to rail against Sarah, the ease of her life, its unearned treasures, the house he imagined to be extensive, the new red BMW he knew about for certain. 'What about you, Phil?' Her voice carried a hint of condescension he could not bear.

'Oo-oh . . . There's the baby. You know . . .' He made a circular motion with the plastic cup he was trying not to crush.

She frowned, as if there was a special gravity in what he said. What was it to her? Was the baby some kind of illness? He felt

131

defensive about Kath's pregnancy, wanting to tell Sarah about the selflessness of parenthood. Now she was smiling, a painted-on expression. But before he could speak, she said, 'Yes, of course. It's a proper grown-up thing, having a child.'

Philip felt his heart pounding. Who was she to lecture him about being grown-up? That was *his* line. She knows *nothing* about such things. She . . . The black beast was stirring in its tarry lair. If people would just stop *putting one over* on him. At every available opportunity!

'Hey, Phil.' Hamid was grinning. 'What did that guy say to you the other morning?'

'Who?'

'After you clipped that car on the roundabout. I heard someone came looking for you.'

Philip breathed deeply. Shelley would pay for this. Pay and pay. Yet all he could say was, 'There was no guy.'

'Aw, come on. I heard . . .'

'Well, you heard wrong, Hammy. All right?'

Tom and Sarah were politely silent, in the face of *more* evidence of Philip's madness. He was getting a name for it. The whole building knew about it. But it could not be stopped, the pressure inside Philip was too great. Hamid was within striking distance. One crack was all that was needed, to blow it, to bring the chaos that might *let out all the poison*. Sarah opened her mouth to breathe. Philip was frightening her. And why not? She had it coming. Tom, though, as if in some bizarre reciprocity of Philip's aggression, screwed up his cup and threw it in the bin. 'Christ, there should be somewhere to smoke in this fucking place!'

Hamid looked at the bin, then at Philip. 'Hey, Phil. Sorry, mate. Just trying to take an interest.'

'Well, don't. Understood?'

Hamid finished his drink and walked away, Tom and Sarah taking the opposite direction, back to Life and Deaths. And Philip was left alone with the hum of the strip lights above his head, the telephones distantly ringing.

* * *

He spent a token forty minutes back at his desk, achieving nothing. There was a corridor of empty air about him, as if everyone knew his mood and chose to keep away. At half-past eleven he went for lunch, leaving the building.

The open air made him feel calmer. Why was that? Might he be better suited to working outdoors? A gardener, perhaps? He could practise in the garden at home, starting with the roses Kath wanted. But the thought of learning a whole new job, from scratch, was beyond him. It was already too late. Nearly twenty-six, and burned out. There was nothing else he could do, other than the rubbish he was doing now. He fell in behind a couple, a lad with gelled hair, metallic grey suit, hands in pockets. The woman was carrying an executive case, black jacket and skirt, sexuality honed into a day-long tease. She was saying, 'If that's what you've got to do to get the job . . .' The lad replied, 'Don't worry about it. You find out if you're suited later.' Business talk, working the angles, the percentages. People with dreams of power, extravagance, things that never entered Philip's mind.

At a pedestrian crossing, people were heading over the road. Philip arrived as the green man disappeared, but there were so many bodies about a new crowd had already gathered, a clot of Yorkshireness, clustering from the pavements, the walkways beneath the scaffolding on a new office development, teeming organic creatures locked in a grid of rational device, the city, the scheme of things. Work. Get on. Hit the deck running and improve your position from there. The green man came back and Philip moved with them, marching to the beep.

He walked through the ground floor of the Bond Street centre, across Briggate and on to the Victoria Arcade. The idea had been to get something to eat while he was out, a proper meal. For the comfort of it. But the cafés and bars all seemed full, and he could not face the queue for sandwiches at Ainsley's. Just could not. He would *perish* in that queue. He crossed over Vicar Lane to the market.

The crowds here, their jostling lower caste, cheered him. Oddly.

He had always liked the market. Then he thought, Maybe this is where I should be. Somewhere I like.

He made his way through the market, looking at the stalls and their owners with a sense of association. All they did was sell things – books, clothes, pet foods. It couldn't be too hard. Of a rougher social order, maybe, but if you paid your way in life, if you were *happy*, what the fuck did it matter what you did? He could do the fruit and veg. His father had been a supermarket manager, hadn't he? He would know about suppliers, all that stuff. And the baby, when it had grown up a bit, could come and help on the stall. Philip slowed with the wonder of this idea. It was his first real sentiment about being a father. Suddenly, in the space of a few seconds, a whole new future lay before him. Pleasing him, no end. To trade dour duty for happiness. To stop being a snob! A joyous possibility, a revelation! And Kath would understand. She had always had a bohemian streak. The idea kept on coming, making his throat dry with anticipation.

At the bottom of the market, his head flushing with possibilities, he turned back up Butcher's Row, the Leeds lads in their striped aprons hanging round the doors of their shops, in the old tradition. A rough lot, but wouldn't they make better, worthier colleagues than those at Pilot? He could not learn butchery, he knew. But he was intelligent. And young! Only twenty-five! He could learn easily. And if it wasn't the fruit and veggies, it would be something else. One of the butchers shouted the price of chitterlings to him, inviting him to come into his shop. Philip smiled broadly in reply, already feeling one of them. If only this guy knew how soon Philip would be his friend!

With a happiness inconceivable a few minutes before, he left the market with the aim of spending the afternoon at his desk, secretly working out the practicalities of such a venture, ringing the council to find out the cost of renting a stall, reading the *Yellow Pages* for ideas about suppliers and what he might sell. A future at last! It could be *wonderful*, Philip thought as he crossed back over Vicar Lane, not seeing the figure behind him, the prancing step of urgency, a man with something on his mind.

Twenty-Five

Merrick caught up with Philip by a fortress of McAlpine scaffolding, halfway along King Edward Street. He stood square in front of him, putting his hands on Philip's shoulders to stop him.

'I was on my way to see you.'

Philip, elated with his new hopeful dreams, did not recognise him at first. He looked down at the tweed jacket and denim blue shirt, then up at the glassy grey eyes. Still not level with the situation, he said a reflexive, 'Hello.'

Merrick tapped his finger on Philip's shoulder. 'My father's in a poor way, Pickles. They say he might not last the week.'

Philip took a step back, out of his hold. 'I'm sorry to hear that.' He could not be bothered with this. He tried to dodge round him, but Merrick moved into his path.

'I want to talk to you.'

'What? Right now?' Philip tried to push past him again. Merrick grabbed his elbow. 'Look, it'll have to wait. I've got to get back to work. All right?'

'You're going nowhere till you've heard what I've got to say.'

Philip shook his head, turning side on, looking across at the people coming out of the Victoria Quarter. His heart was beating quickly. 'Look, it wasn't my fault. You can't blame it on me. There must have been something wrong with your father to start with. Anything might have triggered it off. I'm in insurance. I know about this stuff.' The answer was direct and complete. It had a salesman's gloss, but it pleased Philip, and he gave Merrick a look that said as much.

'I know what you are, Pickles.'

'And what's that?'

135

Merrick curled his lip, teeth clenched. 'You're a rager. A hothead. Racing about like you own the world, like you're the only one in it, the only one that bloody matters. Get behind the wheel of a car and you're an animal. And a coward. You and your type need teaching a lesson. You need putting away.'

Philip smiled sourly, sensing the confrontation sliding into something more solid. He gave a little gasp he could not hide. 'That's a fact, is it?'

'Dead right, it is. And if I have anything to do with it, that's what'll happen to you.'

There was spittle on his lips. His shoulders jerked under the jacket. He had been thinking about this a lot, a realisation that chilled Philip. 'Look,' he said, tilting his head in a gesture of reason, 'I've said I'm sorry about your father. But I really think you've got the wrong end of the stick.' He searched for something else to say, to push their differences into a neutral space, but Merrick turned his head half-away, then lifted his gloved fist. 'You shit! You arrogant piece of shit!'

It was a feeble blow, too preconceived. Philip tapped it away easily. Now the two were facing each other in a self-conscious impasse. A Jamaican guy strolled by, turning and looking at them. Philip, sure of his own virtue at this moment, felt a split-second of pleasure at having gained the man's attention, at the whole of Leeds that seemed to be watching. The immediacy of the situation was becoming more appealing. His manliness surged and he sensed a genuine vehicle for his habitual bad temper. It was the way all arguments should be settled. And with his size and youth, he should come off the better here, no problem. But Merrick backed off a pace, shaking his finger at Philip. 'I'm going to sort you out, Pickles. I'm going to teach you a lesson you'll never forget.'

'You and whose fucking army,' said Philip, his reserve in freefall.

'You'll see,' Merrick said, backing away among the indifferent shoppers. 'You're going to pay for what you've done, Pickles. Have you got that?'

Philip tutted, then grinned for the sake of all the passers-by. But no one seemed to want to know.

The sense of triumph was short-lived.

As always.

At his desk, an hour later, the incident seemed to catch up with Philip, depressing him. How did he get into these scrapes? What if anyone he knew had seen them? It had taken place uncomfortably close to the police station. Supposing Hyder had been about? The fact of tomorrow's court case clattered on top of his thoughts, making him more miserable. It was unfair. He had been in the process of devising a whole new future. A month or two and Philip would have been *reinvented*, then everyone could leave him alone. He tried to keep alive his dream of working on the market, but it seemed no more than a fantasy now, childish and untenable. Besides, if he really did pull it off, what if Merrick ever came walking past his stall? Or any of his other enemies?

The glums were unstoppable. Every few minutes seemed to present some fresh obstacle to his strategies for happiness. He parried calls for premium quotes, suggesting they tried the Pru, or Sun Life. He tapped idly at his keyboard, wiggling his foot against the wires leading to the terminal beneath his desk. He picked up a memo – 'For the attention of P. Pickles'. In the early days, seeing his name in print excited him, validating his existence, like a headline. Now it was only evidence of the company's possession of him. But only his body. His soul was elsewhere, already departed. He picked dirt from his fingernail with a bent paper clip.

Work was an impossibility. It could not be done. He longed to replace the daydream about the market with a fresh hope, something he could develop. Maybe it would help if he listed all the things on his mind, debits and credits, the Merrick thing, Kath, his job, the house, the fucking garden and the fucking decorating, Jeff and his conversation of last night. All debits! The whole chute! He smiled, mortally amused. There had to be something going for him. Across the office Lilian was walking to the door, reading a form, when Howard came barging in from the other side. The door hit her on the head and she screamed theatrically. Sarah, standing by the photocopier, cupped her hand over her mouth. Tom turned his head towards the window, smiling openly. Light relief for everyone. There is a God after all. As Howard fussed round Lilian, Philip felt his spirits lifting.

Maybe the case would go his way tomorrow. There was no reason to suppose it shouldn't. The facts were obvious. Plain robbery. With violence. And then it would be the weekend. Plan a celebration, why not? They had been to Jeff and Tilly's last Sunday, which meant they needn't go again for another month at least. And, of course, Oz was in town. Tomorrow night! Yes! Get steaming pissed! A raft of pleasure coming his way! A galaxy of people on his side! His team! And without his having moved or done anything, there was a huge sea-change in his fortunes. The way things were looking up! Then the phone rang.

'Mr Pickles?'

'Mr Griffiths!' Philip said, too brightly. 'I was going to call you!'

'No you weren't.'

'Honestly . . .'

'Please, no more excuses.' There was nothing to say to that. 'Look, I've decided to take legal advice. If you don't come up with the settlement, within the terms of your policy, by tomorrow . . .'

A blanket of indifference came over Philip. Life was short. They were all going to die one day, then none of this would matter. 'You're lying.'

'What did you say?'

'You haven't taken any legal advice. You're bluffing.'

Through the earpiece alone, Philip could sense the man's face filling with blood. 'Pickles . . .' Everyone was using his second name today. 'Listen to me and listen good.' Fire away, arsehole. 'First, you don't call me a liar. Second, your name is all over this case, and if you don't get it right, you'll be going over the coals. Understood? You'll be hearing from me within twenty-four hours.'

'Yeah, sure.'

'Christ, you're a nasty piece of work, Mr Pickles, do you know that?'

'Yes,' Philip said, sniggering. 'It's a commonly held view.'

'Look, fella, your head's on the line here. You're done for . . .'

'Ah, piss off.'

Philip hung up before Griffiths could reply, and sat back, clasping his hands behind his head, Howard watching from three desks away.

Twenty-Six

Boredom. Even the word was boring. His life was a series of stillborn events. It was the punchline of a joke without the preamble – it would be funny, if only someone could explain it. When he was a child, a youth even, life seemed to promise *everything*. And look at him now! It wasn't like this in the brochure.

No, it wasn't.

Yet might it be the same for everyone? For Howard with his capitulation to the grasping wishes of the company? For Jeff, Merrick, Griffiths? Middle-aged men, all of them, perhaps having spent their youth, like Philip, living through the second part of the joke of existence, then switching, at say the age of thirty, to trying to understand the effortful set-up, with no thread of reason to connect the two segments. Is that what it came to? An endless pratting about on the perimeters of living? Never truly *knowing* anything? No wonder Philip got annoyed sometimes. It was none of his fault, really . . .

'I've ironed your blue shirt.'

'Sorry?'

'For tomorrow,' said Kath. 'I thought you wanted that good blue one.'

'Oh right. Thanks.'

He tried to stir himself from his ruminations. How long had he been sitting there? Hours. Tired, cynical, listless. Maybe he had ME, something he might use as an excuse when Howard asked why he had left work early. God, the look on Howard's face when Philip swore at Griffiths. He just had to leave, before Howard started brow-beating him – something Philip could not face, not in a thousand years.

Kath was sitting on the chair by the fire, sewing buttons on a tiny duvet cover he assumed she had made herself. She looked, it had to be said, nice and demure in her white T-shirt and knitted waistcoat. And the slacks were new, black ones with stirrup feet and a stretchy waist that made the bulge barely noticeable. Her hair was freshly washed too, more natural to the shape of her head. She nipped the cotton with her teeth, her good white even teeth, another of her better features. 'I was looking at the car last night,' she said. 'That bash on the bumper.'

'I know.' Philip lay back on the sofa, closing his eyes. 'I meant to tell you all about it. Honestly. I clipped somebody the other morning, on my way to work. I lost my temper. Going too fast.' The truth came with surprising ease. Just slipping out.

'Was anyone hurt?' Kath asked, flicking a loose bit of cotton from the cover.

'No. It was nothing.' He opened his eyes, expecting her not to believe him. But she was smiling, her hands loose in her lap.

'You're funny, do you know that?'

'Am I?'

'Yes.'

'Oh,' he said, yawning. 'I suppose I'd better try and think of a joke to support that hypothesis.'

'No, you know what I mean.'

'Do I?'

'You're always in a tizz about something. You don't mean any real harm, you just get this bee in your bonnet.'

'Buzz, buzz.' He closed his eyes again.

Kath put down her work and shuffled over to him on her knees. He felt for her and put his arm round her shoulders. He smiled, looking at her. Once he had spied on her through the window of the toy shop, seeing her smiles and her patience with the stupid nit-picking customers. Nice woman. Everyone said. For a moment he forgot his grievances, trusting in the reality of her brown eyes. 'I know what I'm like,' he said. 'It's just that I get bored with everything. I feel like finding a new life. Something . . . interesting.'

She rubbed her hand over his chest. 'Sounds like a decent idea to me.'

'What?'

'A fresh start. Why not?'

Philip sat up. 'Oh yeah. And what about this?' He pointed at her stomach.

Kath laughed. A womanly, reliable noise. 'There's not much point bringing up a child with miserable parents. We have to be happy too.' She kissed his forehead. 'Tell me what you want.' She eased herself up beside him. 'Phil, what do you want to do?'

He grinned, wanting to avoid misery-mode. 'That's just it. I don't know. I don't seem to *want* to do anything.'

'Then do nothing.'

'We need money. Idleness is an expensive career.'

'Well, when the baby's born, I can always go back to work. You could stay at home and look after it.'

'Come off it, Kath.'

'Why not? It needn't be here all the time. We can use childminders. Everyone does these days. And I'd make enough to keep us while you do whatever you want to do. Start a business or something. Work from home. You're a bright bloke, I'm sure you'd think of something, after a while.' She kissed his cheek. 'After you'd got yourself sorted out.'

He pulled his head away. 'You make it sound as if I'm ill.'

'You know what I mean.'

And he did, though this abrupt crystallisation of all the things he had wanted to say to her – all this time, on this very score – seemed too good to be true. Too obvious. 'Oh, I don't know. What would your old man say? And your mother.'

Kath groaned. 'I don't know why you go on about them like you do. What we do is none of their business. It's our life, isn't it?'

'He doesn't like me.'

'Who?'

'Jeff. Tilly's none too keen, either.'

'Oh, for God's sake. Well, keep away from them, then,' she

said, tapping his chest. 'I'll be the one that goes to see them. I can soon make excuses for you.'

Philip smiled. She was saying things he had wanted to hear for months. Yet all he could do was parry them. 'Is that a promise?'

'Yes.'

'I don't believe you.'

'Don't believe me, if you don't want to.'

He looked along her body, its available presence, the bubble breasts, and her wriggling toes. Solitude, the single life, could not be as comfortable as this. And there were some things he rather liked about her pregnancy, not least of which was its evidence of his fertility. He could cut the mustard, and it was there for everyone to see. He hugged her. 'I'd like to believe what you're saying, I just can't. It's not realistic.'

She kissed his forehead. 'Now you're just being stubborn.'

They talked for an hour, Philip wanting to tell her everything that was on his mind, about Merrick, Griffiths, his fears about the case the next morning. Sharing his problems would have been so *healthy*. But he could not make the concession, and he deliberately skirted round his concerns. Maybe, Philip thought, that was the way he was born, with a *preference* for a difficult life. An interesting idea. He might try and work it out. One day.

They went up to bed together, the first time for months. They undressed on either side of the bed and took it in turns to use the bathroom. For all that they had known each other for so long, they were acting like strangers, on a first night, in a hotel where the maid might come rushing in at any second. And it still felt that way when they were in bed, with the light off. Philip kissed her, and made circles on her neck with his tongue. He was trying to retrieve a thread of their old intimacy, running his hand down her body and putting his fingers inside her. 'Will it wake it up?' he said, sniggering. Kath moaned. A good sign.

He would have liked her from behind, a position he had been thinking about a lot, lately, but it might have been expecting too

143

much. He shoved back the sheet and moved over her. Together they made a world of their own, a wobbling Jupiter that made the castors rattle, grinding them through the carpet into the chipboard floor. The man next door would be able to hear everything, but let him, let him listen to what it used to be like to be young. Philip slipped inside Kath, the borders of politeness retreating. This was so good, an earned thing. His body had a natural life he ignored too much. Relax, take it for granted. He tensed his buttocks and worked deeper into her, trying not to think of the baby in there, watching him. He was not quite hard enough. A little more time, more detail to the negotiation.

'Did you really mean what you said?' he asked, in the small voice of lovemaking.

'Mmm. About what?'

'Me staying at home while you went to work.'

'Course I did.' She was wriggling herself up to him.

For some reason, he felt a compulsion to sort this matter out, to fix the idea, and give it an association with this act. 'I'd get incredibly lazy. And I'd only ever see you.'

'That's all right, isn't it? I think that's . . .' She gave a little groan, working herself harder against him. '. . . a very good idea. I could keep you at home all the time. Mmm. Keep you . . . tied up. Would you like that?'

Philip's prick rose harder. 'Yes. Er, no.' He giggled. 'I don't know.'

'I think you do. I think you know it would be good for you, don't you? To have me tie you up, really tightly? So you can't go anywhere? So I have to feed you . . .' She cackled. 'And you'll only get gruel.' Philip had not heard her talk like this for a long time. It was so good. So right. The clutter, the rubbish of daily living should all be discarded in favour of this act. They should fuck all the time. It was a peak experience, only properly known in the doing. 'And you'll never be able to get away. People will want to know what happened to you and I'll just have to say you've disappeared. Then you'll have to be gagged so you don't start shouting for help. Then . . .' Her head was turning from

144

side to side, along a precise diagonal, the moans like little gasps of pain as he worked faster into her. 'Then . . .'

He could not hold back any longer.

When it was over he rolled carefully to his side of the bed. The usual duties followed where he slid his arm under her warm narrow neck, feeling the bones against his skin, stroking her body, kissing her. It was what she liked. She had said it so often. Maybe they should talk some more, he thought, find something fresh that might liven up their interest in each other. But when he opened his eyes, Kath was already asleep, one hand crooked under her breast. Like a deformity.

Twenty-Seven

The verdict, when it came, seemed like just another detail of Luke's life, something to add to the facts of his age, his address, his unemployment. It was nothing more than he had expected, no matter how the brief had tried to talk up that business about his mother having to bring Luke and his sisters up on her own, the deprivation, that kind of shit. Even Luke knew no one wanted to listen to that crud.

Mick had stood there pretending not to be bothered by what the judge said – it was the way he had cracked on the whole trial – but Darren wept a bucketful, his old man shaking his head, looking like death. Luke's mother had said she couldn't face this final day, though he would have liked her there. It might have been nice. Still, it was over now, and he was feeling relieved to get out of the court, to be moving, going somewhere at last.

He looked out of the car window at the rain falling on the fields. They hadn't bothered with a van – maybe they hadn't got one available, or maybe they thought it wasn't worth it for one, since all three of them were going to separate prisons. Until the trial, they had held Luke in a police cell. Another fucking con – remand prisoners were supposed to get their own places, innocent till proven. But they couldn't cope with the numbers. Admitted it. 'Something in the air,' one copper moaned. 'World's going fucking mad. Anarchy, that's what it is.' Luke was there long enough to pass his eighteenth birthday.

He was handcuffed to the escort guy, another in front doing the driving.

'Tough shit for you,' said the man next to Luke, a fat sweaty type. Fucking gorilla. 'If you'd been that bit younger, you might have avoided this place.'

'They'd 'ave put me away anyway.'

'They say the youth custody's harder than stir,' said the driver. 'They don't half make the fuckers jump in those places.'

'Yeah, well,' said the apeman.

Luke did not want to talk. He was concentrating on the countryside, the folds of the land, hedges and coppices, a solitary big house with a horse in a paddock. He was trying to ignore the rain, the cars passing by, the people in them who were not going where he was going. It was getting to him, a shit gloomy mood, a muddy hole. His eyes prickled, and he kept his face turned away.

'Pissing it down again,' said the ape. 'There'll be no exercise today. It's always fucking raining round here.'

'Can I smoke?' Luke asked.

'Can if you want to. Might as well get rid of what you've got now. They'll only have them off you when you get there.'

With his free hand Luke pulled out his packet of Berkeley and lit one. The gorilla pulled out a packet of his own and tapped his mate on the shoulder. The driver reached back and took one. The gorilla lit up, then tapped the 'No Smoking' sign on the window with a smirk, the meaning of which was beyond Luke.

'Twelve years, eh, Lukey? Rather you than me. Still, behave yourself, be smart, and it should only be ten. A mere decade.'

'Fucking less. Seven maybe,' said the driver.

'Well, even seven. A lifetime to a kid like you, eh, Luke?'

'I'll do it.'

'Too right, you will. No fucking choice, old mate!' He laughed, coughing smoke between his stubby yellow teeth.

Luke wished he would shut up. Where he was going he imagined they would all be like him – clever cunts, some a bit more well-meaning than others, but with the same kind of shit underneath. And this one was all shit, nothing hidden. You could tell this was a skive for him, escort duty with someone who wasn't going to be any trouble. An easy day's pay, and he knew it.

'Not much further,' he said. 'Another few minutes and you'll

147

be in, mate. *Inmate*. Get it?' He laughed. The driver looked at Luke in the mirror.

Luke pulled out another cigarette, but the gorilla snatched it off him.

'Not now. We're nearly there. Besides, what's that say on the fucking window?'

They pulled up at the prison gate. The driver got out and knocked on the big metal door. When there was no reply he kicked at the bottom. Eventually a face appeared in the hatch and the door was opened to let them in.

The gorilla got out, Luke shuffling along the seat to stay with him, dragged by his cuffed wrist. In the yard the handcuffs were taken off. Luke's wrist was sore, but he resisted the temptation to rub it. He put his hand in his pocket and followed the driver into the reception area.

There was a long counter with three screws behind it, one at a computer screen, neither of the other two taking any notice of their arrival. 'Today's delivery,' said the ape. 'Fresh from the farm.'

'Well, we're overstocked,' said the man at the end of the counter, not looking up. 'You'll have to take it back.'

The driver handed over a sheaf of papers which the screw signed, giving the top piece back.

'I'll be seeing you then, Luke,' said the gorilla. 'Like I said, be smart. Behave yourself.'

It sounded respectful, though it was only for the benefit of the screws. Luke looked away, wanting rid of him, ready now only for the long sleep ahead. And when they had gone, he felt himself drifting into mindlessness, a detachment from his body as they ordered him to strip in a side room, making him stand up to a lectern, bollock naked while they took his name, date of birth, next of kin. Those details again. Well, they could have them. Let them take them away, literally, with the clothes and belongings they dropped into a black plastic bag.

They took him next door to a shower that smelled of sweaty feet, the white tiles crusted at the bottom with a kind of rust.

As he stood waiting for the water to come on he could hear, through the little open window at the top, doors banging, men shouting, someone singing. The water whooshed out, virtually cold, and he stood there, shaking the water off his head, freezing his bollocks off. Afterwards they handed him his prison clothes and he put them on – a blue striped shirt and too-big trousers with a whiff of piss. A minute later he was led to his wing, the landings filling with men from their work, or classes, or whatever they did. In the cell he was shown his bed and left alone. He looked at the Page Three pictures on the walls, and the two other, empty bunks. He wondered who he would be sharing with, which of the voices that grizzled and bawled outside would belong to the bodies he would be spending tonight with, and all those fucking years to come. Nutters, maybe. He'd heard tales. Then, feeling the weight of the time ahead falling down on him, he wanted to cry. A few tears did come, but he had to wipe them away, quickly, in case any bastard came in.

Twenty-Eight

Philip tried to guess the weather beyond the bedroom window. He was thinking a lot about the weather, these days. Perhaps too much, overrating its effect on his mood. When he was younger he seemed hardly ever to differentiate between summer and winter. An innocence lost. Yet what could he do about it? Nothing. Bugger all. Better to accept life as it had become. Which was . . .

Not so bad. All considered. He stared at the curtains, trying to see them as things he *owned*, as a token of his *real* life, the only thing any sane person should think about.

The curtains were green-striped ready-made polyester things that had shrunk when Kath washed them, so that now they barely reached the sill. They were from British Home Stores. And, yes, when they had bought them he had been sulky, taking no notice of Kath's comments about the enhancing shade they would lend to the wallpaper. Shopping for such *permanent* things, in those far-off, twelve-month-ago days, seemed only to add to the way he thought his youth was draining away. But he was over all that now. As of today. And if Kath wanted to go shopping for more 'homey' things, he would go willingly and enthusiastically. He *owed* it to her, nothing less. All this was down to last night's sex, of course, but didn't that just show how important the act was? Shouldn't they endlessly repeat the process? Fuck for the sake of their sanity? He looked at Kath's back. He wouldn't have minded doing it again, right now, to prove the point, if it hadn't been past eight o'clock. Another time. And soon. Definitely.

He slipped out of bed and went to the back bedroom. As he dressed, he thought about the things Kath had said to him last night and how he might suggest a regular agenda for sex. It was probably just a question of the wording. He knew she would agree, because she was so naturally *amenable*. It was hard to believe he sometimes hated her, he thought as he buttoned the blue shirt. Contemptible, really. And fundamentally untrue. Kath was his greatest ally. He would never leave her. And there would be no more childish silences, rather, they would talk, get everything in the open. Very modern. Wholesome. They *must* get married. Some time.

Mindful of his appearance in court that morning, he fastened his tie carefully, then went back to their bedroom.

Kath was up, and almost dressed. It irritated him. He had wanted to kiss her as she slept, and to get away without the fuss of parting, keeping his new vision of her pure – the resolve to talk, to make their lives more accessible to each other, being something that could wait for the moment.

'I'll drive you,' she said, pulling on her sweatshirt.

'What?'

'Into town. I want the car. I'll go and get it fixed while I'm at it. Then you can get straight off to Oz's after work. All right?'

Philip puffed his cheeks, blowing out slowly. 'I suppose . . .'

'It's not a problem, is it?'

'No, er . . .'

'Right, then. I'll be ready in five minutes.' She skipped past him and into the bathroom.

'There's half a dozen things I want.' She slackened the seat-belt, drawing it carefully over her stomach. 'It's strange, but sometimes I have so much go in me, loads more than when I was working. Then other times, all I want to do is sleep.' The fucking, thought Philip. That's what's giving you all this energy. He considered a strategy for stressing its stamina-enhancing value, and a timetable for fitting as much of it as possible into their lives – a week or two off when the baby came, then a furious and prolonged resumption. For the 'go'.

As Kath started the car, the old man from next door appeared, his white head showing above the raggy brown beech hedge that separated the two front gardens. 'Fancy,' Philip said, wearily. 'I

wonder if he keeps a bloody diary of when we come and go.'
But Kath was smiling, waving at him.

'His name's Boursin. Jean. He's French.'

'French? You're joking! How d'you know that?'

'I've been talking to him for ages.'

'What, does he speak English, then?'

'Course he does.'

'Oh God, I suppose that means I'll have to start talking to him too,' Philip said, sounding more miserable than he had meant.

'You ought to try and get to know him. He's really nice, actually.' She waved again and pulled off the little drive.

Unless he had been drinking, Philip was always an uneasy passenger with Kath. The driving was something he always did. It was a chore, a bit too much of the 'man's' role, but he accepted it, assuming that Kath wanted it that way, given her thirty-two years and the fact that he saw her as fundamentally passive, not militant, the way younger women, like Sarah, seemed to be. Or maybe he had judged Kath wrongly? The things she had said last night, 'I'll keep you tied up . . .' Maybe she was not so old, after all. He gave her a sidelong look, at her little nose and chin in profile, the soft girl's knees. He had a personal stake in her, and sometime soon he wanted it made more frankly known.

The familiar journey passed in silence, Philip watching the road ahead, holding back any comments he might make about her driving. Then, approaching the Cross Gates roundabout, an old Metro skipped across the lanes. Kath shoved her head forward. 'The arsehole! What's he think he's doing? Does he know where he's bloody going?' She stalled at the junction.

Philip felt his heart lurch. 'Shit. Careful.'

'We-ell, honestly.' She slammed the car into gear and shot forward, edging a red van at the side across the lane. Philip looked back, seeing the driver shaking his fist.

When they were on the way again, Philip smiled nervously. That behaviour. Those known symptoms. Even Kath, the nicest of people, with her little white hands clenched round the wheel . . .

It was universal. He was not the only one.

He settled back as Kath followed the rush through Killingbeck. Today, he was a passenger, an innocent man. The sense of calm would follow on, helping in court if he had to speak. He noticed a car on the inside lane, hurrying to keep up with them, swaying towards Philip, inches away. He looked across at the driver, ready with a forgiving smile, a gesture of his new-found tolerance of the stupidity of other drivers. Then he saw the man's face. It was Merrick.

Philip looked ahead, pretending not to recognise him, but feeling the man's mid-life glare burning into the side of his head. 'Christ, they drive like lunatics,' Kath was saying, glancing across. Philip's mouth went moist. A mile to go in the crush of traffic heading to work. A set of lights, two hundred yards ahead, changed to green, the lines of traffic shooting forward. Merrick wiggled his car, a brown Datsun, to within a palm's breadth of their own. Philip risked a glance. He was nodding, yelling something that seemed like, 'See how it feels?' The lights went back to red, two cars in front. Merrick had his fist raised. Kath looked across Philip and saw him.

'Look at that guy! He's a frigging nutcase!'

'He got a bit close,' Philip said, meekly. 'They're like that this time of day. Let him get away.'

When the lights changed, the traffic zipped back into gear, resuming its momentum. Merrick moved away, then drifted back, as if in a waltz. The sweat came like a rash on Philip's face. He could see the Datsun's door handle, less than a foot from his shoulder.

'Bloody idiot! What's he up to?' said Kath.

'God knows. Some headbanger. He's in the wrong. Just watch the road.'

They passed the metal pilings of a set of roadworks. They were getting closer to town, Quarry Hill ahead. If they could get behind Merrick they would be able to make a left, but the two lines were moving at the same speed. Philip keened to take control, wishing he had insisted on driving. Then Merrick came closer, and there was a blunt tap as the two cars touched. 'Jesus! What's he doing?' Kath's pink-trainered foot was trembling over the brake. Philip shook his fist at Merrick, giving him the response he thought he wanted. Merrick answered with a madcap laugh. 'I want to go left! He won't let us by!' Kath was beginning to panic.

'Just keep going,' Philip said, as calmly as possible. 'There's a turn-off ahead. We'll lose him there.'

'But why? Why do we have to "lose" him?'

'Kathryn, just do as I say. Please?'

She was sitting forward, scanning the road, shaking her head. At the run-off she slowed, indicating, crunching through the gears. But Merrick simply barged into their lane, drawing horns from everywhere. Now he was following round the roundabout. 'Take a turn!' Philip yelled.

'Where? Where?'

'Anywhere!'

Shaking her head, close to losing it, Kath shot off the roundabout, catching the kerb. But Merrick stayed on their tail, weaving after them up a side road by a block of flats, tapping their bumper as they slowed to round a parked lorry. 'Right,' said Philip. 'See that junction ahead?' Kath nodded. 'You can stop there.' Kath indicated to pull over on to the pavement, but Merrick had seen it, drawing alongside.

'He's forcing me off! There's a wall! We're going to hit the wall!'

Philip grabbed the wheel. 'Brake! Just brake!'

The car went into a ninety-degree spin, stopping face-on to the low perimeter wall of the flats.

Kath was crying. Philip covered his face, breathing deeply. When he looked up he could see Merrick slowing at the main road ahead, where he indicated and turned sedately away, like a pensioner out for the groceries.

Kath took a tissue from her coat pocket and blew her nose. Faces had appeared at some of the windows of the flats. A group of three boys, on their way to school, bent to look inside at Kath. They grinned, exchanging a few words with each other, looking round again when they had passed. Philip undid his belt and leaned back, sighing. 'Are you all right?' She nodded, wiping her face with the back of her hand.

'There must have been witnesses. Did you get his number?'

'No.'

'Well, we should do something.'

'Just forget it.'

'Why? Why should we forget it? The bastard could have killed us.'

'Kath, it doesn't matter. It's over.'

She was staring ahead at the flats, sniffling. 'Philip, do you know him?'

'I might. It's not worth talking about.'

'You do. You do know him.'

'I said it doesn't matter. Just leave it at that.'

A few people were lingering at their windows. Nosy old sods. They should be used to things like this, thought Philip. It's a rough area. Trouble all the time round here. He would say this to Kath, to defuse the situation. Then he saw her trembling hands and knew anything he might say would sound hopeless.

'God, Philip . . .' she said, closing her eyes, shaking her head.

Darren swept the floor, keeping his eyes down. Strachan and his cronies were hanging round the far end of the corridor, waiting to get back into their cell after exercise. Darren didn't like Strachan. No one liked him. He was a shaven-headed bad-tempered fucker, one of a family of thugs that ruled half of Hartlepool, so they said. They were quiet though, a hopeful sign that they wouldn't take any notice of the kid shoving the brush. Darren swept into the recesses of the cell doors, trying to make himself small, wishing the rest of the cons would appear. He pulled the bin across the floor and emptied the dustpan. Then he heard the steps coming his way and a pair of heavy black shoes came into his downcast field of vision.

'Missed a bit, coffee cake.' It was Strachan. His three mates were watching him.

155

'Where?' Darren said, lamely.

'Here. Look.' Strachan took hold of Darren's neck and shoved his head down.

'I can't see anythin'.'

'Well, you're not lookin' close enough, are yer, fuckin' rainbow. Look at it! Look at the fuckin' filth down here!' He shoved Darren back. 'You're gonna find yourself out of a job, my son, if you don't do your work properly. Am I right?'

'If you say so.' Darren was still holding his brush. His heart felt as if it was spinning on a string.

'I do say so! I do! But, lucky for you, coffee face, I'm gonna help you out.' He went up to the cell door, unzipped his fly and pissed into the corner. He zipped his fly back up. 'There y'are, mate! We've washed it now, 'aven't we!' His mates were grinning at the end of the corridor. Strachan took a menacing step forward. 'Is that better, cup cake? Eh? Is it?'

'Yeah,' said Darren. 'It's better.'

'Good! Good, my son! You're learnin'.' He went back to the others and they disappeared away round to the wing door, business to attend to.

Darren looked at the big puddle of piss. He would not get upset about it. He would not *mind* that Strachan was such an evil bastard. No, he would go and get his mop and clean it up. Stuff like this happens. It was one of those things. That's all.

A hundred miles away, Luke was lying on his pit, looking at the webbing of the bunk above. He drew on the cigarette, and tapped it into the ashtray balanced on his stomach. From outside the open door came the shouting and yelling of the men. They were always fucking shouting. Couldn't they just shut the fuck up?

Couldn't they?

Their bawling was nothing. It was like that all the time. But in the space of two seconds, Luke went from quietly contemplating the mattress above his head to leaping up and throwing the ashtray against the wall. He picked up the one small chair in the place and crashed it down on the sink. On the windowsill was a shoe box containing his shaving gear and soap. He swiped it to the floor then picked up a sheet and tore it in half. It wasn't enough. The fuckers would not be quiet! He pulled the bunk bed over, half watching from some clear space in his skull. How did this get started? How? Was he going out of his mind? Maybe he had to – this was the only way to get rid of the hate, to stop the noise that was booming, inside and out. He picked up the chair again and rammed it at the wire mesh over the window. From miles away, he could hear his name being shouted, 'Old Lukey's throwin' a fucking wobbler! Yahoo!' But he still carried on. He snatched the pictures of women off the walls and ripped them to shreds. Then he shoved at the heap of bedding and belongings on the floor, ramming it up against the door, leaving a space in which he stood with his fast raw breath, wondering what to do next.

Twenty-Nine

Philip drove them through town, the old car's engine seeming to jar his bones. He felt drained, a thickness in his throat. None of this, he thought, would have happened if he hadn't been a driver. Might his driving be a *cause*, rather than a symptom of his problems? Could he get by without it? Thousands of people relied on public transport, perfectly happily, and the carless condition gave you a massive lift to the moral high ground.

'The traffic'll be murder today,' he said to Kath. 'You should go home.'

'I'm all right.' Kath was pale, but she seemed to have recovered her composure. 'Philip, who was that man?'

'Just a nutter.'

'No, come on. Tell me who he is. You do know him, don't you?'

They were at the lights, waiting to get on to Eastgate. 'All right. His name's Merrick. The bloke I clipped the other day was his father. He came looking for me at the office. He's got some bee in his bonnet about it. He's a bit obsessional, if you ask me. Menopausal with it.'

'Oh, I see.' She took a little brush from her bag and drew it quickly through her hair. 'God, Philip, it's pretty worrying, something like that. I mean, how often does this sort of thing happen to you? How many times before have you been in this kind of scrape?'

'It hasn't happened before. It's just this bloke. He's got it all out of proportion. It wasn't my fault. Anyway, the score's even now, I reckon.'

'Why does there have to be a "score"? Why can't you just act like grown men and forget it all?'

'Because . . . Oh, I don't know.' The lights changed and he concentrated on the traffic.

He drove round to the Corn Exchange and pulled up on the cobbles. 'Look,' he said, 'wouldn't you rather just go home?'

'No. I'm fine.'

Philip got out and Kath shuffled over into the driver's seat. She wound down the window. 'You're going to let me know, aren't you? How you get on?' A little pink had come back into her cheeks. She was smiling, but it was a struggle, revealing a vulnerability he could hardly bear to see.

'Yes,' said Philip. 'I'll call this afternoon.' He turned away, not stopping to watch her back into the traffic.

The plan had been to go into the office and while away the hour or so before he was due at the court, making himself visible, a martyr awaiting his mortal pain. But he could not face it. He thought about going for a wander along the Calls, then found himself walking slowly up Vicar Lane, over the road and on to the corner of the very street where Merrick had confronted him less than twenty-four hours before. What if he turned up here? Or might it be good if they did meet again? Right now? They could have it out once and for all, Philip conceding the fear Merrick had induced in the chase, letting him know, for Kath's sake, that he had won. But something told him it would never be that simple, that poison such as that released in Merrick's veins hung around for ever, like mercury. No matter how much he won an argument, it would never be enough.

The sunlight was glinting on the upper-storey windows of the shops and offices, the sky a lovely blue behind the ornate castellation of the market building. Lower down, in the icy air, the buses came along the wet road, heading for Halton Moor, Moortown. Philip stood on the edge of the pavement, wondering what to do with himself. There was time for a coffee somewhere, yet there was a curious barrier to this in his mind, an inability to penetrate the ordinary world. He looked across at the market, yesterday's dream about taking a stall there only dimly recalled. A bloody whim. What had he been thinking about? He stirred

159

himself and walked among the gathering morning crowds up to the Headrow.

There was a computer store near the corner. He went inside without thinking. Two boys were working intently at a screen, on the 'blob', as they used to call playing truant. Idling along the rows, passing boom after boom of electronic mayhem, he came across a Systemax TV Boy-Plus. '100 Classic Arcade Games'. He pressed the select start button, running through the numbers, letting it stop at random. Unbelievably, it came up at InterStellar Cowboy. The jingle came on, more resonant than on the tiny TV he used to play it on. He let it run for a few seconds, then went back outside.

He looked at his watch. Twenty minutes to go. Maybe the case could be heard early? He headed for the Magistrates' Court.

Three Asians were standing outside, a woman and two youths, trying to light cigarettes in the damp wind blowing up Westgate. The woman was joshing with one of the boys about something he should have said, presumably minutes earlier, in the court. The lad puffed the cigarette to life, grinning. More people were coming and going from the orange anthill building, serious faces, everywhere an air of retribution, of being called to account. It was only two minutes from the Pilot offices, yet it was another planet, a complete subdivision of the life Philip saw around him every day, and took only at face value. He hung about, wasting another minute, then went through the doors to the foyer.

The whiteness of the place struck him, its corporate feel, the security man smiling politely, the suited men about their lucrative legal business, skimming off the dross and bringing it to book. Philip looked at the listings on the notice-board. He ran down the names, some of which were repeated a number of times, until he found Carl David Stall. Seeing the name in print gave Philip a dizzying depression. *It had come to this.*

He looked for Court No. 3. A couple came clattering up the stairs, a blonde woman with her hand crooked round the arm of the man, half-dragging him along. 'Five hundred quid for one bloody thump!' she said, in the direction of the security man.

'Fuckin' disgustin'!' Philip felt the weight of her agitation, the breeze as they brushed past him. In this building the wrath of the state was fielded against those who offended its great notion of peace. Philip walked towards the stairs, sensing himself being drawn reluctantly into its interior. Then, in a flash of wisdom, he considered the thousands of incidents that must never make it here – family altercations, piddling thefts, grudge fights. It was only those who took *exception* to these events who ended up here. Suddenly, he wanted to call the whole thing off. He was standing there, the air faintly perfumed and swirling lightly with the constant opening and closing of the doors. He felt a little sick. Go back, why not? But the security man was staring at him and he found himself making his way down the stairs and along to the courts.

The waiting area was open and echoing. It reminded Philip of an airport lounge. He sat down on the end of a row of plastic chairs, near an interview room. A set of big double doors, with small square windows, led to each of the courts. He looked for No. 3, seeing the lit 'Court In Session' sign above it. A youth was standing outside, trying to see in through the small windows. Another youth with him was smoking, despite the notices. There was no sign of Hyder. A copy of the *Daily Star* was on the seat next to Philip. He picked it up and flicked through it. 'Lotto Lulu Lands In Hot Water!!!' 'Wotta Whoppah Wayne's Got!' And 'Raging Readers! *When two pensioners in a Huntingdon library both wanted to borrow the same book, they beat each other senseless with copies of Tolstoy's* War and Peace*!*' Philip put the paper back on the seat and looked around him, feeling fragile. It was not, he thought, how he had imagined it. It was nowhere he could ever have chosen to come. And he looked down at his sweaty hands, trying to think how he had landed up here in the first place . . .

Thirty

It was the end of a working week and he should have been happy. Should have been. Yet his mood was more thunderous than it had ever been before. Fifteen minutes earlier, Kath had phoned him to say the test had been positive. She was pregnant. Wasn't that marvellous? 'Yes,' he said, adding wretchedly, 'I'm delighted for you.'

How could she *do* this to him? He hadn't really wanted her to have a baby. He had only agreed in principle, not *reality*.

He could not go straight home. He walked down to Boar Lane where the traffic was a murderous machine – hissing lorry brakes, buses spewing exhaust fumes, taxis with their fuming drivers, queueing in tens down the slope outside the station. The pubs were filling with braying office workers, people like Philip, off the job, looking to get rat-faced of a Friday night. Him too, why not?

At the corner of Trinity Street an old woman in a filthy checked coat and headscarf stood in his way. 'Fifty p, son?'

The voice, the human contact, cranked up his anger. 'No. Leave me alone.' Seeing an *Evening Post* seller watching him, he tried to make amends, muttering, 'I've nothing for you, love.' It was weak, yet why should people assume they have the right to bother you, to dump themselves into your psyche? Every minute of the day, somebody *wanting a piece*. Couldn't she see from his expression the pain he was going through? The woman ignored his apology and walked on, the newspaper seller giving Philip a blank look. He had to get out of the crowds, find a bar somewhere.

The pavements were narrowed by green wheelie bins over-flowing with cardboard, flapping pieces of shit. Schoolgirls wearing satin American baseball jackets over their uniforms were making their late and sultry way across town, with an eye for the lads. And there were the clammy winter faces of people going nowhere in particular. Philip walked on, stewing in gloom. He did not want to know about having a baby. He was not ready for it. And *never* would be. Kath. The selfish, scheming . . . There were a few pubs up towards the Playhouse, maybe quieter than the ones in the centre. He felt in his pocket for money, finding only change, three quid, tops. He would have to go to the cash machine. Another problem. To add to every fucking . . . He had to have a drink. And now.

Along a side street was the Duke of Wellington, a dive favoured by prostitutes, but at least no one from Pilot would be there. He went down the narrow street and through the door.

It was empty, save for a youth playing a fruit machine, and a young Indian man behind the bar who was leaning on his elbows over an *Exchange and Mart*. Philip asked for a bottle of Bud and drank it as fast as he could, belching with the gas of it. The youth came over to the barman and stood sharing a joke with him. Philip turned his back on them, looking at the television high up in the corner. Snooker. The most boring game . . . He finished the bottle and turned back.

'Another?' said the barman.

'Yes.'

The man brought the bottle, opened it and put it on the bar. 'One sixty, sir.'

Philip picked up the bottle, then took the change from his pocket and counted it on to the bar. 'Well, looks like I'm a bit short.' He grinned sourly. 'You'll have to put the rest on the slate.'

The man picked up the money and counted it. 'No. Oh no.'

'What's up with you?' said Philip.

'It's not enough, mate,' he said, in his Indo-Yorkshire accent.

'For fuck's sake,' said Philip. 'What's fucking four pence?'

'It's the full price, or you can't have it.'

Philip could sense the youth stiffening beside him. He felt himself blushing. He was twelve years old again.

'Give me the bottle back,' said the man, staring at Philip.

The loss of face was unbearable. It had to be avoided. 'No. Tell you what, I'll give you four penceworth back. How's that?'

The youth shifted on his feet, edging closer. 'Oy, mate. I think you should do as he says.'

Philip spun round. 'What the fuck's it got to do with you?'

'You're out of order, that's what.'

'Ah, piss off.' He put the bottle to his lips, but the barman lunged across the bar, trying to grab it from his hand. Philip swung away. 'Get out of it. I've got it, and I'm fucking keeping it, mate.' He headed for the door, but the barman was round the bar, catching up with him before he could get out. They wrestled with the bottle, the foam spilling out of the top. Feeling his grip weakening, Philip shoved it at him, pushing him over a table.

'Hey! Hey!' The youth was shouting, as Philip barged through the door.

He ran back down the street to the main road where he slowed to a quick walk, stalking up towards the Headrow. Four pence. He had lost it, the whole plot, over four fucking pence. Kath. It was her fault. Kath! How could she do this to him!

Youths were skateboarding along the pedestrian ways, weaving in and out of shoppers, one causing Philip to stop, missing him by inches, expertly. Philip looked to the sky, wanting to calm down, then carried on. At the top of Vicar Lane he glanced back, as if expecting to see the trail of his spleen marked out on the cold air. Get cool. Somehow, you have to . . . On the corner a group of leather-jacketed Sikh lads were shouting at the arrival of one of their mates, a youth in a baggy striped shirt and clumping suede trainers. 'He's here! An' he's lookin' right happy!' Further along, two small white boys were sitting in a closed travel-shop doorway, quiet, watchful, the stores around them full of nice bright things, CD players, computer consoles, decent clothes, goods they could not honestly afford. Philip tried to force some sense of compassion into his head, to sober him. Then he saw the old woman who had tried to tap him up, trudging down the Headrow towards him. It was a chance to atone, for the sake of any deity that might be watching. He felt in his pocket. But, of course, he had nothing. Within seconds she was standing in front of him, looking at his waist.

'Any silver, son? Just a bit?'

Philip shook his head. 'Sorry, love.'

The woman looked up. 'Oh, you.' She took a step by him, then turned. 'Shithouse.' Philip bit the lining of his cheek.

The cash machine was fifty yards away, on the rise. He headed for it quickly, trying to forget the old bag's put-down.

He waited behind a well-dressed couple tapping away at the machine. Something about their unspoken politeness soothed him. These were nice people. He belonged with their class, for all its conceit. The couple took their money and moved on. Philip stepped forward, slid in his card and pressed in his PIN number, the machine obliging with a sheaf of eight waxy tenners. Then he turned to find the youth from the Duke of Wellington standing behind him.

'Hey, you were out of order back there, d'you know that?'

'Sorry?' said Philip.

'He's a mate of mine, that Rajiv. You'd no right to speak to him like that. An' he's hurt his back.'

A carelessness came over Philip. This was unfinished business. And he was tired of things being left undone, of always having to suck under. 'Do something about it, then.'

'You what?'

'Like I said. Fuck off.' He folded the notes in his back pocket, hoping this kid in his cheap grubby jeans could see them, something, perhaps, to nark him even more.

'Hey! I wanna word with you.'

Philip began walking away, past a pizzeria with its orange lights and its city-centre smell of garlic and pastry. This guy would not follow. He was street dross, and small with it, barely a match for someone like Philip. In his mood.

Then, in Philip's version of events, the lad trailed him across the next junction, down the dip to the Town Hall, turning left. He must have decided, Philip told Hyder, meekly, to take him from the front by skipping down an alley parallel to where Philip was heading, and reappearing in his path along the quieter street.

And he had seemed to vanish, but it was only to exchange a few hurried words with a man, some other lowlife he probably knew from the dole queue. Then he ran after Philip, catching up with him as he turned off the Headrow.

'You're comin' back with me, you are. You're gonna apologise to Rajiv.'

Philip felt reassured by the surrounding offices, the big buildings whose function this turd could probably only guess at, closed worlds, a part of Philip's middle-class birthright. And Pilot's offices were only a street away. It was his territory. 'Get stuffed.'

'Hey! You're a right clever cunt, you.' He was walking alongside Philip, a bounce in his step. 'I think you could do with a lesson in some manners, you could.'

Philip's head went hot. Fit to burst. He stopped and grabbed the lad's shoulder, tugging him round. 'And who do you think you are, eh? You're nothing! You're a piece of shit! Scum like you shouldn't be allowed to breed. Want a fucking argument, do you? DO YOU?' He glared at him, breathing heavily. This kid was the shit on Philip's shoes, the needle in all his dealings with the world, with the wankers and wasters, the smokers, the drivers who cut him up, the boy who once stole a girlfriend, the critical voice of his father, and maybe even that Luke Coyne kid who had once chased him out of his own house, making Philip quiver and piss himself in the bushes of a neighbour's garden. When he should have been a man. Though Philip was not thinking about Luke now, nor about Kath, nor any of the circumstances lined up against him in his life. He was all front, all here and now. Only and purely mad. He lunged forward, two fists together.

The youth, Carl, fell back in bemused surprise. Philip had caught him softly in the neck. It was an effeminate strike, and Carl swung back with much greater efficiency, catching Philip with a cold thud to his cheek. Philip, in his fury, tried another blow, a cosh to the head, but Carl blocked it, replying with two good boxer's cracks to the forehead and eye. They made Philip's knees give. Suddenly, he was heading for another dimension, somewhere internal, and the ground was the place to get to.

His mind began to draw level with the incident. As Carl's fists rained on to his head, Philip saw that for all that he, Philip, had started this thing, they were both now as bad as each other. The foot came in, a trainered volley to the kidneys, another, and a scooping-up of Philip's tucked-in legs. Carl leaned over and dragged him towards an alley, the place from which, Philip was to say one hour later, Carl had leapt to surprise him in a premeditated attack. Yet, in primitive truth, the only kind that matters, Carl was merely asserting his working-class right for equality, defining subcultural law. And there would have been no comeback for Philip, had Carl not turned this random social statement into something else, an unexpected pay day, whereby he lifted the flap of Philip's jacket and took the fold of tenners from his back pocket. But for that, Philip would have had nothing to complain about. And maybe even that should have been forgotten. Just desserts. He'd *had it coming*.

For a long time.

He sat up and watched Carl fly down the street with a curious running gait, legs lifting upwards and outwards, elbows out, slightly comical. Philip groaned, laughed. And that should have been that.

The first throbs were arriving in his jaw, in the roots and fillings of his teeth. There was an echo in his skull, like a snore. His side was hot, bruising. He managed to stand up, oddly glad that no one was about. Another hour and he could have cleaned himself up somewhere, inventing an excuse for Kath about a door, or that dark flight of stairs in the multi-storey. He straightened himself, rubbing his needled ribs, his nose pulsing across the bridge. He walked carefully along the alley and into the next street, smiling bizarrely, for the sake of the few passers-by. Two more minutes and he would have made it to the car, and a few minutes' sleep perhaps, just enough to get himself together. And no one need have known a thing. But there was a dreaminess in his head, and a man approaching with a briefcase in his hand.

'Philip? Phil?'

'Ah shit. Howard.' Philip stumbled forward still smiling, but with lights burning in the vault of his head.

'Jesus L Christ. Who's done this?' said Howard, putting down his briefcase. 'Shit, Phil, look at you. Look at the state of you.'

'Been attacked, mate. Some bastard . . .' He gestured drunkenly behind him.

Howard put his hands round Philip's cheeks, looking into his eyes. 'Hey, we'll get you fixed up. We'll get you to hospital. Christ, mate. We'll get the police.'

'Anything you like,' said Philip, a warm blackness arriving as he dropped into Howard's arms.

Thirty-One

It was ten-thirty-five, five minutes past the time the case was meant to be heard. Philip stared at the cream-tiled floor between his feet, struggling with the urge to go and look for Hyder. A woman clerk appeared from Court No. 2. 'We're working down the list of non-attenders,' she said to a man hanging around outside. 'Anyone else for Court 2?' she called. Philip considered this business of people not turning up for the proceedings. Maybe it would be called off. Even at this late hour, it may *never happen*. Then Carl came in through the swing doors at the end of the corridor.

He walked straight past Philip, those known feet treading the floor in front of him, a little mince in his walk. A tall man in a dark-blue suit, whom Philip assumed was Carl's brief, was waiting at the far end of the seating area. The two exchanged words, the man laughing, Carl pushing against a pillar as if warming up for an exercise routine. So relaxed. A drag, that's all this was, forcing him to get out of bed early, to get his mum to press his good trousers, to borrow a decent jacket from a mate. He looked across to where Philip was sitting, feebly alone. The brief looked too, a deadness in his eyes, someone who knew all the tricks, the language for reshaping the truth, smug about the fees he was earning for saying the same things, day in, day out.

A woman came and handed Carl a piece of paper. 'Cheers,' he said, loud enough for everyone to hear. He put the paper on her clipboard and signed where she pointed, passing some wisecrack comment that made the woman smile and return a few friendly words. Why did Philip never have this facility? He could have sat there all day trying to think of a joky line to amuse the woman, coming up with nothing. He folded his arms, trying to summon an air of dignity.

At last, Hyder breezed down the stairs and along the wide corridor, his tie flapping over his shoulder. Philip stood, too readily, betraying his tension.

'OK, Phil, we're on next.' He nodded towards the blue suit. 'Cooper's the defending counsel. Our man is Betts. I've already spoken to him. He'll be winding up the last case now.'

A man in jeans came out of the court. A youth who had been waiting for him asked, 'What did you get?' Philip did not hear the reply. Then a clerk came out of Court No. 3. 'Number 6. Carl David Stall. And all witnesses and counsel.'

Philip followed Hyder through to the court, taking his place in the empty public gallery, watching Carl in front of him with a dreamy unrest.

A clerk, a young coloured guy, told Carl to stand. 'Carl David Stall. Is this your name?'

Carl muttered.

'Speak up, please.'

'Yes.'

'And do you live at 52 Monksgrange Road, Richmond Hill, Leeds?'

'Yes.'

'Please give your date of birth.'

'10th April, 1979.'

Philip looked down at his hands, pinching the skin over the bone of his wrist, finding it difficult to concentrate on what was being said.

'The police versus Carl David Stall. The charge is grievous bodily harm and theft against Mr Philip Pickles.'

The sound of Philip's own name brought him tiredly to attention. He looked at the magistrates, their theatrical presence at the head of affairs, two men and a woman. The man sitting in the centre seemed to be in charge. He looked an old-fashioned patrician Yorkshire type, right-wing, no-nonsense. He nodded to a middle-aged, balding man Philip guessed was Betts, the prosecuting counsel.

Betts got to his feet. 'On the night of December 8th last year, Carl Stall observed the plaintiff Mr Pickles getting money from a cash machine in Leeds city centre. He then waylaid Mr Pickles as he was walking along Queenside, a street not a few minutes' walk from this building.' The magistrate nodded. 'Stall then attacked the plaintiff, a vicious assault resulting in multiple injuries – heavy bruising, various abrasions – which naturally left Mr Pickles in a state of considerable pain and distress. Stall then relieved Mr Pickles of the eighty pounds he had seen him withdrawing from the machine. There were no direct witnesses to the incident, but the accused's flight was recorded on a closed-circuit camera of the Nightvision Securities company . . .' He paused, puzzling over his papers. 'Er, further such evidence is, I believe, available.' He rubbed the wrinkles under his eyes, and continued. 'Consequently, Stall was identified by Mr Pickles and, since he is known to the police – there is a record of theft from a department store two years previously – he was successfully apprehended three days later.'

The magistrate looked at Cooper. 'How does the defendant plead?'

Cooper stood. 'Your Honour, the plea is guilty.' Philip dared not believe this. It could be over within seconds. It was almost too easy. 'At least to the charge of theft. But I ask that a number of complicating circumstances be taken into account.'

'Go on.'

'The first is that my client made no attempt to resist arrest, nor to deny the charge, despite the fact that there were no direct eye-witnesses to the incident. Secondly, he has a long-standing medical complaint, namely diabetes, a condition severe enough to merit daily injections of insulin . . .'

Philip knew to expect, by legend, a measure of whitewashing, but this seemed laughable. He looked at the ceiling, vaguely hoping to lead the court with a show of indifference.

'The upshot of this,' Cooper went on, 'is that when Mr Stall's blood sugar is not absolutely controlled, as happened on the day of the incident, his judgement is not all it might be. It has also severely limited his chances of any kind of career.' He paused, a moment when the magistrate looked over, the tip of his tongue between his lips as if he had heard it all before, ten times a day. 'There is also the point that Mr Pickles had rather foolishly drawn money from a machine on the Headrow, and in counting it openly on a busy street, did all but brandish it under the defendant's nose. This, on a Friday night when all manner of people, as we well know in this court, are heading for town bent on who knows what indulgences and mayhem.' Philip felt his heart tipping to one side. He had been too optimistic. 'And at this critical time we have a well-to-do, professional-looking man all but flaunting his affluence . . .'

Betts stood. 'Sir, I object. Mr Pickles is a clerk with an insurance company, earning less than fourteen thousand pounds a year. The picture of him as a well-heeled, er, yuppie type is a bit fanciful to say the least.'

The magistrate was nipping a hair from his nose. He rubbed his fingers and nodded. 'Just the facts, Mr Cooper, thank you.'

'I withdraw the aspersion, though I think it's fair to say Mr Pickles was rather asking for it. He's no stranger to this city.' He paused, swallowing for effect. 'The next point I would like to make concerns Mr Pickles' frame of mind before the incident took place.' There was a touchable silence. Everyone wanted to hear this. 'Sir, this man was seen minutes before haranguing an old lady who asked him for money in the street, when he could simply have ignored her. Prior to this he had been in the Duke of Wellington pub where he was seen by Carl Stall to be acting in an aggressive manner, refusing to pay the full amount for his drink, and hurling abuse and insults of a racist nature at a member of staff. A tussle then followed whereby Mr Pickles pushed the member of staff, a Mr Hatad Rajiv, over a table, before storming out of the premises in a fit of rage.'

The word 'rage' made Philip's insides shrivel. Hyder looked round. Philip shrugged, stupidly.

'Do you have witnesses to this behaviour?' asked the magistrate.

'Yes, sir. Mr Rajiv is waiting outside. I understand he's just arrived.' The call went out for him.

Philip was squirming, guilt hanging over him like a blanket. He leaned forward wanting to speak to Hyder, to try and find some excuse, but the policeman was looking fixedly at the bench. Rajiv sidled into the room, gingerly taking his place in the witness box. He was wearing a pale-blue shirt and tie, no jacket. He seemed older than Philip remembered and he wondered if it really was him. Cooper asked his name and he nodded. 'Mr Rajiv,' Cooper said, 'do you see Mr Pickles in this court?'

'That's the guy.' He pointed, drawing the eyes of the whole court towards the public gallery where Philip was sitting, massively alone.

'He comes in the pub in a bad temper, demanding drinks and throwing it back like there's no tomorrow.'

'How would you describe his mood? As a kind of rage?'

'Yeah. That's about it.'

'And he refused to pay the full amount for his drink?'

'That's right. I remember it. He wanted another bottle of Budweiser. He didn't have enough money, so he starts getting abusive, calling me a black . . .'

'Go on.'

'A black cunt.' He looked down at the floor of the court.

'That's a complete lie!' Philip hissed at the back of Hyder's head. 'A bloody lie!' Hyder scratched his ear, not turning round. Philip glared at Rajiv, then at Carl's scandalous impassivity. These two knew each other. They'd cooked the whole thing up between them.

'Did you,' Cooper went on, 'worry about your safety at the start of this altercation?'

'Sure. He's a lot bigger than me. He starts banging his fist on my bar.'

'So you attempted to get the bottle of lager back from Mr Pickles when he refused to give you the full amount?'

'It's my job. I went round to try and get it off him and he shoved me over the table.'

'Did you report this matter?'

'No.'

'Why not?'

'Because it happens all the time.'

'But it's no pleasant matter, is it?'

'No. It's not.'

'And this was what time, about ten to six?'

'Yeah. It'd be that.'

'And there was no one else in the pub, apart from Mr Pickles, the defendant, and yourself?'

'No. There was nobody else.'

'Thank you, Mr Rajiv.'

He was led to a chair where he sat, studiously avoiding looking at Carl. Cooper carried on. 'Sir, having witnessed Mr Pickles' behaviour towards Mr Rajiv, Carl Stall followed the plaintiff with the intention of challenging him about his manners, though he received only a torrent of abuse, in which Mr Pickles said, among other things, "Get a life, you piece of shit." An argument followed along the Headrow and into Queenside, whereby Stall attempted to get an apology. Pickles then pushed him away, a gesture which the defendant – a man of poor health, you'll remember – took to be threatening. A fight then ensued in which Mr Pickles got rather more than he had bargained for, and in which the money became scattered on the pavement. My defendant, given his problems, felt unable to resist the temptation and he pocketed the notes before running away.' Cooper took a deep, weary breath. 'Sir, my client pleads guilty to the charge of theft as it stands, but I think the circumstances of the assault require special consideration. Mr Pickles had been drinking, and he is clearly a man of uneven temper, given to unsociable outbursts, perhaps rage . . .' Again, that word. '. . . for all we know. On paper, Carl Stall is guilty, though in principle it would seem six of one and half a dozen of the other.'

The court seemed to shuffle collectively, realigning itself against

Philip. Heads turned in reflection, the magistrate tugged his lower lip. And, for all the bending of the facts, Philip knew this was essentially the truth. Cooper's statement was a brace, tightening around his head. In complete knowledge of himself, his ways, Philip looked at Hyder, at the back of his clean neck, miles away now, it seemed.

The magistrate was frowning, knowing he had to respond to the stiffened atmosphere. 'Well, your point needs to be substantiated, Mr Cooper. And since Mr Pickles is actually here in court, we might, Mr Betts, ask him to step forward and answer this, um . . . aspersion about his behaviour that night. Perhaps that would be agreeable?'

Perhaps nothing. Perhaps you could all go and *fuck yourselves*.

As Betts stood, dithering with the idea, Philip lifted his heavy weight and made his way to the door, his footsteps, soft as they were on the carpeted floor, hugely amplified in the court's watching silence.

Thirty-Two

Darren, on his knees, pinched out the little weeds with his fingers. He liked doing this. Anything like this. It surprised him. He had lived in that flat with his old man all his life and never had anything to do with growing things. Now the outdoors suited him no end, miles better than the workshops where they made chess boards, kids' toys whittled from scraps of wood, spice racks you couldn't imagine anybody wanting. For the cons, doing that stuff was just a way of earning their allowance, or scoring points for parole, though one or two really got off on it, like Darren's cellmate, Henry, who made wire men in stooped-over poses, calling them 'Anguish', or 'Innocence', or 'Paranoia'. Fucking things – they were stuck all over their 'pad', making weird shadows in the dark. Darren didn't get the point of any of them. Nor did anyone else, though no one said anything – they meant too much to Henry, who was a bit of a grizzler. Anything to stop him harming himself, Darren would say. More than once he had told Henry he would be better off out here, getting some fresh air. But they were always watching Henry in case he did something stupid, and besides, you had to be a Green Band orderly to get this job, which meant they trusted you enough not to make a mad leap for the wire. Henry was too screwed up for that kind of freedom.

They were turning the big flowerbeds, Darren and Ray. Pat was behind them, minding the barrow, his turn for a smoke. Pat didn't put as much effort in as the other two, maybe because they were younger – Darren was twenty-four, Ray about thirty, and Pat was way past fifty. He only had a few months before he was up for parole. Juicy cunt. And he was more than happy just to let the time pass, no ripples, minding his own. 'Hey,' he called from behind Darren. 'You know that fella, came in last week? What's his fuckin' name?'

'Zachary,' said Ray, as he humped a spadeful of earth over.

'That's it. Fuckin' Zachary. What sort of a name's that? Anyway, he's had that fairy Wayne after him. And d'you know what Zachary says to get rid of him? He tells him he's got Aids. Fuckin' Aids!'

Ray said, 'Is he positive?'

Darren laughed, but Pat either didn't hear, or did not get the joke.

'No, but,' said Pat, 'if it's right, if he's brought it in here, a prison for fuck's sake, they should tell us. Nothin' against the bloke, but if it's right that he's got Aids, there should be some fucking place for him. Know what I mean?'

Darren thought about this. His father had told him Mick had the same disease. Darren hadn't seen Mick since the trial, though he heard he had been taken down to Leicester. The old man thought Mick had turned out queer, saying maybe he'd been one all along. Darren suspected that it was his father's way of turning him against Mick, particularly since, in less than twelve months, Darren might be out of here. Maybe that was Sam's worry, that he might go looking for Mick again? Fucking no way. Not a chance.

There was plenty Darren had not known about Mick, such as the news that he had been inside twice before – once for posing as an insurance collector, once for house-breaking. It came out in court. So too did the fact that the 'dibbles' had been alerted by some security code set off by the supermarket manager pressing one lousy button on his mobile phone. They were on the way before they had even reached the bastard supermarket. Mick hadn't known what the fuck he was doing. A complete amateur, it turned out. But, balls to it now. Darren didn't care any more. It had all been a stupid mistake. Just that, no more. And when he got away from here he had made a vow to get things right and that certainly meant avoiding Mick, though he did wonder about Luke, from time to time.

Ray tossed the trowel down and stretched, dark-blue pads of sweat under the arms of his baggy shirt. He took his place beside the barrow, a hint that Pat should now do his bit. But Pat did not move. All morning, and he had done fuck all.

'Compassionate pardon,' Ray said, wetting his cigarette paper, moving his head from side to side as he licked, an odd habit he had.

'What?'

'If he's really got Aids, he'll die soon anyway. What's the point in keeping him banged up in here?'

'Fuck knows.'

Pat's failure to move was making Darren uneasy. He could have done with a break himself, but if the screws saw them all standing about together, they might say something. And he did not want to lose this job. He turned to look behind him. 'Look, Pat, are you fuckin' doing anything today, or what?'

'I'm coming. Fuck's sake, what's the rush? You should make this spin out. No cunt's bothered how long it takes.'

Pat brought the long-handled trowel and lazily turned the spots Ray had just cleared. But Ray was not bothered – he was staring towards the main gate where a Group 4 'cattle wagon' had just pulled up. Pat stopped to watch. 'Jesus. How many more?'

Yells came from the punishment block. 'No vacancies!' 'We're full for the bastard season!' 'Is there a Tommy Maloney with you?' They yelled all day and night sometimes, whether there was anyone there or not, bawling over the grass to the fence, over the razor wire, where only the rabbits would hear them, or occasionally the farmer who ploughed there, turning his tractor, laughing at the comments, the loony-bin howls. Inside, though, it was different. Some of those who shouted from the windows didn't say a thing indoors, and others were nice as pie. But those who went on all night, banging at the doors . . . They got so mad about things. Darren could not see the point. It put him on edge. Couldn't they see that prison would be a piece of piss, if they could all just get on together?

Ray doffed his smoke, nodding to Darren to take his turn by

the barrow. But the scene by the gates was a magnetic distraction. Four men, handcuffed in pairs, were being brought from the van. 'Designed for two hundred and fifty, this fucking place,' said Ray. 'And how many's here? Four bastard hundred. At least. We'll be kippin' on the fucking landings next.'

'Maybe they'll give us a tent out here,' said Darren. 'If we play our cards right.' No one heard him. He went to stand with the others by the barrow and skinned up a smoke.

When the men had gone inside, the din became fragmented, prisoners shouting to each other, or no one in particular. Darren looked out over the sun-soaked countryside, knowing every hedgerow, every tree and palm-print of land. Out here you could work on your daydreams. His latest was to get out of the country, as soon as he was away from here. He had never been abroad in his life, but he liked looking at pictures of the Mediterranean in magazines from the prison library. It gave him fantasies that went on for hours, about travelling, working his ticket across Europe till he got to some holiday place in Spain or Greece, somewhere hot with the white beaches and the blue sea you could see in those photos. Maybe Luke would fancy it too, if he got out at the same time. In Darren's imagination, the only future he had, he often thought about meeting up with Luke again. After all, Darren owed him plenty. Wasn't it his fault for getting him involved with Mick? So, maybe he could make it up to his old mate and they'd get it right this time.

Get a life. Or some such thing.

Thirty-Three

'So, how'd it go, Phil?'

Howard was standing with his hands on his hips, shirt-cuffs fashionably rolled halfway up the forearm.

Philip stared hard at the Quality Street tin. 'All right, I suppose.'

'So what did he get? Must have been a black-cap job. Hanging at dawn?' He was wanting recognition for his part in the affair. Always on the grab. Always.

'I don't really know.'

'What d'you mean, you don't know?'

Philip shuffled his chair up to his desk. 'The case was more complicated than I thought. Maybe he got away with it. I couldn't say.' He could see Howard's bald head in the corner of his eye, the buzzing overhead light creating a downy halo.

'But you must know what happened.'

'I said I don't know! All right, Howard?'

'Hey sure, Phil. Sure. Steady away, mate.' He still did not move. 'You're OK, aren't you, Phil?'

'I'm all right, Howard,' Philip said, stressing each word slowly. 'Never . . . better. The tops.'

'Right. Well, if you want to talk about it some other time . . .'

'I doubt it.'

'Right. Er, right. I'll leave you to it, then.' He took a step back. 'There's the Griffiths thing to carry on with, if you're up to it. I know it's boring, but we're close to a result.'

'I'm up to it.' Philip banged the keys of his computer, bringing it to life. 'It'll be sorted.'

'Great. Fine.' Howard moved on, talking quietly to Tom, then leaving the office.

For the next forty minutes Philip looked at his screen and the papers on his desk, capable of nothing, the trappings of his job around him like badly fitting clothes. No one was looking at him. They knew he was in a state. Always something nettling our Phil. He left his desk and went to the coffee machine, then realised he had no change. He walked along the corridor, trying to connect with the place in some way. But he was an absence, rooted elsewhere. Not belonging.

There was no thinking about what had happened that morning. No way back. And no way forward, except from moment to stiff moment. Through a part-glazed door he saw Tarquin at his desk, spinning a set of keys on his finger, laughing with a girl opposite. A steel shutter seemed to drop in Philip's mind. And he thought . . .

I want my own back.

He went to his desk and pulled out the Griffiths file. Howard had put a memo from the legal department on the top. The words 'clearly shows an intention to take her own life . . .' caught Philip's eye. He ignored the rest, retaining only this phrase to nurture a principle. Think of the poor woman's suffering. And what about the kids? Grown-up maybe, but she was their mother, all the same. A time to prove his *good self*, to show that the world deserved better than to be judged by Pilot Insurance Services. It would be a rite of passage, something just. At last.

He looked around the office then took a claims authorisation pad from a drawer. He laid it precisely on his desk and filled in Griffiths' name and address with a cool attention to neatness. He looked again across the office to where Sarah was leaning over Tim's desk, brushing her hair behind her ear, querying something.

A second of rationality. He had not yet done this mad thing. There could still be a way back. But then, I *want* to do this.

He had forged signatures before, in the days when he put his mother's signature on a set of poor school reports. And that time when he had copied Kath's in front of her, as a joke. He was practised in the art of deception. What did that say about him? Never mind. He took an old stationery request pad that was meant for scrap and copied Howard's signature from a claim form, four times. The last one was almost there, the flourishes close, and that awkward seminal curve at the bottom of the 'F'. The next attempt would have to be it, to make it as natural as possible. He put the claim authorisation form on the desk's hard surface and, in the square for the supervisor's assent for payment, made his facsimile of Howard's signature.

He was excited. A good sign, a symptom of being alive. For once. He picked up the form and headed across the office. As he reached the door he heard his phone ring, but, already remote from his usual obligations, he ignored it. Back in the corridor he was wildly in tune with his surroundings, completely different from the way he had been only minutes before. This was drama, deliciously subversive. He should have done it a long time ago! Then, halfway up the stairs, he saw Howard appear through the door at the top. Philip hurriedly rolled up the form.

Howard sauntered down the stairs, pulling on his jacket. 'Is that the Griffiths report?' There was a gruffness in his voice, as if he had been considering Philip's rudeness over the court case and had now lost patience with him.

'No.' Philip said. 'Something else. Just cropped up.'

'Oh. OK.' Howard shrugged himself into his jacket, brushing the sleeves. 'Right, well, you'll get on with the other business today, won't you?'

'Yeah. No problem.'

Philip carried on up the stairs, hearing Howard pass through the fire door below.

He could still turn around and no one would be any the wiser. But the momentum of his actions was now purely external, beyond reservations. And the fact that there was no one waiting at the Accounts office window only seemed to confirm that what he was doing was right. The floor space was inviting him. This was *meant to be.*

There was a new woman behind the glass partition. White permed hair, glasses on a loop. A temp maybe, a cluck without doubt. Philip nodded to her and handed over the form. 'It's to go out straight away,' he said, contriving an authority he hoped she might not challenge. 'Urgent. Days overdue.' He leaned on the shelf. 'Harry'll take it.' Harry Turling was one of their oldest reps, and a dead hand when it came to finding new business. He would not question the delivery of a cheque. In fact he would be pleased by having such a simple job to do on a Friday afternoon. Anything was better than selling. And he was the one who had sold the policy in the first place, failing to get a proper health check on Griffiths' wife. It would be a relief to Harry to get this business finished with, his oversight forgotten. For a moment, Philip wondered about this. How had he worked out Harry's involvement without thinking? Had it been in his mind for some time? Was this further evidence that this was *bound* to happen, that it was an unstoppable, fate-driven, DNA-coded certainty?

The woman flipped over the triplicate copies. 'Sixty-five thousand. It's an awful lot. Doesn't this need to be counter-initialled, on the bottom copy somewhere?'

Doesn't this need to be counter-initialled? Philip stifled the impulse to do a mime of her cluck's voice. 'No. It's down to Mr Freeman and myself.'

She was pressing up the wattle under her chin. 'I should ask someone, really.'

Philip took a deep steadying breath. 'There's nothing to it. It's standard procedure.' The woman was still staring at the form. The situation was closing in on Philip. A trickle of sweat ran in the hairs of his chest. His arms were hot. 'It is rather urgent, love.' The door whined open behind him, brushing the carpet. It was Tarquin, carrying a sheaf of papers, and wearing his suit jacket, trying to look as if he was on the job, for once. He stood behind Philip, a pestilence bound up in this morning and its grand plan.

'I should wait for Sandra,' said the woman. 'She'll be back in an hour.'

Philip squared himself up in front of Tarquin to stop him hearing. 'It has to go now. Really. I'll take full responsibility.'

She looked from the form to Philip. 'And you are?'

'Phil Pickles. Life and Deaths. And this is a matter of . . .' He smiled sarcastically.

The woman shrugged. 'Oh well, if you're sure.'

'Oh, I am, love. I am. Now, the cheque, if you don't mind.'

'Sorry?'

'You have to make out the cheque and I countersign it.'

She was reaching under the counter when the phone rang in the office behind her. 'Oooh . . .' She went to answer it. Philip heard the words, '. . . she's left me on my own, you see. I've got people waiting.' He turned round and looked at Tarquin, knowing he had to acknowledge his presence.

'All right, Phil?'

Philip nodded. It was an incongruous thought, but in this small gesture Tarquin seemed to want to put right their little difference from Tuesday night. If this wasn't happening it might even have been worth exchanging a few words of conciliation. But it was too late for that. Way too late. The woman came back to the window. She reached under the desk, lifted out the big cheque book and ran it under the computer franking machine. Philip hunched himself up again to stop Tarquin seeing the figures. Then the woman was staring at the cheque, putting her stupid glasses on. Philip held his breath to resist the urge to tell her to get on with it, to stop holding up the world, to appreciate how lucky she was to have a job . . .

She signed and passed the cheque under the glass. Philip countersigned. 'You'll be able to get hold of Harry now. If you're sharp you'll catch him before he goes to the pub for his lunch.'

'How?'

'Just page him,' he said, turning away. 'He'll know what it's about.'

'Hey, Phil.' Tarquin put his hand on Philip's shoulder. 'We're up the Crack again after work. If you fancy it.'

He looked genuinely modest about the offer, as if someone had said something to him about the other night, Howard, perhaps, though in the midst of his tension Philip could not resist the bonus of a dig at him. 'Sure. Why not, Tarkers, old mate?' Tarquin spotted the slight, shrugged his shoulder and stepped up to the window.

Back in the office the first lunch-takers were making their way out. Philip went over to his desk. The computer was still on. He had a blazing wish to type his resignation into the all-department memo section, the words, 'Fuck off, the lot of you', high on the list of things he wanted to say. But it might have spoiled the Griffiths scam, that greater, more important treachery. So, it would have to be simply this, the turning-off of the computer, the taking of his jacket from the back of his chair, a calm walk from the room. And, as he left, the world of Pilot Insurance seemed to close its doors silently behind him.

Thirty-Four

In the fresh air, the sense of relief was tremendous. The streets of Leeds felt good, accessible, the sudden pace of Philip's day lifting him way above himself. Even the shop signs seemed to have come to life – Boots, Argos, Going Places. *Going Places!* Sound. He wanted to run down to City Square, smiling instead of avoiding people's looks. Now he was free, everyone seemed so *interesting*! And wouldn't it have been good to have someone to talk to, a soul to whom he could declare that he no longer belonged to the society of scurrying office workers, with their dead eyes, their crappy suits. To tell someone that all they needed to do, ever, was to be themselves.

And to *act* on it.

It was uncanny, a roller-coaster ride. But tinged with aggression, and a wish for confrontation. With a leap of adrenalin, he hoped Merrick would appear. Wouldn't it be great? With this sureness of himself, Philip would rip him to shreds! And stamp on the pieces!

What a day. And no longer a Pilot employee. He'd really gone and done it. Kath would understand, if no one else. She would be *proud* of him.

'Look, calm down and tell me that again.'

'I've walked out. That's it.'

In the taxi on the way home he had planned all the things he wanted to say, setting them in order of philosophical importance, ideas about choice, change, the wisdom of impulse. Yet it all seemed too extravagant now. Kath's infuriatingly quiet presence, her ordinariness, did not permit it.

She was wearing a coat, as if she had just come in. It was a new coat, navy and red reversible, roomy, no doubt the latest thing for mothers-to-be. She took her cigarettes from the cupboard over the cooker and stood, waving the packet as she spoke. 'This is unbelievable. It's your job, Philip. You can't have just done something like that. How could you? What's been going on?'

Philip laughed. 'Oh, come on!' He wanted to tell her about the Griffiths business, but it would have taken too much detail, detracting from his high. 'Nothing's been going on! I've had enough and given it up. It's like we said. Like you said. Last night. Remember?'

Kath shook her head. 'Oh, Phil. Honestly.'

'Honestly what? Don't you remember what you said? About you going to work and me looking after the baby? About me setting up some sort of business?' His elation was on the verge of converting to anger. 'And the things you said you were going to *do* to me?'

Kath rubbed her face, looking out at the back garden. 'God, Philip . . .'

'God what? For Christ's sake, Kath. Sometimes you're just so . . .'

'So what?'

'Jokeless. You've no sense of humour, that's what.'

She closed her eyes and pushed back her hair. 'This is supposed to be funny, is it? Look, what's happened to make you do this? Was it the case?'

'No.'

'Well, what happened? What sentence did he get?'

'I don't know.'

'What do you mean you don't know? Didn't you go?'

'I went. I just didn't stay till the end.'

She looked at him, her head to one side. 'Why not?'

'It was too boring.'

'That's ridiculous! What do you mean, it was too boring?'

'Like I said.'

Kath paced in a half-circle, made for the door to the living room, then turned back. 'Christ, Philip, I can't stand this any more. You're going off your nut. If it's not one thing it's another. All the time, nothing's ever right. And all you can do is get mad at everything. It never bloody ends! Why can't you just accept things and live like anyone normal!'

The power of her voice cowed him, threatening to defeat him. He said, 'What's normal?'

'For God's sake!' She was shrieking. 'Taking life a bit at a time. Little by little. Having patience. Look at what you've done, what you're like! You've walked out on your job. You walked out of the court case. And what was that business with that man this morning?'

'What man?'

'Fucking hell, Philip! The one who was trying to kill us both!'

'That? It was nothing. Believe me.'

'Nothing?' She threw the cigarettes on the draining board. 'Jesus, what are we going to do now? What's going to happen to us?'

He looked at the new coat, seeing it as a symbol of her increasing remoteness from him, the line of her life diverging from his. They could go no further together. It was an ordinary fact and he wanted to tell her so. He took a step towards her. They were two feet apart, silent, save for Kath with her hand over her nose, sniffing. For a second he saw the fragility of her wrists, the softness of her forehead. There was nothing he could say. Plain cruelty was beyond him. He eased himself past her, careful not to touch. 'I'm going out.'

'Where? Where are you going now?'

'I'm going out with Oz. You know I am.'

Kath took a tissue from her pocket and blew her nose. 'The car's still at the garage,' she said, her voice going watery. 'Mum's picking me up to go and get it. She won't be long. Why don't you wait?'

'No. I don't want to. I'm going to get changed, and I'm going out.' He was halfway across the living room. He turned, wanting to say something placatory, but she had gone out into the garden.

Thirty-Five

Kath was being so negative. He couldn't *breathe* near her. Couldn't she see how good this was making him feel? Could she not see the *funny side* of it all?

Some people. Honestly.

Rather than ring for a taxi in her presence, Philip walked into the village to the phone box outside the hairdresser's. He paced up and down, waiting for the car, ready to give the driver hell if he did not show in the next fifteen seconds. Then he saw the woman from the Spar, clacking down the steps from the shop. Wasn't life just like this? He ducked behind the phone box.

It was too late. She was standing in front of him.

'Hello-oo!' she said, buttoning her bristly old bag's coat. 'Thought it was you. I saw you from the shop.' Philip was pondering her spindly legs and fat ankles. 'You won't have time for standing around soon,' she went on. 'Not when that baby's here. You won't have time for anything. I should know . . .'

'Piss off.'

Her dentured smile twitched into a parody of itself. 'Excuse me, young man?'

'Like I said. Mind your own fucking business.'

Her hand went flat over the top button of the coat. 'Good heavens. Well . . . Pardon *me* for breathing.'

'Why don't you stop altogether, do everybody a favour.'

As he was saying these things, Philip wanted to laugh. They were needless, he knew, and he almost did not want to say them – they were simply an alternative to the tedium of being polite.

'How rude! I've never been spoken to like that in all my life.'

'That's a surprise. Maybe you should get out more.'

'Oh, really!' She looked down at her sleeves, as if trying to find something in her appearance to reassure herself. 'Well, young man, I shall not speak to you again, if this is what you're like.'

'Do that. It suits.'

It was too much, and he knew it. She walked away to the dip to the green, her look fixed in front of her. Philip would not go to heaven. Not now. Ah well, fuck it. Another bridge burned. That was all. He stamped on the paving flags, dancing from one foot to the other. Seconds later, the taxi appeared, cruising along the edge of the green.

There was a fug of cigarette smoke in the car, a freshly doffed tab end on the dashboard. The driver was a big Leeds man with greasy blond hair, combed back fifties-style. His neck was fat and suntanned in the open white shirt collar. Philip sat beside him, wondering if he should tell him about his exchange with the old woman, perhaps inspire some blokish sympathy. Or maybe not. Some Leeds men had an old-fashioned respect for women. This guy might love his wife big-time, or his mother, perhaps with the kind of maudlin Yorkshire sentiment that Philip found nauseous. And if he knew what his passenger had just been saying, he might want to rip Philip's head off. Philip stared out of the window saying nothing until, as they skirted round Chapeltown, the driver remarked on a knifing the night before. 'Drugs, drugs, drugs,' said the guy. 'Everythin's fuckin' drugs, these days. Bloody nutcases.' Philip replied with a grunt.

Five minutes later he was outside the big Victorian terraced house where Carla, Oz's nineteen-year-old sister, lived with her baby son. Philip had been to the flat before and, for some reason, it impinged on his daydreams. When he was imagining the life he really wanted, being the bachelor he had never been while he was with Kath in Manchester, this was the kind of flat he saw himself living in. Yes, something like this, the single existence, without the shackles of a job, impending parenthood, the fucking mortgage. Here, in student Headingley, he would be like these *young* people, with no life-plan, only a week-to-week existence, the future massively empty, and kept that way, every option permanently available.

He went in through the porch and climbed the stairs. The rumble of reggae behind a closed door and the smells of herbs and stale fat only served to develop further his wish for a life of his own. It would be the answer to everything. If Philip had that he might even, weirdly, *not* have given up his job at Pilot. He may have actually worked harder, climbing the ladder. Thus, in these few moments, the crystallisation of all his problems, in a single body, a name: Kath. She was the *complication*, the one thing keeping him from *accepting* happiness.

The landing at the top was dark, though he knew the right door. He knocked, and when there was no answer he thought about breaking in, or leaving a note and going to sit in the Cygnet at the top of the road, pleasantly contemplating his sudden, and startlingly genuine, lack of a future. He knocked again, harder, and he was about to leave when he heard the creak of a floorboard and a sniff at the other side of the door.

'Who is it?'

'Oz?'

His friend opened the door. 'Ah shit, it's you.'

'Mate! Good to see you!'

'I thought you weren't coming till tonight?'

'Afternoon off!' Philip trailed him into the living room.

'Oh, right.' Oz scratched the mess of his hair. His shirt was open, revealing his narrow white chest. There was dope smoke on the air, the television on MTV. Oz began tidying up, half-heartedly shifting magazines, picking up a cereal bowl and puzzling where he might put it.

'What's going on here, then?' Philip said, in their old joky rap. 'Look at the fucking state of this place!'

'Bit of a blow,' Oz said, half-asleep. 'You know how it is. Anyway, how are you, mate?'

'Great! Never better!'

Oz was still standing in the middle of the room, holding the bowl. 'Ah, fuck.' He put the bowl down on the arm of the settee and went to the bathroom.

Standing there alone, Philip felt annoyed. He had imagined his oldest friend would be ready to receive him, to share his day of revolution. But he was not. At this moment he was in the toilet, farting.

In the pub, an hour later, this impatience was still there and Philip found himself looking at Oz, his straight laddish brown hair, the whippet leanness beneath the purple silk shirt that hung almost to his knees. He had showered and it seemed to have made his skin even paler. At school Philip had always, in secret conceit, thought himself a touch superior to Oz and his council-estate upbringing. Looking at him now, hunched over pie and chips, pausing between chomping mouthfuls to take in his surroundings with those watchful, self-contained eyes, the divide seemed even greater, spilling over into their respective adulthoods. But Philip knew that there was plenty to admire in him – the easy-going life, the way he drifted from job to job. And tiny things, like the way he had slobbed out of the flat, leaving the door unlocked, something Philip would never have done. Oz never gave a shit about anything. It was an art that was hard to imitate.

'I've got this gig for the summer,' Oz said, livening with the food. 'Up the coast, working on the gas.'

'What, the fucking rigs?'

'Nah. Where the stuff comes ashore.' He picked up the salt and showered it over his meal. 'It's contract stuff, working on the conduits or some such fucking thing. This guy I met up in Scotland. He's got me in on it. And, get this – seven hundred a week!'

Philip had always envied this in Oz, his failure to succumb to the burden of something as boring as a career. He just refused to fall for it, unlike Philip. 'Sounds all right.'

'Better'n fucking all right, mate. Three months of that and I'm away to Magaluf for the winter.'

'Why not?' Philip said. He wanted to ask if he could join

him. But something was in the way. They were schoolmates, not workmates. They only met now to compare notes, to rekindle an effortful nostalgia, old adolescent jokes and shared experiences barely worth remembering. It was a shame, Philip thought, wondering how he might turn it round and make them as close in adulthood as he remembered them being as boys.

'So, how's the office?' said Oz, wrapping his tongue round a forkful of pie.

'It's crap, basically. Sick to death of it.' It did not seem the moment for telling the absolute truth about his day. Oz was not up to being serious right now, the dope no doubt lingering in his veins.

'Ah, bollocks. Can't be that bad. Regular, if nothing else.'

'Yeah, well.' Philip reached for his glass.

'And how's the lovely Kathy?'

'You taking the piss or what?'

'No.' Oz licked his teeth and wiped his chin with his hand. 'Should I be?'

'Well, she's pregnant, isn't she?'

'So?'

'So it's a fuck-pig, fuck-up situation. I'm done for. Middle fucking age, that's all there's left for me now.' It came out heavier than he had meant, the unspoken events of the last few hours perhaps pressing on his mind.

Oz laughed. 'Don't try and tell me it was a fucking accident!'

'I'm not. I just don't fancy it, that's all.'

'Christ, Phil, lighten up! You'll love it! They're great, kids are. Take our Clara's young 'un. And our Marion's two. Love 'em to fucking bits, me.'

'Only because they're not yours.'

'Piss off. Anyway, what're you worried about with Kath around?' He lifted a bottle of Miller Lite to his face. 'She'll make a brilliant mother, her.' He belched and put the bottle to his mouth.

Philip curled his lip. How would he know? He had only met Kath twice, and he was drunk both times, the second occasion when they had just moved into the house and Oz had spent an hour heaving up his guts before crashing on the floor in the spare room. He tried to think about Kath, and their row a few hours earlier. By now, he should have had it in some perspective, yet it was still a sore, a piece of undigested material that the lager would not melt. He emptied his glass and went to the bar.

The Friday afternoon workers were wandering in, guys from the building sites, on a flyer, filling the brown vinyl wall benches, claiming their territory here with a smoky unchallengeable ease. When Philip got back to his seat, Oz was talking to one of them, his back to Philip. It was another source of annoyance, a display of Oz's connections in this world. Philip drank quickly. When Oz had still not turned round he nudged him in the spine. 'Are we out of here, or what?'

Oz looked at Philip's empty glass. 'Shit. Er, yeah, I suppose.'

'Come on, then,' said Philip. 'For fuck's sake.'

They headed for Hyde Park, Chapeltown's nephew, with its streets of rising red-brick back-to-backs, sociologically sited clumps of newer council houses, and more student life, its light-heartedness mingling uneasily with the angry humour of the local talent. They were roughing it, getting wasted, tacitly drifting to the pubs where they first got served as sixteen year olds. Philip was not keen on the nostalgia trip, but this suited him – he was keen to avoid the town centre and anyone who might be around from the office. He still had not mentioned the Griffiths story, nor his walking out, nor Merrick, nor the Carl business, about which Oz knew nothing. He wanted to but, as the drink set in, it seemed a point of vague integrity to keep the news to himself.

They went from pub to pub in the winter dark. When Oz wanted something else to eat – where did he put it all? – Philip forced down half a sandwich, preferring to make himself drunk enough to have to spend the night at the flat, a finale which was not yet an explicit understanding. They did not actually say much to each other, Oz playing the fruit machines, falling into more casual conversations with people he half knew, yet Philip was glad to be with him. This was his friend, his fucking, fucking old pal. And they were out on the town, all grown-up now.

In the Fairfax Philip went to the toilet. As he pissed he could hear a man spewing in the cubicle. A few minutes later he saw the guy leave the toilet and go to the bar to order another drink. Oz came back with the latest round, dropping like coal into his seat. 'Nearly done for, mate. 'Bout shagged.'

'Right. Know the feeling,' Philip said. It was half-past ten. He edged himself round and, for some reason, the movement seemed to loosen a sudden impulse to tell Oz everything about his day. They were men now, weren't they? They *should* be able to talk about serious things. But how to start? 'Listen, Oz. Do you get mad sometimes? I mean really raging? Out of your fucking head?'

'What, you mean like that cunt Powell, the head of fucking science? Fuck, remember . . .' It was a belated attempt at reminiscence.

'No. Not like him.'

'Remember that cunt? I mean when he threw that fucking flask at Chuckles. And the next lesson . . .' He was snorting with laughter. 'The next lesson . . .'

'I know, I know. We all sat at the front in crash helmets.'

'That's it!' Oz was slapping the table, laughing.

They had recounted the story dozens of times. Every time they met. 'No, that's not what I'm talking about. Listen . . .'

'And then . . .'

'Oz, just listen. What I'm on about . . .'

Oz controlled himself. 'Yeah, sorry, mate. What were you saying?'

'What I was trying to say was, I just get really uptight sometimes. You know, raving.' As a solitary statement it sounded stupid, wankingly confessional.

Oz was looking at his glass. He had bought himself a rum and black. 'You wanna do drugs, old mate.'

'Nah. Bollocks.'

'No, really.' He put his arm on the back of Philip's seat, leaning closer. 'E's, they're the thing. You don't hate anybody with a few of those inside you. Or a bit of whizz, or a bit of weed. Better than the piss, any day. Do drugs, Phil. They're great. I love 'em.'

Philip looked at his glass. 'I don't like drugs. I don't agree with them.'

'You should, mate. They're not half as bad as people reckon.'

Philip went silent. It was a deflating exchange, seeming to put a new barrier between them. He was scratching for a way to bring the conversation round to what he wanted to say when the door opened with a blast of cold air. Oz put his hand on Philip's arm, as if trying to stop the talk going any deeper. 'Hang on, old son. We might drop lucky here.'

Philip tutted, wanting to try again to batter his way through to his pal's attention. Then he glanced up at the two girls who had come in.

One, he did not recognise. The other was Sarah, in a black spangly dress, looking older, more worldly than she did in the office. All his memories of secretly watching her seemed to curdle in Philip's head, her presence here a mockery of his day, and the significance with which he had imbued it. He tried to hide his face, but she had seen him the moment she set foot through the door.

Thirty-Six

A song came on the juke-box, some anthemic Oasis number – 'Stand By Me', or some such fucking . . . It made a group of students in the corner bubble to life, wailing along to the words. Philip watched Sarah follow her friend to the bar, his drunkenness souring, the atmosphere in the pub seeming to change, resettling like a shaken blanket.

'I'll take them both,' said Oz, unable to take his eyes off the two women. 'Whoa, steady on. They're coming over!' And, to Philip's shrinking pleasure, Sarah came and sat down across the table from them.

'Hello, Phil. Not seen you round here before.'

Philip reached for his drink. 'No. You won't have.'

Sarah's friend tottered up behind her. 'This is Romana.'

'Hiya,' said Romana. She had stacked-up black curly hair, her full body teemed into a short lime dress, her thick upper arms dappled by the cold.

'Now then, Romana,' Oz said, beaming.

The discourse Philip had planned for the next half-hour went flat in his head. Instead, the information was about to be piss-takingly imparted by one of his workmates, a failed conquest to boot. There was a temptation to walk out. But there was also a creeping curiosity to find out what had gone on at Pilot that afternoon.

'Had a good day at work?' he asked.

'No.' Sarah pushed her hair behind her shoulder. 'Actually, I went home at lunchtime.'

'Oh?' Philip wondered if she was making this up, embarrassed by his behaviour, perhaps, and not wanting the responsibility of being the first to confront him about the Griffiths business. Or maybe it was even bigger than he had imagined, with the police out there, looking for him.

She was leaning round-shouldered on the table, turning the stem of her glass in her fingertips. There was a slight malaise in her smile. 'Problems, Phil,' she said, addressing the glass.

'Oh? I'm sorry to hear that,' he said, not meaning it. He was looking at Romana, her thick black eye make-up. Fucking tart. He dragged his gaze away and rested his hand on his chin, looking beyond Sarah's shoulder. 'Is the boyfriend not out tonight? What's his name? Mike?'

'He's the problem.'

'Ah, right.'

Oz was chatting to Romana, making instant headway, the girl possibly looking for relief from the gloom her friend was oozing.

'Well, I'm sorry,' Philip said, trying to rouse some feeling, wondering if it might really be true that she had not been at work that afternoon. If so, it might suit him to forget about the whole affair, all his problems, until the morning. He was tiring of the evening, its disappointing agenda.

The Oasis crooners rested their voices, their silence revealing a new disturbance, a tall Jamaican by the bar getting some serious rise from two white men. Philip watched them, on the black guy's side, bitterly resenting the racist implication that had been made against him that morning. That just was not true. He should have stayed to challenge Rajiv's statement. But it was too late for thinking about it now. In an attempt to distract everyone's attention away from the argument, the barman called for last orders. Sarah turned to look at the bar. 'Do you want another drink?'

'Not really. Anyway, you haven't finished that one yet.'

'I know. I can't seem to get drunk.'

Romana went to the bar, Oz following.

Philip looked at Sarah. 'Have you two split up, then, you and this Mike?'

She smiled. 'Looks like it. I think we've got the "responsibility" problem on our hands.'

'Ah well, that's men for you,' Philip said, getting more interested, though still watching the argument. The two white men were stalking out, stern-faced, leaving the black guy shaking his head and rolling a cigarette.

Sarah seemed not to have noticed the incident. 'What is it about men and a few simple bloody duties?'

'Can't take it,' Philip said, as the two men left, one of them kicking the door frame. 'Growing up. It's a big step. Not everyone's ready for it.'

'But you're all right.'

'Am I?'

She had her elbows on the table, her head resting on her palms. 'Course you are. Steady as a rock, you. You've got the house, a baby on the way. You're good at your job.'

Philip laughed. 'I'm not so sure about that.'

'Yes, you are. You're always on the case. A bit grumpy maybe, but you know what's what.'

'A bit grumpy, eh?' He laughed. 'Some might put it more strongly than that.'

'Who? Tarquin? You don't want to worry about that little wanker.'

'I don't. Life's too short.'

Sarah smiled, her bottom lip flaky, with a little crack in the middle. She had not made the effort to get dolled up for the night like her friend. She should have. The glums did not become Sarah, and Philip felt like telling her so. 'You're in control,' she said, stretching out her wrists, rolling them on the table. 'I wish Mike was. He can't seem to decide from one minute to the next what he wants. Sometimes it's an outdoor job, sometimes an office, sometimes bloody travel . . .'

Philip nursed a secret disappointment. She might have been talking about him. And when she found out the truth . . . But she need not know that just now. He wanted to preserve her good opinion of him. 'What about those foreign trips he goes on? That stuff you were telling us the other day?'

She shook her head. 'That wasn't work. The idea behind that

was to go and look for work. His father gave him the money, the sap. Only today Mike decides it's a new car he needs instead, so he spends it on that.'

'But you've got that red BMW. Fuck's sake, Sarah, what's wrong with that?'

'Not good enough. When Mike gets something he really wants, his first thought's not, Isn't this great! It's, How can I get something even better? I couldn't see you doing a thing like that, Phil.'

There was a slight tic of the shoulders. Drink was her weakness, he could see that, and the access it gave her to a surprising depressive tendency. It was how she had been that night when he had tried it on with her. 'You're all right, you, Phil,' she had said then. 'You're a copper-arsed, fully paid-up member of the adult race.' If only he hadn't dived for her that moment. God, the timing of it. With everyone watching. What else could she do but push him away, cackling with embarrassment?

She was frowning at her hands, clicking her thumbnails together. Oz and Romana came back. They had been too late to get served at the bar. Oz was saying something to her, making her laugh. 'Hey, Phil!' he said. 'Looks like a club now! You on, or what?'

'Sure,' Philip said, reaching for the glass he now saw was empty. He sat back, smiling gently at Sarah. 'Why not?'

As they were leaving a police patrol car pulled up, its two occupants, a regular constable and a woman special, getting out and going into the pub through the main double doors. Philip thought about Oz and his drugs, wondering if that was why he and Romana were walking quickly ahead. Sarah seemed less steady on her feet, planting her black wedge heels deliberately, one in front of the other. Philip thought she was putting it on, and when she slipped her hand round his arm, it felt even more of a con, but good, comfortable. Halfway along a terraced street a car came zooming up the road, followed by a police motorcycle. Oz, thirty yards ahead, turned to cheer them on.

'God, Leeds,' said Sarah. 'It's a shithole. Really, it is.'

200

'Oh, I don't know . . .'

'No, I mean, don't you ever think about leaving? There's loads of better places.'

He grinned. 'Sure, I think about it. On an hourly basis, some days.'

'Why don't you just go then? Why not just fuck off and start somewhere new? There's nothing holding you back.'

She was projecting her gloom on to him. 'I might. One day,' he said. 'Anyway, why don't you move away, if you hate it so much?'

'God, I don't know. Sometimes I think I'll be stuck at Pilot till I'm old and grey, sucking up to Freeman till I'm pissing sixty. A cluck like Lilian.'

'You won't be like that.' They were rounding the corner of the street, the lights of the city centre in view. Philip wanted to deflect her dreary mood, though he knew equally that there might be something to be gained from keeping it going. 'Have you really split with that guy?'

'Ah shit, he won't leave his folks' place. Not till he's got someone who can do his washing, make his meals, wipe his arse like his mother.'

Philip laughed. 'I don't think that's you, somehow.' He was being seduced by her closeness, the warmth of her hand on his arm, seeing her silence of the last couple of months, all the imagined slights, in a different light. He had got it wrong. She *liked* him, really.

Up on Hyde Park Road they could see a group of youths running, scattering across the road to the park. A siren sounded somewhere nearby, followed by another.

'Something's going on,' said Philip.

'Well, if they're hassling the dealers round here, they're in for it. I should know.'

'How's that?'

'My folks live in Woodhouse. That's where I am now. Back with them.' She laughed. 'Sponging.'

Oz and Romana had stopped, jokily tugging each other in

201

different directions. Then Oz looked back and pointed along the next street. Philip waved in reply.

Sarah had both hands on his arm now, leaning more heavily. He could feel the softness of her breast through the sleeve of his jacket. It had been a long time since he had touched a woman other than Kath. Years.

They were heading down to Burley Road. Philip looked ahead at the lights of the old factories and works that spread down to the canal. Beyond was the rise to Armley and the hills of Leeds to the west, the blocks of flats standing like cigarette packets, the streetlights strung between them, in necklaces. It was as bleak as could be, yet the hum and heave of life seemed everywhere, determined to renew, to lift the *weight* out of Leeds.

If only he could see things this way *all the time*.

They turned the corner. Oz and Romana had disappeared. Sarah chuckled. 'You know, sometimes I think I owe you an apology.'

'For what?'

'The office party.'

Philip had hoped she would not mention it, preferring his newly optimistic view of the incident, and life in general. 'Nothing happened. We were both a bit, well, too refreshed, if I remember rightly.'

She gave a snorting laugh that unnerved Philip. 'I know. Still . . .'

'Still what?'

'Ah, well . . .' She sighed, winsomely. 'You're a nice bloke, Phil.'

'So they say.'

'No, really. You're fanciable.'

'Come off it. You're taking the piss.'

'It's right!' she said. 'I could go for you.'

'Yeah, me and Paul Daniels.'

'No! Honestly! Only . . .'

'Is this the punch line?'

'No. What I mean is I'm no home wrecker. And I like Kath. She's nice.'

'You've never met her!'

She giggled. 'I know! But I feel as if I know her.'

'That's daft.'

'It's true! I'm jealous of her.'

'What you're jealous of is what you think is security, a steady going on. That's what you want. But it's not like that, really. The arguments, drawing up battle lines. Rows about money.' He didn't know why he said that. One thing he and Kath never argued about was money. Sarah was flustering him. 'Put it this way, it's not what it looks like.'

'Ooh! Don't tell me that!' Her voice had gone childishly hoarse. Philip looked at her face. She was crying. How long had that been going on? 'I want to believe it's possible, that people can be happy. It *is* possible. I know it.'

They had stopped. She was looking up at him. No force on earth could stop him kissing her.

After a full minute she hugged him and rested her head on his chest. She seemed about to say something when Oz came running back. 'Hey, we're round here. The Paper Wall.'

'Right.' Philip kissed Sarah's hard forehead and they walked, holding each other tightly, along the road and round the corner to the side-street club.

There was a queue of about twenty, girls with bare shoulders and tiny clutch-bags, the lads in overshirts. They made Philip feel old, though he was oddly glad about it. To the side of the door was a pair of drunks who had been refused entry. They were doing a sort of pissed-up country dance, the bouncers watching them, not letting anyone else in until they had gone. Sarah was still leaning against Philip. She made a small 'mmm' sound and appeared to be falling asleep. Then she stirred herself, shaking her head. She let go of his arm, scratched her knee, and went over to Romana. Oz turned his back on them to talk in Philip's ear.

'Nice one, mate. She's a looker, yours. Does she work with you, then?'

'After a fashion.'

Oz grinned. 'A couple of hours in here, then . . . Listen, I've got a couple of pills if you fancy getting up a bit, you know, dropping the booziness.'

Philip smiled, saying nothing.

The two drunks were moving away, weaving along the middle of the road, singing about the IRA. One of them gave out a long loud belch, then they ran to join a group of men at the end of the street who had stopped to greet them with a loud, unlikely cordiality. The queue shuffled along, the bouncers frisking for knives, perhaps hopeful of finding a gun. Oz turned and winked at Romana. Sarah was smiling at Philip.

This was it. Redemption. A rancorous old score settled. He could be *himself* now, he thought. The queue began moving freely. They would be inside within a minute. Oz shivered in the cold, drawing his hands up into his sleeves. A wedge of strobe lights was pulsing at the end of the red corridor, a rave voice soaring, 'Whoa whoa whoa, Yea-ah!' over a one-note electronic bass line. Philip reached into his pocket for his money, then left it where it was.

'I'm not going in.'

'Eh?' Oz was frowning, a cloak of light and sound around him in the doorway.

'I'm away. Off.'

'Aw, fuckin' hell, Phil.'

'You go in, if you want to.'

Sarah and Romana were at the window, sorting out change for the entrance money.

'Come on, Phil. Are you light or something? I can sub you, if you want. I've got plenty.'

'No. It's not that.' The woman was waiting for them at the window. Sarah and Romana had disappeared inside.

'What then? What's up with you?' Oz said, further annoyed by a couple who had dodged past them.

'I'm past it, mate. Knackered.'

'Ferk-off, sad bastard. Look, you've got it on a plate. I saw the way she was looking at you. How can you say no? What's wrong with you?'

'Nothing. I'm fine. Sorry, Oz.'

Philip turned away, brushing past the waiting hopefuls and walking down the street with his hands in his pockets. When he reached the end, he looked back. The tail of the queue was being swallowed by the door of the club, with Oz nowhere to be seen.

Thirty-Seven

He wandered back towards Headingley, cars speeding by with kids hanging out of the windows, the music like a crack with a baseball bat. Yet it felt good being out on the streets, and even his fear, as he saw a large group of men hanging round on a corner on the Otley Road, inspired a sensation that Philip found healthy. It was a hard-core internal experience, a message from the heart of things.

Back at the flat, he put the television on. *Butthead*, as if on cue: 'Uh-Huh, Uh-Huh.' First class. Like the old days, the good times surgically removed by the conventions of modern life. Alone, he could make a better fist of it, aloof from the world, sidestepping its crappiness. The single life. Yes!

Maybe he should have gone into the club with Sarah. Certainly, he would have liked to have spent the night with her – though in his present state he could have managed nothing. Perhaps that was a possibility he could store for a later date, when he had retrieved his independence. The new, younger Philip he saw himself becoming would have no trouble knocking over a piece like Sarah. Absolutely not! It was going to be so good. He felt as if the future was here already.

He opened all the cupboards in the kitchenette, finding tinned tomatoes, baked beans and corned beef. Enough to make a sloppy hash. There was a can of Stella in the fridge and he drank it while stirring the car-accident mess on the dodgy-looking Baby Belling. Leaving it to simmer, he opened the balcony window in the living room. The air was needle-cold and in the street below a gang of skimpily dressed girls was walking along the middle of the street, laughing and falling into each other, led by a raucous transvestite in a twenties sequined dress and feather boa. Philip grinned, loving it, this ferocious pursuit of a good time, made racier by the sirens of the patrol cars on their night chases, and the police helicopter winding towards Chapeltown.

He went back inside and poured his meal into the cereal bowl Oz had left on the draining board. He left the balcony window open to listen to the sounds of the city, until it started to hail and he had to force it back against a sudden gust of wind. This achieved, he turned the electric fire on full, half-hoping the meter might run out, so he would have to feed it again, just like the old days. Then he sat in front of the television, eating his mush with a spoon, watching a spoof chat show, laughing out loud at the jokes as if in the presence of all the new friends he imagined he would soon be making. Now and again he looked around at the flat, delighting in everything, the crappy glossed-over anaglypta walls, the Japanese bamboo lampshade, the red shawl wall-hanging that must have belonged to Carla, the sagging second-hand settee with its split armrests, the cobwebs and trash of a life lived only in transit. And that's what life was – a temporary thing.

Wasn't it?

The sound of reggae bumped against the floor from the flat downstairs. Music. Something else Philip had given up on, too readily. But it was never too late. In fact, it was inevitable that he had to find it again. Without it, this turning back from the impasse of adulthood, he would go mad. And wasn't his bad temper, weren't his ranting, raging ways, evidence that this was already happening? He had never been like that before. Not when he was young. He was a good boy then, kind and thoughtful about his fellow man.

A *nice* guy. Uh-huh?

He turned his spoon in the pink mess, forcing himself to eat. But it was awful and he knew what was coming if he persevered with it. After one more brave mouthful he went back into the kitchen and tipped it in the bin. In a cupboard, he found more Stella. Two cans. Perfect. One for now, one for later. He opened the first and drank deep to flatten his heartburn, and a threat of hiccups that might prove fatal. Back in the living room, he hunted round for a bluey video. Oz must have had some. But all he could find was a sad-looking row of Disney stuff that must have been for Clara's baby girl. He left well alone, not wanting any reminders about parenthood, or any of *that shit*. Then the noise below seemed to lift a decibel or two, a girl and a boy shouting at each other over The Wailers. Philip stamped on the floor. 'Shut it! Noisy bastards!' When there was no response, he turned up the television, feeling it only reasonable that he should be able to compete. This, in turn, brought a knock on the wall from the next-door flat. 'Aah, give over! Miserable old fart!'

Turning, he stumbled over the settee arm, landing on his elbow on the cushions, though managing to keep the can held upright. 'Not a drop spilt! Not a fucking drop! Did you see that?' He sat back, laughing.

This was the life. The dog's bollocks. You had to admit.

Thirty-Eight

Luke put his money in and it dropped out. Again. The sixth bastard time. He threw the handset at the wall. 'Hey, stupid,' said Butcher, who was watching him. 'People wanna use that.'

'Fuck off.'

The poison was in his blood now. He could taste it on his tongue, like salt, his chest booming, his breath fast and wet. He had a fucking *right* to ring his mother. Why was the bastard phone not working? It was never fucking working. He stormed up the stairs. In this mood he felt so strong, so fucking pissed off, he could pulp anyone. At a moment's notice. Not even that long.

On the landing below, he spotted the white shirt of a screw. He leaned over the balcony, shouting through the suicide mesh. 'Hey, Hughesy! Fucking phone's bust!'

Hughes looked up. 'Maybe you haven't paid the bill, Lukey.'

'Bollocks. Well, can I go down the gym, then?'

'Leave off. It's not open. If you want to go, you go down when everybody else does.' He made this loud, so everyone got the message. Piece of shit. 'What's up with you, Luker? You know the rules.'

'Just checkin', mate. Just as long as I know. Anyway, you get that fuckin' phone fixed.'

Hughes pulled a face and turned his back. Luke walked on, fast, banging his heels into the metal landing, fists tight at his sides. Hughes turned to watch him again, no doubt thinking he might put this in his report for the night staff. The cunt. Six years Luke'd had to take this shite. It was a vendetta against him. Totally personal. And all he'd wanted to do was ring his mother. Someone should *pay* for that. It was *owed*.

He went to the far staircase and down, four at a time, to the ground floor. There, almost running, he paced the perimeter where Hughes could not see him, slapping the walls, the doors, no one taking any notice. Nobody giving a fuck.

Christ, all he'd wanted was to talk to his mother. A fucking simple thing like that . . .

Into the toilets, three lads standing there, up to some trade or other, all wearing blue-and-white striped shirts, just like Luke's, like every fucker's. 'What you bastards lookin' at?' One of them, a handy-looking twat Luke had not noticed before, took a step to the side. Ready for it. But Simmo, a big soft cunt, in for fraud, stood in front of him.

'Lay off, eh, Luke?' said Simmo. 'We're busy here.'

Luke felt the hissing mist in his head. He hit the tiled wall with his fist, booted a washbasin, and left, running the length of the ground floor, back up the stairs, up the next flight, and along to the high meshed window at the end. He grabbed at the wiring and pulled himself up, kicking and ranting, wanting to smash his head through to the outside, wanting to be out, out of his head . . .

A pair of arms circled his waist, heaving him into the air. 'Gerroff me! Cunt! Get off!' If he could turn round he would smash the bastard to smithereens. Regardless. But the arms were heavy and strong. Man's arms, Luke just a boy. Along the landing, kicking and shouting, then in through the pad door where those fat arms dumped him on the bed.

It was Terry, his cell mate. 'Stupid pillock. What're you playin' at, acting like that? You'll get your fuckin' brains knocked out, carryin' on like that.'

Luke smashed his fists on the bedhead, banging his head on the pillow.

Terry was standing near the door, watching him. 'All right, pal. Let it out. Better the bed than some cunt else.'

Luke turned over on his back. He lay still, his blood cooling. Easy now. Feeling better.

For the moment.

A last kick at the iron rail at the end of the bed. To let it be *known* how he had been feeling. To make it a fucking fact.

'Time for a smoke, eh?' said Terry.

'Yeah. Yeah, right.'

Terry sat down at the tiny table between their beds, keeping one eye on the door as he warmed the dope with his lighter, picked a corner off, and sprinkled it into the tobacco. He rolled up, lit it, took two deep drags, and passed it to Luke.

'Who was it, Lukey? Who got your fuckin' goat this time?'

'Nobody. Just this place. It gets to me, sometimes.' He took a lungful, holding it till he coughed, his eyes watering. 'It's this fuckin' shithole. Fuckin' everything.'

'That's all right, mate. Same for everybody,' Terry said in his soft Scots burr. 'You get depressed.' He waved his arm, gesturing at the walls. 'You get these fuckin' moods. Who wouldn't? You just have to learn to keep out of their way, let them pass.'

Luke took another deep draw. The wacky-baccy. A life-saver. Smack was even better. It made you feel so in tune, and so out of it at the same time. But there was just never enough of the damned stuff. Never enough of anything.

Terry was smiling. 'Is that better, son?' Luke nodded and handed the joint back. Terry put it between his fingers and made a chamber with his fat cupped hands, sucking deeply to get a good big chestful. Luke watched him. He was all right, Terry. A good mate. Forty-five, seen fucking everything. In for GBH and two charges of aggravated theft. Yet you never saw him get mad. He was a wise old cunt, always talking about the mistakes he had made, and how he was going to go back on the bins when he got out. Best job he'd ever had, he would say, boring Luke to fuck, truth be told. But Terry had taken it on himself to keep an eye out for his young cell mate. Sometimes Luke resented this, seeing himself as very much his own man. Still, he knew enough to realise he could have done a lot worse than having to spend his nights with this guy. 'The old lady's comin' tomorrow,' Terry said, picking something from his nose and looking at it. 'Maybe she'll have a little lump for me. Could do with it. Gettin' a bit scarce round here.' He took one more drag and handed over the last of the joint.

Luke took the stub. 'It'd be handy.'

'Yeah, but we keep it to ourselves, Luker. Right? You can get your fuckin' throat slit round here for a fuckin' two-quid deal, just of this fuckin' stuff. So there's just you an' me. Right?'

'Right, Terry.' Luke drew on the hot end, grimacing as the smoke burned his throat. He heard this talk every time from Terry – his worry over the dope he was holding, about being sliced up for it. Luke forced one last scorching drag out of the joint, tasting the roach, then put it out. Lying back he tried to think of better things, of having a wank later, or tapping that ponce Pugh for something decent to eat, getting it on the slate. And there was always the telly room till ten. But, after he'd given the come-on to that guy with Simmo in the shithouse, it might be wiser to give the bottom landing a miss for a few days.

Terry tidied his stash away, pressing it into the radiator cap and screwing it back tight. Then he sat on his bed, red in the face, smiling. 'We can 'ave a game of cards, if you like.'

Luke did not want to play cards. He wanted to do fuck all. But he felt he owed his cell mate something. He swung off the bed. 'Sure. Why the fuck not?'

'Good,' said Terry. 'Good lad.'

Thirty-Nine

In the flat below there was a rattling of plates and cutlery, and the voices of the young couple, with the deep, erratic tones of the hungover. From the street below the balcony came the shuffle of footsteps, the odd car passing. It was two in the afternoon. Philip's bladder was up like a football, his head dull with the debris of a headache, the worst of which he must have slept off. He stirred himself from the settee and went to the bathroom, pissing mightily, feeling grimy in the clothes he had slept in. He tried the old Ascot water heater above the sink. After a few seconds it had failed to light and he wondered if it might blow up. He turned it off and rinsed his face with cold water, drying himself on a filthy pink towel on the edge of the bath.

He made toast and tea, something to mop up the last of the booze in his veins. He stood munching the toast, looking out of the kitchenette window at the sunny winter's day, feeling odd, as if he did not really know who he was. The rest of the day lay before him, its agenda undecided. All those ideas that had been swimming in his head last night seemed flat and ghostly now. He was going to leave Kath. But to do it in cold blood? Should he wait for a moment of provocation, with his growingly famous bad temper at the ready? How long might that take? His fingers were greasy with Flora. He rubbed them, wishing an answer would suggest itself.

From the bedroom next door came the sound of Oz stirring and coughing. He came out in his dressing gown and went through to the bathroom, giving a weak wave as he passed. When he came back, he sat down on the settee. 'Ah, fuck,' he said, yawning. He rubbed his face and lit a cigarette, resting a bare white foot on the coffee table. 'What's the fucking time?'

'Quarter to three.'

'Shee-it.'

'I didn't hear you come in,' Philip said, feeling a sudden black curiosity. Was Sarah in the bedroom?

'It must have been gone four. You were out on your back.'

'How'd you get on with those two then?'

Oz grinned. 'All right, I suppose.'

'What's that mean?'

'I mean it was OK.'

'You mean you scored?'

Oz threw his head back with a laugh, showing his furred tongue. 'Yeah, mate! Quite a result!'

'Which one?' Philip asked, forcing a smile.

'Well . . .' Oz grinned. 'When I say I scored, it was more of an undecided result. It needs to go to a replay.'

'What's that mean?'

'Goalless draw. Nil–nil.'

'You mean,' Philip said, quietly pleased, 'you didn't have either of them?'

He sniggered. 'Fucked off, didn't they. Got inside and couldn't find them any fucking place. Not till the end, anyway. I ended up talking to this guy I know, then I saw them leaving. That mate of yours, what's her name?'

'Sarah.'

'Yeah, her. Drunk as a twat. She eggs this bloke on, then she's crying, shouting at him to fuck off. Is she a prick teaser, or what?'

'That's about it.'

Philip was glad that Oz had not made it with Sarah. If he had, their relationship could never have been the same again. Oz was wiggling his finger in his ear. Philip felt a revived appreciation of their old friendship.

'What're you up to, today?' Oz asked. It sounded a little as though he might want rid of Philip.

'No idea. Haven't made my mind up, yet.'

214

Oz looked at his outstretched feet, then across at Philip. 'Is everything all right with you, mate?'

'Tip-top. Why shouldn't it be?'

'I don't know. You just seemed in a strange mood last night.'

Philip did not want to talk about his life right now. It was the wrong time, and he realised Oz was not the wise counsel he was looking for. They were mates and, as such, they did not talk about things of too personal a nature. It would have been naff, unmale. 'I've got a bit of pressure – work, Kath and the baby. And her folks. All that bollocks. Nothing I can't handle, though.'

Oz stood, stretching as he walked back to the bedroom. 'Well, don't let the fuckers . . .' he said, yawning, 'grind you down, old chum. It's not worth it.'

'I know,' said Philip, clasping his hands behind his head. 'I know, mate.'

Twenty minutes later he was walking towards Headingley Lane. The sun was warming the roads, making the plastic guttering click along the roofs of the tall old houses, streets he knew better than he gave himself credit for. He felt remarkably at peace with himself, with only the moment to consider. If he could just keep it like this, with time in its place, beneath his foot like an accelerator pedal you could simply caress or leave alone. Maybe if he was rich? He could sort everything out then. But the making of wealth took so much effort, and a particular bent of personality. Philip was not greedy – it was one of his finer qualities, he believed. He wandered over the big green spaces of Hyde Park, dodging the kids' footballs, and the dogs running all over the shop.

The university was ahead. He slowed, sensing something ethereal about the block buildings in the late sharp sunlight. He smiled to himself, once again nostalgic for his younger days, regretting his flippancy towards his studies, the way he had only ever done the bare minimum, enough to get him through the boredom of the work. Then there had been his job, and more crushing tedium. And more wanting out, no end to his dissatisfaction. But what if he backtracked on all this, and started again? What about being a *mature* student, in every sense? He saw himself before an interview panel, good-humouredly admitting his failure of attitude while he had been at Manchester. A wholesome contrition. Could he pull that off?

The possibility excited him to a point whereby he wished he was heading for an interview that very moment. A graceful loss of face was all it would take. And as for choosing a course, there were a thousand post-grad things he could *make* himself interested in. Pure study. No people, no hassle. And hence, no more rage. That was what had been the matter all along. He'd taken the wrong turning once or twice, and stopped *being himself*. He walked under the Inner Ring Road, taking a vicarious pleasure in the graffiti – 'We are born. We consume. We die. Think about it.' Three male students passed by, badly dressed, idling away the weekend, seeming framed in the reference on the wall. A set of wankers, really. But was that so bad? He quickened his pace, anxious not to hang around too long, in case he saw anything else in the students that might put him off his wished-for future.

He crossed the road to Calverley Street, past the Infirmary, and on over the Headrow where the shoppers were milling in their thousands. Then, steeling himself, he walked down from the Headrow and past the Pilot building. It was a test he felt he needed. He looked up at the locked glass doors, and the third-floor window of Life and Deaths, a skin of detachment already satisfyingly formed between this old world and the brave new life he was heading towards. Bloody Pilot. It was as if he had never set foot in the place. And now, to cement his pact with the future and, intrinsically, his past, Philip wanted to go further back, to regress to his youth.

To go home.

Forty

'There's talk about the open prison. Might be in with a chance. It's early, like, but you never know.' Darren took the Lambert and Butler his father was offering, stretching his fingers to hide the tenner rolled up beneath it.

'Sounds good.'

In a flush of gratitude for the money, Darren added, 'It'd mean weekend leave an' all. Some sort of job scheme. All that stuff.'

'Aye, well, it'd not be too soon. You've kept your nose clean. Earned your chance, 'aven't you?' Sam said, rubbing the stubble under his chin with the back of his hand.

The 'open' was something Ray talked about a lot, probably wishful thinking, but that was better than nothing. And Darren really was due for his review. 'I've never understood why you have to be here anyway,' Sam said. 'You're not like this lot. You're a good lad. Quiet, like. And they're makin' you serve every minute of your sentence, looks like to me. And for what? Because you fell in with a bad 'un? It was a first offence too, that's what I could never understand.'

Darren slipped the ten-pound note into his pocket, broke the filter off the cigarette and lit it. 'It was the goin' rate. No way round it.'

'I know, but what good's being done by you're still bein' stuck in here? Nothin' was taken, in the end. And that couple, they probably forgot all about it the week after. They'll be runnin' round, free as birds,' he said, with an odd, one-eye-open frown, the wrinkles deep on his shiny tanned forehead. 'Bet if you asked them, *they* wouldn't be bothered if you were out now.'

Darren could see this same line of talk up the Green Leaf club of a Sunday dinner. His father was looking round at the other

217

cons and their visitors, no doubt after tales to take back with him to the same place. Still, why not? Nothing much went on in his life. Darren liked seeing him. He was a good old fucker, and he could easily have not bothered with his son again, after what he had done. And he was Darren's only visitor, truth be told. 'What you been up to lately, then?'

'Bit of this an' that. It's a quiet life now, since they retired me. Mind,' he chuckled, 'best job I've ever had.' Then he turned to look at Atterby, a con who fancied himself as a drug dealer, big-time. He was a Londoner and he was laughing with some bloke who had come to see him, his voice dominating the room. Noisy bastard. Sam smiled weakly, then sat forward. 'I saw your mother the other week. I rang her up and asked her if she minded me goin' round.'

'Aw, Dad, 'onest. Why d'you bother? What's she ever done for us? We always managed without her.' It was the ten thousandth time Darren had said this, yet what else could he say? 'She'll only disappoint you. Whatever you want from her, she won't give it you.'

'No, I think she was pleased to see me. Really, son. And she asked about you, course, wantin' to know how you were gettin' on.'

Darren humphed. 'Not much to say, is there.'

'We-ell, it's something to talk about. And she's interested.'

'Yeah, so interested she walked out when I was four.'

'You're bein' hard on her.'

'She asks for it.'

The talk stalled, as it always did at this point. Darren wondered what went on in the old man's imagination, how he could ever believe Darren might forgive his mother for the problems she had caused them. Now Sam was smiling, a bit sad, turning the cigarette packet over in his hands as if looking for something to read on it. Darren wondered if he still listened to the two tapes he had of his mother singing. She made them fucking years ago – stuff like 'Killing Me Softly', all that shit. She could croon a bit then, it was true, though her voice probably sounded like an old frog's now.

Sam put the cigarette packet down. 'I saw Luke's mother the other day. She says he's all right, but I don't know. He's in Durham, she says. What I can't see is how come he shouldn't be getting out the same time as you. How come, when you're talkin' about maybe going to an open place, he's in this higher-security joint. He must've done somethin', but she wasn't saying what.'

'Dunno.' Darren put out the cigarette and slipped the butt in his pocket. 'You don't get to hear much in here. Nothin' that you can rely on, anyway.'

'Aye, well. I just thought it was strange, that's all.'

'Maybe she doesn't want to say.'

'Maybe, yeah. Maybe.'

The bell went and the wives and mothers scraped their chairs and put on coats, some wanting to hang on, scrounging every second, kissing the blokes like they wanted to be eaten by them, half of them hiding some guilty secret about what they were up to outside. Darren's father stood up. 'So I'll see you then, son. In a fortnight.'

'Yeah. Thanks, Dad. That'll be nice. An' I'll let you know if there's any news about the review.'

His father nodded, his eyes half-closed, giving Darren the impression that he did not really believe him. 'I'll see you, son.' And he made his way through the smoky air to stand silently in line as the visitors were checked out of the door.

Forty-One

'Your mother's out. She was off to Ian's, then she was going to meet Eileen.' Philip's father led the way through to the back room. 'Kath not with you?'

'No.'

'That's a shame. You should've brought her. It would be nice to see how she's getting on.'

They lived in a bungalow now, three streets from the old house. They had reduced their lives in a way Philip found both predictable and appealing. They'd done everything, kids gone, work finished for them both, a pension, nothing else to do but eat, sleep, take holidays in Malta, Florida this year. God, the freedom. If only you could get it without being old. His father sat down at a VDU on a big table, returning to a game Philip must have interrupted. 'P-tang!' he said. 'Do you know it? I was up to level five the other day, but I can't get past the swamp. There're these things that spring about. They're not reasonable, really.' He tapped the pause button. 'I suppose there must be some trick for getting them, though I'm damned if I can work out what it is.'

'I didn't know you were into computer games?'

'Why not?' He swerved with the control stick. 'Ah, shit . . .'

The screen flashed bright orange and he sat back, staring at it for a few seconds, weighing up the possibility of starting all over again without, Philip assumed, appearing rude.

The table was the glass dining table from the old house, covered in a big blue cloth. It stretched the length of the wall in here, filling half the room. To this day Philip could never look at it without remembering what that boy Luke had done that night. There was no stain, but it would be for ever in his mind. Sometimes it felt as if a little clock had stopped in his head, stuck at that time, yet his parents didn't seem bothered at all. 'You've never got rid of this table, then?'

'Nah. Why bother?' He was wearing jeans and a red Wrangler sweatshirt, the sleeves rolled up to his elbows. He bent back to the screen, as if deciding to allow himself one last go. 'Though I suppose it's a bit big for here.'

'That's not what I meant.'

He pressed the buttons perfunctorily over the first level, deliberately ignoring Philip. It was annoying. He had always been too dismissive of this particular subject, assuming everyone was as self-reliant as him, not once talking it through properly with Philip, thinking his son was eighteen years old at the time. A man, according to his generation. Once, his father had even said he just thought of those kids as chancers – they were broke, they had crappy lives, and he could hardly blame them for wanting to have a go. It was too rational for Philip's taste – no wonder he had never told him about Carl. Yet why couldn't they talk about such things? Even now Philip could feel an old ghost of a wish to thrash out his feelings about that night seven years ago – it would have been such a good way to get on to the subject of the million things on his mind. But his father seemed to want none of it. As fucking usual.

'Aaah!' The white, former-supermarket-manager fingers shot into the air. He had lost on level two. He turned off the computer and stood, stretching his arms and arching his back. 'So how's things with you? Are you in the car?'

'Got the train. The car's in the garage. Actually, I was thinking about giving up driving for a bit, seeing if I could manage on public transport.'

'Oh?'

'Well, I thought it might be worth a try. Less expensive, for one thing.'

'You'll need it for the baby. Everybody needs a car when they've got kids. But I can't say I blame you. The roads are hell, these days.' He was looking out at the garden, rotating his

221

hips to ease some stiffness in his back. 'D'you know, I turned into Broadway the other day and this fella just gets on my tail, flashing his lights, the horn going. The bugger was right up me. I think he reckoned I'd taken his ground. Or I wasn't going fast enough. I thought he was going to have me off the road. God, men in rage, though I suppose the women can be just as bad, you know, road raging and all that.'

Philip looked at the carpet. 'There's a lot of it about,' he said.

'Sure is. You see it everywhere, in the pubs, even in the queue at the post office. They're like kids!' He chuckled. 'You were a bit like that when you were little. Couldn't wait for anything, your tea, opening your birthday presents. Still, you've grown out of it, and that's all that matters.' He rocked forward, getting some movement into his back. 'Your mother'll be bloody annoyed she's missed you.'

'It was an impulse thing. I was out with Oz last night. I stayed over at his sister's place, then I thought I'd come and see you.'

'Oz, eh? You still see him?'

'Yes.'

'That's good. I liked old Oz. What's he doing now?'

'This and that. Bumming around.'

'Hah. Bumming around, eh? Good old Oz,' he said, grinning. 'Anyway, how's your job?'

Philip joined him in looking out at the garden, knowing it was all right for Oz to be fooling around with his life, but for him it was a different matter. 'Poor really.'

'Oh?'

'Well, I fancy a change.'

'Doing what?'

'I've had this idea for doing a bit of study instead.'

'What's that, then?'

'Post-grad.'

'What, you mean going back to university?'

'That'd be it.'

His father raised his eyebrows, head on one side. 'Fair enough, I suppose. If that's what you want.'

'I think it is.'

'Mmm, well, education. I've always thought it's just for the teachers, myself. Yet they all seem to want it now, employers I mean. You need a degree to pull your own pisser, these days, it seems. But what about money? You'll be needing plenty of that soon.'

Philip shrugged. Like he did when he was eleven years old, trying to sidestep some uncomfortable misdemeanour. What was he doing here? What had he been hoping for? Guidance? Some sort of blessing? He was still looking out of the window, at the laurels and cypress, the roses pruned into neat stubs. This was the moment for telling his father the truth, for saying he was through with insurance. And the house. And Kath. And there would be no grandchild . . .

'Shall we go into the kitchen?' his father said. 'I'll put the kettle on.'

Despite being six inches taller than his father, Philip felt small as he trailed him to the kitchen.

'Can you get some sort of allowance for this post-grad stuff?' his father asked, filling the kettle.

'There'll be something, I hope. There's a few bursaries knocking about. I might get one of those.'

'Are you sure you've thought this through, Phil?'

'Absolutely.'

'I mean, children cost the earth. I was reading the other day, a kid can cost up to two hundred grand, from cradle to being a man. Two hundred grand!'

There'll be no child. Say it. It would be a bit cruel, that's all. Like all major life changes, they take some understanding at first. But, tiredly, he said, 'Sounds a bit of a big estimate.'

'That's what I thought. Still, it's plenty dear enough. Everybody knows that. Fancy a sandwich?'

'No.'

'I'll have one, if you don't mind.'

'Dad . . .'

'God, life for young people, these days. Everything's money. And work's so bloody hard to come by. That's the problem. More work and there wouldn't be half the trouble there is nowadays. D'you know there was something going on up Hyde Park way last night? Again?'

'No. I was up there myself. I didn't see anything. Listen . . .'

'It'll have been drugs. Always is.'

He was doing this on purpose, knowing Philip had something momentous to tell him, and not wanting to hear it. How often had it been like this, over all these years? When would he let Philip speak his mind, *allow* him to be a *boy*?

'Dad . . .'

'What is it? Ecstasy? Whizz? What's that? I've heard somebody on about that.'

'It's . . . I don't know what it is.'

'Smack. What's that? Heroin? The names! It's another language!' He leaned on the worktop, chuckling. 'Smack, crack. Crack cocaine . . .'

'Dad?'

'Weed. Ganja . . . They're the same, aren't they?'

'Dad!'

His father looked at him with a plainness in the eyes, an arrested expression. 'What, son?'

It was the moment to go for it, to get him to *understand* Philip, for the first time in both their lives. Yet the opportunity seemed to be flustering him. 'Look, can I stay here tonight? I fancy staying here. Is that all right?'

'You want to stay?'

'Yes.'

The kettle was rattling on its stand. 'Oh, I don't know. Your mother's bringing Eileen back. She's supposed to be staying here the weekend. Not that I'm bothered myself, mind. The old natterbag gets on your nerves after a while.'

'Couldn't she stay some other time?'

His father wrinkled his mouth. 'It's a bit short notice, Phil.

You should have let us know. Anyway, what about Kath? Where's she?'

'She's . . .' Off the agenda. History in the making. I'll tell you this now. And I'll tell you how I've had to make my own way in life, the whole blasted way, *without your help*! But . . . 'She's at her folks' place. She's gone there.'

'Oh, I see. Well, if only we'd known! Christ knows I'd rather have you round here than bloody Eileen any day of the week. But she is your mother's sister. You know what it's like.'

'I know,' Philip said. 'It doesn't matter.' He closed his eyes, the occasion gone. His father could offer no comfort. Had never been able to, would never. And if not him, who could Philip turn to in this shit-faced world? It was enough to make him want to spit and swear and rant and . . . But he could not. Not in his father's house. He opened his eyes. 'Is the tea ready then?'

Forty-Two

Luke woke with the remnants of a dream in his head, and a burning hard-on. The dream had been about him being back at school, working away, being friendly with everyone and winning approval, particularly from Oakesy, his old RE teacher. This guy had once got Luke on his own after a class and slammed him up against the wall, telling him that if he fucked up one of his lessons again he would flatten him. It had made Luke feel bad, though he never told anyone about it. Now, as he looked at the square of windowed light on the far wall, it seemed like this dream had sorted all that, giving him a vision of being someone nice, creepy maybe, but likeable. And there'd been girls in it too, lasses he used to fancy yet with whom he could never risk the loss of face by saying he liked them. That was a good experience too, in the dream. Lying awake, it was like he'd become someone else. He felt happy.

Inside.

He stayed quiet half the morning, pretending to be this new person, thinking it could not be too difficult just to get on with people – Terry was always saying it was as easy to like people as to hate them. In the laundry where Luke worked, he decided to try and apply this new way of behaving.

His job was to bring the skips from the lift and empty them, sorting the linen into piles and placing it by the appropriate washer. There were three big steel-drum washing machines, and they were tended by a shit-mouthed, pizza-faced bastard called Tanner. Normally Luke acted busy round Tanner, so he didn't have to speak to the cunt, but this morning he was going to say something to him.

'Are you all right, Tanner, mate?'

'What the fuck's it got to do with you? D'you want to suck my fuckin' dick or summat, Luker?'

Luke lifted the heaps from the trolley and put them to the side of the steaming drum. 'What's it taste like?'

Tanner laughed. 'Peaches and fuckin' cream! Specially the fuckin' cream! Come on, then. Here y'are.' Tanner unzipped his fly and pretended to pull out his pisser.

'Ferk-off.'

'Hey!' Tanner announced to the rest of the room. 'Luke's gonna suck my willy! Lukey, Lukey, Lukey! My honey-bunch!'

Luke finished emptying the trolley, hauled it round and headed back to the skips. That Tanner was a piece of shit. It was a mistake to talk to him. But Luke still felt that sense of serenity, of being centred in himself.

At dinnertime he sat with Terry, the talk coming easily, about the older man's English course he was doing, and the meat – was it pork, or had the governor's fucking Alsatian gone missing? And throughout the afternoon Luke still felt good, as if he had been visited by God, or an angel. Or some such.

At four o'clock, they packed in work and went back to their wing. Luke usually liked this couple of hours, idling about, maybe a game of pool, if he could get one. But he felt restless, wanting to communicate his feelings, for someone to notice how *good* he had been.

He had been waiting to get on the pool table. The game was taking too long. He *couldn't* wait any longer. He banged his heel against the wall, stalked off along the recreation area. And into the toilets.

All Perry had done was to walk into the pisser while Luke was trying to get a single minute alone. Was it too much to ask? Sixty fucking seconds? But there was Perry, a smallish man in his thirties, a petty thief Luke hardly knew, and he was just standing there, a piece of cat-meat in this cube of space, the area around Luke's body that, for one pathetic minute only, he wanted to keep to himself.

'Mate?' said Perry.

'You what?'

'Mind if I use the crapper? I mean, is this your fuckin' office now, or what?'

'Are you gettin' at me?'

'Oh, fuck off, Luke. It was a joke. Christ, you're a touchy cunt.'

Luke could not believe what Perry was saying. Couldn't the guy see what a changed man Luke had become? Why was it that no one *ever* saw anything decent in him? In a split-second the air had turned sour. Luke was massively his old self, snapped out of his vain good intentions. Perry went into the cubicle, but Luke grabbed him from behind. 'Say that again! Go on! Call me a cunt!'

'Fuckin' hell, Luke. Gerroff.'

Luke dragged him to the floor. The first crack to the middle of his face was delicious. It felt pure. Perry slammed back, 'Oww! Oh!' He had taken Luke's private territory, the only thing Luke owned in the world. And he had not *paid* for it. Luke went in again with the fists, racing for a greater, gluttonous satisfaction, the repayment of all that was *owed* to him. 'Hey! Hey! Yer bastard!' The guy had lost his identity, his voice nothing against Luke's easy superiority. As Perry tried to get up a kick at the shins took his legs, and he was back down on the red tiles. Then Luke was on him, banging and banging at the head, each crack the retrieval of some ancient injustice, settling the score. He thumped and kicked and stamped, wanting to take his face off, feeling a meaty release with each wet contact.

When Perry stopped groaning, Luke stood back, wiping his mouth with the back of his hand, feeling dizzy. Yet there was still more to do, more of this satisfaction to be had. His strength reviving, his arms hot and ready, he looked around at the doorless toilets, the metal piss-trough. The pipe over the trough was the only grabbable object in the place. He got both hands round it, jumped up and pulled, his feet against the wall like a monkey. Superhuman strength. It came away in two sections, water gushing from the cistern as Luke fell flat on his back.

All his weight thudded on to the tiles, but he was on his feet in a second, the water spurting on his head. 'Bastard! Look what you've done to me!' In his hand was the lower foot-long piece of pipe that had come out of its housing.

Perry was crawling on his side to the wall, moaning. Luke, with the water dripping off his face, went over to him, wanting the game over, to take him apart and scatter him round the floor in pieces he could gloat over. He brought the pipe down three times on the bloody mess of hair, but it was nothing, barely a knock. The pipe was not heavy enough. He turned it in his hand, holding it like a dagger, jabbing it into the side of Perry's head, into his stomach and the corrugation of ribs. He was in a new rabid extension of the process, wishing the pipe was a knife, that it would penetrate the body so he could rive the heart out, all the innards, seeing the different sections as facts, as evidence of the damage the world had inflicted on him. He rammed the pipe into the flaccid arms, the buttocks and hips, but it would not cut, would not make the body fall into separate kickable parts. With a yelp of frustration, Luke threw the pipe across the floor and dug his fingers into a cut on Perry's neck, wanting to rip him open. The flesh would not tear. Luke dropped and hit him with his knees, tiring now, wailing as he heard the voices approaching from outside. Those who would soon interfere and pull him away. Like they always did, when Luke was on the brink of his own absolute fulfilment. In the few seconds before they came he slapped at Perry's body, chopped with his bloodied wrists, and shuffled forward to fall on him, to get the last out of him. For what it was worth.

Forty-Three

'Stupid cow. She 'ad it coming.' The taxi driver pointed at the woman he had just cut up. 'Look at her! What's she doing? Lookin' for her bloody granny's house?' He sat forward and made a lunatic dash into the outside lane, going for his horn, raising a finger at a lorry driver who shook his fist at him. 'Jesus! They wanna read the bloody *Highway Code*, some of these prats.'

Philip was sitting tight, his hands clammy on the side of the seat. He wanted to tell him to calm down, to make some soothing comment on the finite nature of life, and he was thankful when they were moving away from town and the worst of the traffic. Then the driver actually slowed down, laughing. 'All in a day's work, eh?' Philip said nothing.

A few minutes later they passed by the village green and on to the estate, the afternoon light fading, a pink ribbon of twilight visible above the half-built homes beyond the older ones. At the house, Philip gave him a tenner, his last note, and waved nonchalantly about the change, for some reason feeling he needed to placate the guy. He got out and took a deep breath of the cold air, looking around at their street, the gardens, all its arid familiarity. There was a light in their front room, and on the landing, but no car on the drive. He walked round to the back of the house. In the dim light beneath the kitchen window he could see a few dark shapes, like little refugees bundled together against the cold. With barely an interest he bent down and saw they were rose plants, five, each in a plastic pot, triangular labels fastened to the stems with green plastic twine.

It melted his heart. A few roses. Such a small wish. For once, he was glad to be home. He was tired and his defences were down – he *wanted* Kath to have his baby, and for her to be *allowed* her happiness, with him an agent for its existence. This was the real future, he thought as he yawned and felt for the key in his pocket. And it was something which must be said before he changed his mind. He put the key in the door, then realised it was not locked. Inside, he turned on the kitchen light. There was mud on the coconut mat behind the door, and a few smears on the cushion-floor leading to the living room. On the draining board was a basket of washing, its stale soapy vapour on the air. 'Kath? Kathy?' The receiving silence was self-contained. No one home. How annoying, when he had made up his mind, a few seconds ago, to tell Kath he had decided to mend his ways, perhaps to apologise for his anger the day before. There was even a joke on the tip of his tongue: 'I think it must have been the peanut butter! I've been overdosing on it!' But in the living he room he was further irritated by having no audience for his new resolve. His good humour was being thwarted, and there was nothing worse – it would give him time for a change of heart, a reversion to the old flaky Philip. *Honestly, Kath, you're never around* . . .

The phone rang, startling him. He went to the little table by the window.

'Is that you, Phil?'

'Jeff?'

'Where the fuck have you been?'

Philip felt his loathing of Jeff instantly revive. He wrestled with the impulse to hang up. 'Out and about. Is Kath there?'

'No, she isn't.' A sigh. 'Look, I think you'd better listen. There's a problem.'

'And what sort of problem's that, Jeff?' Philip said, confident it would be nothing of importance.

'There's been an accident.'

The words had no immediate meaning, Philip's conditioned irritation with the man still lingering.

'What, with the car?'

'No. She's fallen down the stairs.'

These words had more bulk, a resented significance. 'When? I mean, where?'

'Your place. She was digging the garden. She was wanting to plant some roses or some such bloody thing. She felt dizzy and went up to the bathroom. Only she didn't make it to the top of the stairs. Christ, Philip, couldn't you have dug the fucking garden for her?'

'Hey, hang on a minute . . .'

'No. You hang on, mate. That's not all. She also said something about some guy trying to shove you off the road, when she was driving you to work, yesterday morning. That shook her too. Fuck's sake, Philip, you wanna get a grip on your life, d'you know that?'

It was all too much. Philip had had enough. He could not *believe* that this was true. Time to tell Jeff he was through with Kath. That would shut the fucker up. 'Look, Jeff . . .'

But there was no beating him. 'Last night she was saying she didn't feel right. And this morning. I told her to stay with us, but she said you'd be back by dinnertime. Where the fuck've you been? I've been trying to get hold of you for hours. Don't you tell anyone where you're going?'

Philip was holding the handset tight in his fist, shaping up for his defence. Then he saw muddy footprints on the carpet and, through the hall door, a mark on the wall. A glimmer of the seriousness of it all was sinking through his thick hide, though on the surface he was still looking to save face. 'Where is she now?'

'Tilly called round on her way back from town. Bloody good job, eh? She got an ambulance. They took Kath to L.G.I. She's on the admission ward, unless they've moved her.'

Philip moistened his lips. His eyes were prickling, the information getting to him. 'What about the baby?' he asked, lamely.

Jeff paused, then said, more calmly, 'There was a lot of blood. We don't know yet. Look, I think you'd better get yourself over there, Phil. Now. Visiting might not be all night.'

Philip looked again at the marks on the floor and wall, feeling suddenly, awfully human. 'Where's the car?' he said, his voice cracking. 'There's no fucking car!'

'It's here. I took it to the garage myself. It's sorted. New bumper. Look, I'll come and pick you up.'

'No. Er, no. It's all right, Jeff. I'll get a cab. It'll be quicker.'

'You will, won't you, Philip? I mean, you'd better . . .'

'Yes! Fucking yes!' He banged the phone down.

By the hall door was a box full of junk from the back bedroom. The stupid stolen telephone was sitting on top, unbearably revealed. What else had she been doing besides digging the garden herself? Throwing his things out? What had she *decided*? He looked away, along the length of the living room, at the dead television, the flagging spider plant beside the fire, the hated dralon suite. Kath's crumpled shopping bag was by the armchair, her pile of crappy magazines on the table, the bits and bobs of a modest life, the hopes of which she had pinned on a *wanker* like him.

In a daze, he decided to go upstairs to change, to try and get the idea planted in his head, struggling with the dreadful notion that this was something that, in the nether regions of his soul, he had *wanted* to happen. But at the foot of the stairs he stopped. The mark on the wall was a shoe scuff, impossibly high. And on the carpet there was a crimson stain, reaching to the edge where it ran in a red biro line along the skirting board. He wandered mindlessly to the kitchen, wet the dish cloth and went back. Dropping to his knees, he rubbed madly at the stain, then stopped, wondering why he was doing it. A door slammed across the road, beyond their own mock-Georgian front door. And Philip looked at the cloth, the redness on his fingers, and wondered who to blame.

Forty-Four

The train slowed into Whitkirk and Cross Gates, rolling past the blocks of flats and the council estates with half the houses boarded up, or their roofs burned out. But it looked so good!

Darren still could not believe his luck. When he had talked to his old man about the 'open', and weekend leave, all that shit, he'd never really believed it himself. Yet now, here he was on weekend leave, three weeks after being moved from Hull. In your dreams, you didn't get a break like this. You just didn't. Had he been smart? Had he? All those years of playing it by the rules. Roughly, anyway. And now . . . Pay day!

He was fascinated by the people around him, couples of all ages, men in suits, kids running up and down the aisles. A tiny girl came up to him, holding something that looked like a digital watch with no strap. 'This is my pet.' She pushed it under Darren's nose. 'Look, he's asleep now. When he wakes up he'll want feeding. Or. Oor-rr . . .' She giggled, her hand over her mouth. 'He might want his mess cleaning up!'

'Yeah, right,' said Darren. He knew he looked a miserable bastard – he just didn't know what else to say. When the mother called her back to her seat, he looked out of the window at the 'Jesus is Alive!' sign above the Leeds Christian Centre, and Queens Hotel ahead. Almost there, home. He fidgeted in his pocket for his ticket. He had been scared stiff of losing it and getting into bother. That would be proper shit, after a result like the one he'd had. He found the ticket, picked up his old duffel bag, and joined the people getting off the train.

The open spaces of the station were scary, the people rushing about dizzying him. He hung around by the Traveller's Rest kiosk, wondering if he should buy something for Sam, though the old man probably wouldn't mind if he didn't bother. He looked around, opening up to his arriving sense of freedom. There were plenty of gloomy faces – the droopy twats – but he ignored those, looking instead at the smilers, the up-beat, wishing they would congratulate him, share his buzz. He pulled up his trousers – they were too big, and the shirt was like a fucking tent. It was the same clobber he had been sent down in. The rest of his stuff would still be at the flat. There was a pair of Joe Bloggs jeans he had thought about often over this last seven years. He'd bought them the week after he started work on the site. Nothing special, but hardly worn. He'd have those out first thing, soon as he got there. He walked out of the station, wondering about getting the bus. How much would it cost? Did they still go from the same place, opposite C&A? He decided to walk.

The rough fabric of the seat makes Philip's buttocks itch. Like bus seats everywhere. Why can't they make them out of something more comfortable? Then people would *use* public transport . . . This was a stupid idea, he thinks, wishing he had the car. Two lads get on at the next village, boys who'll soon be old enough to drive. And will they be bothered about what their cars do to the environment? Of course not. Fuck the moral high ground. They lumber past Philip to the back of the bus.

On the outskirts of town more people get on, up for the night, creatures from old Leeds, with pale skins, things from under rocks. Lampoonable. Philip just doesn't need to be here, among *this*. He's a *modern* man, capable. Though look at the way he's *fucked everything up* . . . He watches the other passengers, a vague regret sticking to his ribs. In his roiling view of them now, they do seem to have life worked out, after a fashion, working their own groove, bugger what anyone else thinks. If only *he* had learned, somewhere along the line of his twenty-five years, to take life in his stride, sit out his time on this planet. Why take *exception* to people, the way he did?

He tries to think of Kath. It's a copper-bottomed certainty that

Tilly will be there with her, filling in for the no-win boyfriend, a role snatched with malicious glee, the longer they wait for him, the greater her self-righteousness. If Jeff and Tilly would only mind their own bloody business . . .

Five minutes later he's off the bus, feeling better. This is Leeds of a Saturday night, with its hair done up, club capital, the industry of the day replaced by a city of the imagination, bleakly famous, feared. Where everything might be possible, and is sure to end in frustration.

Two men are making their way through the crowds on Boar Lane. One is big, with a shiny shaved head. He is wearing a new-looking suede coat, matching sandy boots. He draws all the looks, with nothing for his greaseball mate in a scuffed leather jacket. For some reason, they walk either side of Philip, the big guy chewing, making the veins ripple on his temples. He says, 'Usual tossers around tonight.' Then laughs. Philip feels protected by his own problems, his gloom. They are not interested in him. It's just a matter of geography, their being next to him. They pass on, taking the piss elsewhere.

On Albion Street, on the pedestrian way, three youths approach, their faces in chip papers. One has the drunk's one-leg-straight, one-leg-bent stagger. He lets the paper float from his hand and it flaps round Philip's feet. He looks at Philip. 'Cheer up, cunt.' The price you pay for being alone. Philip walks on, hearing more churning banter. The punters. Northern to a fault.

A lone car is parked outside a shop. A girl peels off from her mates to scramble up the boot and on to the roof. She jumps on it till it dents, clumps down the bonnet and returns to the gang who seem barely to have noticed her antic.

The clock above Boots says it is not yet eight. Philip wants a drink. But that will mean going to the cash machine. Might Pilot have frozen his account? Only one way to find out. Needs must. As they say. On the Headrow he heads for the machine, forcing away every thought about that night with Carl. His heart lifts when he sees there's no queue. Fate, perhaps, on his side for once. He keys in his number, presses the buttons and, more joy, gets the fifty quid he's asked for. Maybe he should take everything, empty the account. Later, perhaps.

The Infirmary is only a hundred yards away, across the road and up. A minute to get there, even less. But there's time for a drink, surely, something to steady the nerves. He goes into the Henry and buys a bottle of Bud. He's never been in here before and it's surprisingly empty, though tediously fashionable – all lasers and screens. Whatever happened to the traditional British pub? Philip's empty stomach curdles with the first few swallows, but halfway down the bottle he's getting a direct hit. Worth it. Feeling better all the time. He buys another.

Bodies appear through the door, people his own age, cherry-faced, dressed to the nines, and older ones, slower, rueing the fact that they have just not won the lottery. Maybe next week. Soon there are plenty of people, each entrance pointing up the fact that Philip is alone, of a Saturday night. Time to leave.

He heads down Westgate, not looking at the Magistrates' Court. Each step takes him in the opposite direction to the hospital. Another drink before he can face that. In the next bar he pretends to be looking for someone. He wishes Oz would appear, then, in a belated insight into the night before, he thinks that he does not really like him any more. They're different people now. End of story. Sarah, if she was about, might be a better prospect. There'd be no fooling around this time – a few drinks, back to her place, and the world would be remade, no messing. But there's no sign of her. As if . . . He gets another bottle and stands by the fruit machine, watching this place filling like the last, as if the whole of fucking England has decided to meet in Leeds, eight o'clock for nine. Yet he's feeling more comfortable now, virtuously lazy. And sick of being miserable. Would someone please tell him a joke? He looks around, thinking, This will not do. Just one more drink, a pint perhaps, then that will have to be it. Out, then. Find Kath and get things sorted. Then at the bar there's a tap on the shoulder. The touch draws a lightning anger. He'll flatten the bastard . . .

'Well, well, Phil. Fancy you being here.'

Fate again. The fucking genes. What chance did he have in this life? 'Howard?'

'That's me, Phil.'

He's wearing an expensive-looking black leather jacket, red-striped shirt, Levi 501s with a thick leather belt. There's a woman with him, and a couple standing back. Howard mutters something in the ear of the woman Philip assumes is his wife. Then he steps round to Philip's other side and leans on the bar. 'Something going on out there. Cop cars all over the shop.'

'Is that right?'

'Yeah.' He looks back and around, then edges closer, his after-shave pungent as sulphur. 'Look, Phil,' he says, the black eyebrows knitted with a spivvish conspiracy. 'What was all that yesterday?'

'Sorry?' Philip says, slurring, aware for the first time of a creeping drunkenness.

'Come on. You know. The Griffiths job. What were you playing at?'

'Oh that!' Philip grins. 'Well, old mate, I just thought he kind of . . . deserved to win!'

Howard shakes his head, smiling. He takes a cigar from his pocket, flicks off the cellophane. 'Look, I know you've been having a bad time lately, but Phil, for fuck's sake . . .' He lights the cigar, spits out a speck of tobacco.

'I know. Lost it, didn't I? Well, it doesn't matter now.'

'Come again?'

'Well, that's it, isn't it? I'm a free man now, aren't I? No more Pilot. The world's my lobster, and all that.'

Howard looks across Philip, seeming not to be listening. His wife and the other couple have moved into the centre of the room, hopeful of a table near the fireplace. 'Look,' he says. 'It's dealt with.'

'What's that, Howard?' Philip smiles, eyes half-closed to exaggerate his drunkenness.

Howard touches the dent in his nose, and draws on the cigar. 'I've covered it over. Harry queried it with me. I told him last week we weren't going to pay out. At least not the full whack.'

Philip put his drink down. 'Since when did Harry start checking up on things?'

'What?'

'I don't believe you, Howard. What happened to that cheque? I authorised that.'

'Yeah, and you'd no business to. It's in the fucking bin. I told everyone there'd been a misunderstanding, crossed wires and all that.' A surprising bottle of Spoof arrives for him and he takes a swig. 'Look, Phil, this may be none of my business, but does this have something to do with the court case?'

'Does it, fuck. I walked out. I don't care about the case. I don't know anything about it.'

'I do.'

'What?'

'It was in the *Yorkshire Post* this morning. They said there wasn't enough to convict him on the attack. They just did him on the robbery. Bound over for a year, two hundred and fifty quid, plus costs.'

'Fancy.' Philip took a drink.

'Come on, Phil, what's going on with you? Look at you, look at the fucking state of you.'

Philip laughed. 'I'm fine, Howard! Just fine, mate!'

'You could have fooled me.' Howard took another swig, looked behind him at his wife, then stared ahead at the top shelf behind the bar. 'Anyway, I've saved your bacon.'

'You've what?'

'Like I say. The Griffiths business. I've smoothed it over.'

'Howard! How do you know I wanted it "smoothing over"? Ah, Jesus.'

'Don't be stupid, Phil. We all have these bad patches. Things just don't go right, I know. We all go through it. It's stress, that's all.'

'Stress?'

'Yeah, right. Stress.' He stood back, pointing the bottle neck at Philip. 'Just remember you owe me.'

'Are you sure about that?'

'Damn right you do.' He draws on the cigar, taps it on the ashtray.

Philip chuckles sourly, shaking his head. 'Jesus fucking Christ, Howard.'

Howard finishes his drink, checks his wife isn't looking, and asks for another. 'What're you doing here, anyway?'

'On a night out. All right?'

'You want to watch it, you know, boozing on your own. It's a bad sign. You're too young for it.'

'Bollocks.'

He gets the drink, turns away, then seems to remember something. He puts his fragrant face close to Philip's. 'Anyway, Phil, Monday morning, you come and see me and we'll have a natter. Just you and me,' he says, pointing the bottle neck at Philip. 'Right?'

'No.' But Howard is already moving away, weaving his sharp black-leather shoulders through the gathered bodies. When he sits down, his wife sneaks a look at Philip. She knows about him. She must read the *Yorkshire* fucking *Post* too.

Philip leans back on the bar, the space Howard left already filled by a man waving for attention. Philip wants to speak to him, to solicit sympathy from a stranger. But his head is a mess and he says nothing. Standing upright he downs his drink in two and heads for the door, avoiding Howard's look from across the room.

No one home! Where was the old fucker? Hadn't Darren phoned Sam to tell him he would be home that night? Where was he? Didn't he *believe* him? Darren had left his bag with the neighbours, a young couple with two screaming kids. What else could he have done? He couldn't have left it outside the flat door, not with the thieving bastards round there. Now he wished he'd brought it with him. They'd be going through it now, sure as fuck. They'd find the weekend leave pass from the prison. What a stupid wanking mistake! What was he like?

He'd gone up to the Green Leaf, but they hadn't seen the old man for weeks. The silly old get. Where the hell . . . Now Darren was walking the streets, and not caring for it, the groups of kids hanging about in gangs much bigger than he could ever remember. Yet what the fuck else was he supposed to do?

Cool it, that's what. He wandered back towards town, shivering, the wind blowing through his cotton bomber like a knife. He wondered if he should go and see his mother to see if Sam was there. In the mood he was in, he would have it out with her right now and tell her to stop leading the old man on. Darren would be out for good soon, and she could piss off out of their lives altogether. But what if he went all the way to Beeston and found out she'd moved? For fuck's sake.

Fuck's sake!

He looked in a travel agent's window. Two weeks in Palma – two hundred and seventy-nine pounds, half-board. It meant nothing to him. All those daydreams, meaningless now. He moved on and stood outside a pub, feeling in his pocket. Three quid. All he had, and maybe no place to fucking sleep, either. He turned away from the door.

Philip starts laughing. He's still a Pilot employee! He still has not left Kath! What do you have to do to get a result these days? Murder someone? With the city behind him, he walks on up Park Lane, the people passing townward, their laughter more diminished the further he goes, as if he's penetrating their circles of reserve, heading for the dark heart of Leeds.

Standing on a footbridge he watches the lines of traffic beneath him, the whizzing dots of light like the symptoms of a fever. Now he either goes back to find Kath, or he goes on drifting through the streets. Looking for . . . Fuck knew.

He walks on, finding another pub. He doesn't even look at its name, just enters, nodding to the bouncers. And it will do, somewhere to stand till he drops.

'Pint, mate. Lager. Carling'll do.'

The barman puts the glass under the tap, watching the punters who are kneeling on the seat by the window, looking out over the stained glass at something happening in the street – flashing lights, a stone or two flying through the air.

Forty-Five

Luke drew on the cigarette and bit at the smoke as he blew it out. He could have used a joint, a fix. Any fucking thing – being without was driving him round the bend. He rolled on to his side. The meal they had brought him was still on the floor, untouched. He wanted it, but he would not eat it. What else could he do? What other point could he make? He looked at it – pie and mash and green beans. Fucking filth, anyway.

He turned over and looked at the wall. 'This is the place AFTER hell.' He had read the graffiti so many times it had no meaning. Now all he saw were patterns, differing depths of scrawl. Someone came along the corridor, looked through the peephole, closed it. Fuck knew who. Luke couldn't care less. It was as if he was slipping inside himself, way down. Nothing else for it, just this waiting, for the next day, the next fucking minute, and for the news, some time, about whether or not he had killed that guy, that fucking Perry. Luke couldn't be bothered either way. If he'd done it, he'd done it. If not, he might even regret it.

Half-sleep, the only kind you could get with the fucking light on all day. He closed his eyes . . .

And for a moment it's a hot afternoon, by a river. A rod tip wavers, there's the tug, a flash of silver on the water, and Luke shouting, 'Got one! Got one!'

He wakes up. Somebody walking on his grave. Some cunt. It was the lack of drugs, giving him nightmares. He could do without that. Maybe he should bang and shout until they brought him something, anything. But it wouldn't do any good. They never gave you a fucking thing. You never got what you wanted, ever, in this bastard life.

*   *   *

243

He'll never make it to see Kath now. An absolute fact. He looks round the pub. This is it, he feels like announcing, the place where he'll descend into damnation. Some of the people have left, away up the clubs, or looking for adventure among whatever's going on out there. Philip looks across the room seeing four girls at the far end of the bar, a couple in a corner, a few others standing around on the red carpet. He closes his eyes, and when he opens them, everyone seems to have changed places. He grins, looks harder, and spots the straying cuff of a denim jacket, black-trainered feet and tight buttocks. They are features from a halted life, details he cannot quite trust. Carl David . . . ?

But it's true. A prince of a moment. Meant for Philip.

He's with a mate, like everyone – you don't hang around here on your own. Philip tries to hide behind two men and a woman at the bar, though he can't resist watching.

Carl's friend, a lean, older white guy, is joshing with a group of teenage girls. He laughs, makes an open-armed gesture. Then he hands Carl his pint and drops to his hands and knees, crawling among the fag ends and trampled crisps to look up the girls' skirts. He sticks his tongue out like a dog. The girls squeal. Pleased with the joke, the man gets to his feet.

For Philip, there is only this horrible fascination. And a needle in his stomach. What would it be like to settle this score? How much was he *owed*? A lot. A fucking awful lot. More than people could ever know. He wraps his hand round his glass, knowing it is stupid, yet wanting it, wanting to do *something he will regret*.

Glass in hand, he walks over, knowing his brains are in his knees, yet unable to stop himself. Carl sees him, seeming to take two seconds to recognise him.

Philip sways. 'Rem . . .' He burps with the lager, a little acid in his throat that he swallows. 'Remember me, shithouse?'

Carl is calm, as if he had already seen Philip and decided to make nothing of it. The wiser party, as before, and now. Yet there's a half-smile, a show of those straight meat-tearing teeth.

'Are you listening, or what?' Philip says. He tips the drink from his glass on to the carpet.

The girls are on the move, wanting none of this. The friend puts his face near Philip's, his hand on the arm holding the glass. 'We heard. Now fuck off.'

'I'm fucking – going nowhere.' Words from a limited script, but good enough for this place. 'You're a piece of shit, you. D'you know that? Got away with fucking murder, you have.'

Carl shakes his head. An affectation of weariness. Philip, with the coiled-in petulance of an infant who wants to strike his mother, shakes off the man's hand, draws back the glass and lunges. But the man grabs Philip's arm with pitiful ease, wringing it, making him drop the glass which bounces on the carpet without breaking. 'Fuckin' tosser! Is this him, Carly? That cunt from yesterday?'

Smiling, Carl says, 'Yeah, this is him.' Philip pulls his arm away, wobbling on his feet. Carl points at him. 'Tell me what I've done to deserve a twat like you. Go on, tell me!'

Philip kicks out, pathetically, a yard off his target, lumbering like a wounded bear. 'You prick, you . . .' He launches himself forward again, then he is suddenly looking at the ceiling, hands grabbing his neck, finger stubs in his throat, tipping him backwards and letting him down to the floor. Philip spins round on his side, bicycle-kicking. But he's weak. All his life, he's been soft. The bouncers pick him up – a wordless, efficient procedure – and they carry him out and roll him on to the pavement. Philip's head catches on the sandpaper surface of the flags. He groans and lies on his back among the stones and bits of glass, looking at the stars and a night that's a million years old, as the door slams behind him.

Darren could hear the sirens all over the city, and there was the glow of a fire somewhere up Hyde Park. Was it like this every Saturday night, these days? Fucking lively, that's for sure. He decided he would just have to hang around outside the flat until the old man came back, or perhaps try and break in, or throw himself on the mercy of the couple. Then he saw a figure ahead, sprawled over the pavement. He stopped, wondering if he should turn around. Trouble was the last thing he needed. But this guy might want his help. A point to be scored, maybe. Whatever. He went up to him and leaned over.

'All right there, mate?'

There was something familiar about him, as if it was someone Darren should remember, though the face was older now, and he was fatter round the belly.

'I said, are you all right, mate?'

'Piss off, lowlife.'

Darren straightened up. 'Fuckin' charmin', pal. Only askin'. Know what I mean?'

'Get out of it! Go on, fuck off!' He wheeled round on his side, trying to kick Darren.

'Hey, please yerself, mate. Right?' Some people. It was the last time he'd try and help anybody. They were more civil inside. He walked away, breaking into a run before the police appeared, hoping to fuck that the old man had shown himself back at the flat.

Philip hears the man running down the street. Inside the pub, the lights dip behind the stained-glass windows and an angry voice calls for drinks to be finished. Philip struggles to his knees, his face chafed with cold. He feels the wet graze on his head, looks at the blood on his fingers. His own. *Someone should pay for this. Someone . . .* Ah, what the fuck.

He gets to his feet and stumbles to a shop window where he throws up. Two women pass, taking no notice. He straightens up and starts walking, defying his dizziness, along the street and round the corner to a deserted crossroads at the foot of a short rising road. He stalls, feeling faint, his knees weak as he sees a dozen or so bodies running haphazardly down the hill. At the top, seventy yards away, is a van with a hot glow underneath. Philip watches, trying to stay on his feet. A single flame licks round the exhaust then suddenly spreads in a sheet up the back doors, spoiling and licking. A car passes, slows, accelerates away. One of the youths turns as he runs, laughing. 'The bastard's gonna blow!' They all turn, their faces and fronts illuminated by the fire that whooshes into a mushroom around the van. 'Yes! Yess-ss!' As they disappear, Philip wonders, with a remote moral sense, how things ever end up like this. All he wanted was a quiet life, with good things happening to him, and nice things happening to other people. It wasn't right, all this.

He's still standing there when a small boy appears alone at the top of the hill. Philip watches him go up to the fire and throw a half-brick at the hulk of the van. It hits, sending up a shower of sparks, and the boy dances, waving his arms as if he's scored for United.

The police helicopter circles overhead. Philip stumbles over the crossroads and round to a street of shops where three youths are ramming a rubbish bin through the window of an electrical discount place. They prise up the grille like it's made of cellophane and, though the alarm is going, they calmly help themselves to the stuff inside. Then they're walking openly towards Philip, their arms laden with boxes of camcorders, radios. 'What you lookin' at, wankface?' Philip says nothing.

His head is spinning again. He staggers to the end of the first row of shops, finding an alley. He wanders down, stooped, cursing in the dark as an ambulance speeds down the street behind him. He looks up at the side of the building, not knowing where he is. At the end are two big wheelie bins. Philip drags himself along, bouncing off the wall. He hears a groan in the dark, a shred of humankind that inspires a familiar indignation. Leaning into the shadows between the bins and the wall, he finds a body and drags it to its feet. 'Out of it, shithead.' From the body's lap the tackle of its indulgence – a syringe and bits of silver paper – rattle on the ground.

It's a boy, fourteen years old. If that. For a few seconds the two are looking at each other. The kid seems genuinely frightened, then he's scrabbling around on his knees for his gear. 'Fuckin' watch it, can't yer?'

'Piss off out of it,' says Philip.

'Hey, live an' let live, mate. Christ's sake.' The kid gets his things and heads for the end of the alley, sniffing, muttering about not being able to get a minute's peace these days.

Philip watches him go then falls into the boy's nest among the heaps of rubbish, moaning, before the lights went out, 'Someone'll pay for this. One day . . .'

And that was Philip. A modern man. All the rage.